Secret Language

Secret Language

Neil Williamson

NewCon Press
England

First edition, published in the UK June 2016
by NewCon Press

NCP 095 (hardback)
NCP 096 (softback)

10 9 8 7 6 5 4 3 2 1

Cover art and layout by Andy Bigwood

Interior layout by Storm Constantine

Contents

For Emma

Introduction

As a lad I had a passion for spies and espionage. From colourful books full of shifty, sneaky cartoon figures I learned about disguises and fieldcraft, and most of all how to write messages that no one else could read. I spent hours playing with invisible writing, code wheels and substitution cyphers, making the most banal (and, at that age, probably puerile) messages exciting because only I could understand them. Keeping secrets.

Now skip forward a few decades.

There's a conventional wisdom that writing fiction should be an act of communication. A dialogue – a communion – between author and writer, and if something isn't clear then the writer must have in some way failed in their job. Of course, up to a point, this is true: the reader has to be able to follow the basic action and, when the story is over, they should have a reasonable appreciation of what the point of the whole exercise was. But, for me anyway, that's where it ends. Nuance, subtext, meaning? Those are all worked into the messages that we spend hours crafting, hunched alone in our garrets over our ancient enigma machines. Creating riddles wrapped inside mysteries. I don't write to communicate. I do it simply for the joy of making cool, new things. And these things are constructed from all sorts of observations and memories and bits of my own hopes and fears, and... well, who can ever know everything that a writer puts into their work? Most of us barely know ourselves. And who knows what you will discover on reading these stories? It all depends on your individual make-up of personality and experience: the keys you bring to the reading experience. And if that wasn't bad enough, I then feel the need to package everything up as Science Fiction or Fantasy, extra layers of substitution and misdirection that may make a piece incomprehensible to a layman, but will offer richness and wonder to those steeped in its lore. Ultimately, a writer has no control over who reads their work. So, all you can do is write your cypher, leave it to be found, and let what happens happen.

I've a tendency to attribute this attitude partly to being a musician. There are few more direct artist/audience dynamics. During a gig you know instantly whether an audience is getting what you do. If they like it, you can build it into a great experience for all concerned. If they don't, there's very little you can do to stop it sinking. You don't worry about communing with an imaginary listener. You just put your songs out there and see whether the heads nod, the feet tap... or not.

Music is something I think about a lot. It is, along with mathematics, one of the few modes of expression that could be called a universal language. Music has the power to convey mood and emotion directly without needing to be processed or translated. I believe it's one of the great gifts of human culture and, unsurprisingly, it features in quite a few of the stories in this collection. Both "Pearl In The Shell" and "Killing Me Softly" are warnings against throwing away the wonderful music culture that we have, while "The Death Of Abigail Goudy" features a composer obsessed with the sometimes bizarre causes of death of classical greats and paralysed by the fear of never producing her own ultimate work.

A few years ago now I wrote the first in a series of occasional stories set in a Musicals world, the sort of place where people sing instead of speak to each other and the music that is ever present in the world acts to direct people's lives, a force of destiny. For those interested, the first story in this sequence, "The Last Note Of The Song", a pirate musical, can be found in the ebook edition of my first collection, *The Ephemera*, but the others, including a piece original to this book, "This Is Not A Love Song", are included here.

I'm not only obsessed with music. I'm fascinated by how we consume stories too, and there are several pieces here, such as "Deep Draw" and "Lost Sheep", that are stories about stories, their ubiquity and necessity in terms of how we make sense of our lives. Because that's what we do, we humans, we tell ourselves the stories of ourselves. The harshest, truest ones we edit and encode to make them palatable to ourselves. Often we tell even more sanitised versions of these to those close to us. Sometimes we don't. Sometimes we *can't*. The dynamics of what people say to each other interest me. What we share in public, what is private and what is true. In stories such as "The Posset Pot", "The Bed" and "The Secret Language Of Stamps", I've tried to explore what happens when, even with the best will in the world, people fail to communicate with each other. In a new story, "Silk Bones", I examine what happens when we try to keep secrets from ourselves.

Ultimately, stories aren't about truth. They're about hints and glimpses for most, with only the rare reader having the keys necessary to understand everything. All we writers can do is make our messages and hope that when people translate them through the code wheels of their own experiences, there's enough there to provoke some thought, or at least provide a little entertainment. So, I'm going to place this book inside a briefcase and leave it under this park bench. Then I'm going to get up, button my raincoat, set the brim of my fedora, and walk nonchalantly away, without once looking back. And, should you come along and find it, I hope you enjoy it, at least.

Neil Williamson
Glasgow
April 2016

Deep Draw

"Say, son. Do you want to hear a story?"

Fat fingers tugged the sleeve of my shirt. Under its Angelino camouflage, the old fellow's face was *brimming*.

Did I want to hear a story? As if the timing of me coming by his table was a coincidence.

The tropical storm raged against the windows. Reflected in the streaming glass, the airport hotel bar was all but empty. Just a few desultory sots spending an unplanned evening away from home. Sitting in their self-absorption, stirring who knew what stories. I could have chosen any one of them to tap, but this old West Coaster was ready to spill. It was obvious from the second he walked in, grumbling about the flight cancellations, complaining that people didn't get treated like this in LA. A stream of babble directed at no one in particular until he found his way to the bar and asked for a whisky. *One of the good ones.* By which he meant a conspicuously expensive scotch, but I've been a barman a long time: when a customer demands a drink you don't give him the one he asks for, you give him the one he needs.

For the sake of appearances, I hovered, rubbed at an imagined speck on the mouth of the water carafe I happened to be holding. "If the manager catches me slacking off –"

His eyes crinkled. "You're not worried about your *manager.*"

"No." I placed the empty carafe on the table, sitting it just so behind the bright distraction of the candle glass. "No, I'm not."

"My name is Vincent Deluca," he said once I was seated and he had my full attention. "I'm a Hollywood man."

He wanted me to be impressed. I've served water, in all its forms, everywhere from the banks of the Ganges to the highest table on Olympus. And even Olympus struggled to match Hollywood for misplaced self-importance. This introduction wasn't a pleasantry, it was an establishment of our dynamic; high to low. And that suited me fine.

True to form, Deluca didn't offer to shake my hand. Neither did he ask my name. I could have told him: *Ganymede.* But to do so would have changed the gradient between us before the flow had even started. So, instead, I replied with an indulgent smile.

"Forty five years in the movie business," he said. "You know what it takes to last that long in Hollywood?"

I refrained from rolling my eyes. He really wanted to bang the *Hollywood man* thing home. The cinema is a useful tool, but not one I hold in much regard. At its best it is capable of piquancy that almost echoes truth, but at its worst, like chick-lit novels and soap operas and sci-fi shows and *bandes desinée*, it generalises and dilutes. In my experience, the majority of Hollywood men treated story like a cheap currency, squandering it disdainfully.

The only tales of value are true ones. Those treasured by the gods are unique. They are seldom spoken, and to obtain them takes skill.

"Oh," I said lightly. "I'd imagine: pluck, luck, and a ruthless streak that'd make Chuck Bronson look like Little Orphan Annie."

He liked that, gave me an appraising look that took in the ambrosia blond of my tied-back hair, the sandstone stubble on my chiselled chin, the old Adriatic eyes. He leered like a man half his age. I didn't react to that, kept my expression friendly but neutral. He'd promised me a story. I wanted him to focus on that.

"Damn fucking right you do." He spoke *sotto voce* into his glass, sipped, then took a moment to appreciate the scotch blossoming in his mouth. It made him cough; a dry, indelicate hack. He wiped his lips on a napkin.

"So, this story." He was ready at last. But first, another look, a different kind of appraisal. "I guess you're not old enough to remember Sandie Laurence? She was an actor, early-to-mid seventies –"

"Sure, I've heard of her," I lied. I didn't want to be here all night. "YouTube, yeah?"

Deluca grunted. "Well, then you know Sandie." He relaxed in his chair. "Terrible actress. Terrible. *Abysmal.* But talent is overrated. She was a looker, and she had one skill: she could cry. Jesus, could she cry. So, she had a career. Started off in the soaps and cop shows, moved up to TVMs. Frightened hooker in *Ironside*, aggrieved widow in *Columbo*. You'd know her face for sure. It'd be the one with tear-tracks through her make-up. Anyway, her modest skills earned her a studio contract, and she starred in a string of moderately successful weepies. She even made the long list for Love Story before they gave the part to Ali. You get the picture. Anyway, at some point she started to believe she *was* something, and then she started to behave like it too. We're not talking Lyndsey Lohan, but throwing trailer fits, holding up production, demanding changes in the script. Pain in the fuckin' ass. You know what I'm saying?"

As I nodded, I glanced at the carafe. The glass had begun to mist inside. It might have been caused by proximity to the heat of the candle, but it wasn't. "Directors stopped wanting to work with her?"

He snorted. "Damn fucking right. But around about the time she started acting up she also raised her game. Those tear-jerkers started getting respectable box office. There was even a whisper of an Academy Award nomination. So, the studios wanted her. For a while."

"Until?"

"Until her last film. Another trashy piece of emotional blackmail. We're talking doomed relationship, terminally ill child, and a whole load of that love-and-peace shit. Well, it was the seventies. Picture was called Franco's Wish. Had a budget too; Martin Schiller directed, 2nd unit location filming in Spain for the *dego* scenes. Shit as the script was, that movie could have made her. Instead it finished her."

Deluca rolled his glass again. Shark-grinned into it as he sipped, savoured, stretched out the moment. Just a hint of a cough as he drank the whisky down. He was hitting his stride now.

"So this was, let me see, spring seventy three? I was still new to the business, but I'd got myself a job as an assistant to a producer named Harold Gravey. That was really his name. For a while the girls in the office tried to stick me with the nickname, *Biscuits*, because I was always tagging around after him. But fuck that, right? It didn't even work. Anyway, what assistant meant – taking calls, running errands, driving people from airports to hotels to studios. Yada, yada. And on the location shoot for Franco's Wish, I was the kid who got to run around after Sandie Laurence. And, man, she was hard work." He put on a voice, thin and screechy. "Vincent? Vincent! Come here now."

His impression sounded exactly like Bette Davis calling for her sister in *Whatever Happened To Baby Jane*. Like he couldn't remember the difference between memory and the movies. Or maybe he just thought it sounded more dramatic. The false note irked me. It diluted the truth so prized by my customers.

"So, one day we're shooting exteriors in a vineyard up in the hills off the 101. This is one of her big scenes and the director's setting up for a sunset shoot. I'm sent to get her from her trailer to run through the scene, and she tells me: 'Tell that man', that was what she called Schiller, *that man*. 'Tell that man I don't want to do this scene today.' Now I know what Schiller will say. He'll hit the fucking roof to hear this now. Once the sun starts to set we've got maybe a thirty minute window before we lose the light. But I trot off dutifully and tell him. And then he comes to her trailer and they have words, and when he's gone she calls me in and says: 'You've got to get me to a telephone'. Like that. Wide-eyed and deadly serious. Like she's in one of her crappy pictures."

Deluca spread his hands. "What am I to do? I'm eighteen years old, but I do happen to know there's a house close by. The people that run the winery, right? I sneak her over there in the studio car and she turns on the movie star eyes and, of course, she gets her phone call. Fifteen minutes later we're back in her trailer. It's starting to get dark. Schiller's been over twice and Sandie's promised she'd be there shortly, but that she's not ready. Not yet. So we sit."

Deluca laughed dryly. "At least I sit. Not Sandie. But she's not prepping for the scene, she's not using the method, she's not doing mantras or any of that calming, holistic shit. She's pacing and she's smoking like a three alarm fire, and every two minutes she peeks through the curtain. And she's making me nervous too. I mean, I'm just a kid, right? I'm shitting bricks thinking I'm about to have to deal with a highly paid movie star's full blown nervous collapse, you know?"

"Then there's a knock at the door, and Sandie composes herself. 'Let her in and wait outside,' she says. I open the door to an extremely unhappy young woman. I just stand there like a sap, trying to work out how a woman dressed for working on the farm – there are sawdust sprays on her blue jeans, oil stains on her plaid shirt – and in an obvious fucking rage can possibly look this beautiful. The object of my absorption, of course, doesn't even see me, just pushes past me to confront Sandie. I'm smart enough not to hang around, but before the door closes I see the visitor dump a grocery sack on the table, and say: 'You can't keep on doing this.'

"Whatever passes between them doesn't take long. Sandie's visitor soon storms out of the trailer again and takes off in a muddy Dodge truck. And *poof!* Sandie appears at the trailer door and announces she's ready. Anyway, long story short, right? They shoot the scene and catch the sunset and she's stunning in it. Stunning. The perfect combination of melodrama and real emotion. How she managed to bring those marshmallow lines to anything approaching life is a miracle. But she did. Exactly what the director's looking for. Everyone goes home happy, right?

"Hey what are you doing? Are you even listening to this?"

I'd only diverted my attention from the great impresario for a second. Just long enough to check the carafe again, satisfy myself with the drips streaming down the inside of the glass. "Course I am." I smiled reassurance. "Everyone's happy. Right."

"Wrong, wise ass." Deluca pulled a face and I thought for a second I'd blown it, but the rain, the whisky, an audience... The story was flowing too well now.

"Sandie wasn't happy at all. She was a wreck. Everyone could see how much the performance took out of her. Possibly even earned herself some respect among the crew. I knew there was more to it, of course, but had no idea what, and Sandie wasn't in the mood for sharing.

"Well, the rest of the shoot was in the studio in Burbank, and everything returned to normal pretty fast. Sandie reverted to being a bitch and the crew to being frustrated. She never once mentioned what happened in the vineyard, and it wasn't my place to ask. I was just there to deal with her shit.

"Of course, it happened again. She'd been putting off the scene where the husband leaves her. Kept begging Schiller to postpone it until later in the schedule; which he did, bending over backwards to oblige her until they couldn't delay it any longer.

"So, same routine: Sandie confines herself to barracks and won't come out for anyone. Outside her locked dressing room door we can hear her going through her lines, trying a hundred ways to say the same words. Then, for almost a whole day, there's silence, until finally she comes out and once again she summons the visitor.

"'Where's the fucking bitch this time?' When I meet the young woman at the studio gatehouse, she's no less beautiful and maybe twice as angry. I escort her to Sandie's dressing room and they have a real screaming match in there, but I'm fucked if I can make out any details. I'm thinking the visitor is her supplier, of course, but people in that line of work are seldom so reluctant to deliver. Unless Sandie wasn't paying her bills, but then you turn up with a thirty-eight and guy named Angelo, don't you? Anyway, when the visitor leaves and Sandie toddles off at last to do the scene, I search the dressing room but the only thing that wasn't there before is a grocery bag with a Goody's soda bottle in it. And there's nothing more suspicious in that than a dribble of water.

"So, Sandie does the scene. Unbelievable. Nails it first take. The actor playing the husband barely keeps it together. Everyone's in tears. Even me."

"All from a little water?"

That made Deluca laugh so hard he started to cough again. He shook his head, red faced.

"Are you all right?"

"I'm fine," he choked. "Fine. Just a little inoperable cancer."

"That doesn't sound *fine*."

He wiped his lips on his napkin again. "Son, I've got the best doctors in the world. I pay them to tell me it's fine. You understand?"

While he gathered himself I glanced at the carafe again. The water that hadn't been there before. Then I asked: "And the third time?"

"How'd you know there was a third time?"

"There's always a third time in stories."

Deluca's nod acknowledged that. "Heh, well, it's the last day of the shoot. There's a mixture of relief and apprehension on set. Everyone's glad the beast is almost in the bag. They know it's not Oscar material, not even with Sandie's waterworks, but all that matters is getting it wrapped now. And she still has the final scene to shoot. The one where the kid dies. Oh, hey, really that's not a spoiler if you ever watch it. It's pretty much obvious from the opening titles, I promise you.

"Anyway, same routine. Come the big moment, Sandie delays. Everyone has a go at getting her on set. If Schiller had any hair he'd have been tearing out by the roots. Eventually, I go to her: 'Sandie, this happens every time. Just call her and get it over with.'

"Her face is like stone. 'Vincent, I mustn't do that. I can't.'

"'I know you want to be free of whatever it is she's got you dependent on.' I guess I'm still convinced it must be pills of *some* sort. 'But you can start over tomorrow. Today, you need to shoot this scene.'

"Sandie just sits there. 'You don't understand.'

"I stretch the telephone over, put the receiver in her hand. 'Call her.' And when she makes no movement, I take it back. 'I'll call her. What's the number?'

"'It's disconnected.'

"I can see that she's absolutely lost.

"'What's her address? I'll drive there and get what you need.'

"Five minutes later I'm running red lights with a scribbled address taped to the dash. The name that goes with the address is *Megan Kirkhope*. I toss the name around all the way out of the city and up the 101, trying to make it connect to something, but come up empty. Kirkhope's place is way up beyond Santa Barbara, and then further on still, north through the forest almost as far as Bakersfield. The house is far from being worth the drive. A shell of a place. Paint faded and scabbed. Junk on the porch. A wood pile with a litter of saw debris.

"Megan appears before I've even got out of the car. Arms folded, fingers twitching like they're wishing for a shotgun.

"'Miss Kirkhope, I'm –'

"'I know who you are. And who sent you. Just you run back to her and tell her no. Not any more.'

"So, what can I do? I'm eighteen. I don't care particularly about Sandie or even about whether the picture gets finished. I just care about making a name for myself as a guy who can get things done. So, I lie. I tell Kirkhope about how I'll be fired if I return empty handed, about my sick widowed mother, my brother in rehab, his jailbird wife and his kids in state care and already getting into trouble with the law. I lay it on like ketchup *and* mustard. When I'm done, she laughs in my face.

"'You call *that* a sob story? Try being an adopted kid discovering age nineteen that your *real* mother is every inch the Hollywood actress you'd dreamed she'd be and that she's also a wheedling, manipulative bitch who forces you to do unspeakable things for the sake of her career.'

"To say I'm surprised is an understatement. Sandie Laurence is this woman's *mother*? Kirkhope has to be older than me by at least a few years. Sandie's official studio age is thirty, but even if that's an underestimate, it can't be by much, which would have made her a mother – I'm guessing here – at twelve, thirteen at the oldest.

"Megan can see I've done the math and am already on to the

supplementary questions. 'No, I *didn't* track her down to blackmail her. She found me. I'm the secret well of tears she taps into every time she has to blub on screen. Why she couldn't have left me as the lost baby of a child mother, why she had to go *further*, I don't know. But, well, here we are, fuck it all to hell.'

"She goes inside, leaves me in front of her porch trying to gauge the potential value of what I've just learned. It'll ruin Sandie's career if it comes out she has a secret adult daughter, but she's pretty much on her last chance as a viable property anyway. Hell, Kirkhope probably told me in the hope that I'll spread it around.

"She's inside five minutes, maybe ten. When she emerges again she's holding one of those grocery sacks. She hands it to me. I feel the bottle inside, liquid sloshing.

"'Tell her...' Kirkhope's been crying. 'Tell her this is the last. Tell her there's no more. It's dead.'

"'Tell her what?'

"'Tell her it's *dead*.'

"And she turns her back on me and slams the door."

Deluca looked to me for a reaction. "Well, what do you think of that?"

"That was pretty rude, I guess."

"Damn right it was rude. But that's not the end of the story."

"No?" *Not by a margin.* The carafe was barely two thirds full.

"So what happened?"

"Well, obviously I get back to LA in time to stop the crew from packing up. Sandie practically assaults me. 'Did you get it?' she says. 'Oh, you *angel*, you got it.' Then, once she's discarded the bag, even as she's glugging back the contents. 'Is this all there is?' So I tell her what Megan told me: *it's dead.*

"And right at that second everything changes. She's no longer a movie star. And I'm no longer a kid at the bottom of the studio food chain. I have power over her and we both know it. So I tell her she needs to go and do the scene now. And just like that she goes and does it. And again, she's amazing. Heart wrenching. You'd almost believe she actually had real talent all along."

"And then?"

"Well, that's it. It's a wrap and everyone breathes a huge sigh of relief and moves on with their careers. The picture does moderately well and Sandie... well, Sandie retires gracefully from the business."

"But that's not the end of the story either," I said. "What about the bottles?"

Deluca sipped his drink. Nodded, appreciative that I'd been paying attention. "The water was just water, you know. Came from a local stream. Sandie claimed its purity helped her centre herself but really she used it as an excuse for contact with Megan. To sharpen up the memories and the guilt of giving up her baby. A shot of nitrous for those tears."

I waited.

"What? There has to be a *point* to the story? Son, this is true life, not the movies. Well, if there *has* to be one, I guess it's use *your advantages wisely*. See I didn't blab what I'd learned to the rags. Where would that have got me? But a quiet word in the right ear got me the right promotion at the right time. And every now and again I used it to demonstrate I understood discretion. And that, let me tell you, is a rare commodity in La-La Land." Deluca expanded in his chair then, smiled like a proper fat cat. "Son, I was a junior VP before I was twenty five."

"And as such a *paragon* of discretion, you're telling me this story now because?"

His Cheshire smile melted. "Hey, I'm passing on hard-earned wisdom here. A little gratitude?"

"That's not the reason." I placed my palm against the window, removed it. Rain ran through the fading print of my fingers the way water permeates everything. "You're telling me this now because it's raining outside and it's warm inside, and those are always the right conditions for telling stories." I nudged his whisky glass. "And you've been drinking, of course."

Deluca peered at the glass. "What do you mean? What's in there?"

I shrugged. "Just whisky. Fermented grain and water. Mostly water." The *source* of that water was another matter, but he didn't need to know about that. "But then so is everything." I lifted the carafe. It still wasn't quite full. There were two empty inches in the neck. I placed it down in front of him. In the candle's illumination the water took on a shade of darkling aquamarine, a sheen of peach. Like a sunset over the ocean.

Deluca gaped.

"The water wasn't *just* water. Tell me about what happened when you followed Megan into her house."

Deluca looked at the table top, at his glass, at his over-neat fingernails. He refused to look at the carafe, at the droplets of condensation coalescing into a burgeoning drip. But I knew he could feel the pressure of it.

"I don't want to." The words seeped from his lips.

"But you will. All stories have to be told. That's how the cycle works. You human beings. Seventy per cent water? You're all water carriers. Drinking it, using it to live, pissing it back out into the world again. Same with stories. Stories need to be consumed and absorbed and retold, distributed from speaker to listener. Even the secret ones. The deep, still water that doesn't see the light. The pure stuff. You had to know what was in those bottles, didn't you?"

Deluca looked bewildered. He'd thought he'd been telling barroom brags. Showing off with his Hollywood connections, trying to impress the cute blond waiter into after-hours drinks, a blow job in the men's room.

"You've never told anyone the whole story have you?"

He shook his head. "No one would believe me."

"You wanted to keep it for yourself." I tried not to chide. He didn't deny it anyway.

Deluca took in a thin breath, let it out through his teeth. "Megan didn't invite me in. But she didn't forbid me either. You're right, I wanted to know. I followed her inside."

He'd closed his eyes, drawn in to the memory now. His lids shivered like beetles under parchment. "I found her in the kitchen, in sunlight, rinsing a bottle in the sink. It was a Goody's green. I remember the label, that old fashioned boy's face, soaked and beginning to peel. I guessed Goody's must have been her favourite soda. She had more bottles lined up on the window sill. All the flavours. She had a stack of grocery bags too, smoothed flat on the kitchen counter. That was the kind of person she was. Thrifty but proud of the fact. She wasn't lying about not being a blackmailer.

"I watched her. In that light, the tap water frothing out of the overfilled bottle neck was like diamonds cascading over her hands." Deluca squinted. "Does that sound fanciful? It's how I've always thought of it."

"If that's what it looked like, then it's true."

"Megan let the water run like that, full force. It sprayed all over but she relished it. She didn't acknowledge my arrival in the kitchen, but she knew I was there.

"'Manolo came here the same day as Sandie,' she says. 'The self-same hour in fact that she arrived out of nowhere and started spewing up twenty one years of stewed guilt. I don't know if you noticed but this place is hardly on the beaten track. I don't get two visitors a season never mind the same hour. But the funny thing was, I was waiting for him. I didn't know it but I had been for a long time.'

"Megan allows the bottle to fill one final time. She towels off the outside and goes through to the adjoining room. After the bright kitchen, the parlour next door is like a cave. The lights are off, the curtains drawn. There's a smell of dust, and another smell too, a sweet-sour funk like bad milk.

"Megan is bent over a couch, and she's whispering to the occupant, helping them to sit up, to drink from the bottle. There's a sound of wet snuffles and hasty, desperate glugging. She places the emptied bottle on a side table, next to a plastic funnel and a washcloth.

"'Manolo,' she says. 'This gentleman is from my mother's movie.' The fat guy on the couch straightens up. He has dark hair that tangles in the blanket tucked up around his chin. His burnished, Hispanic skin has a sickly pallor. His wide eyes are soft like liquid chocolate. They glisten. And he wheezes when he breathes. It might be because he's out of shape or it might be because he's ill, but mostly it's because he breathes through his trunk."

The word was barely spoken. It condensed, it seemed, out of Deluca's breath. He looked to me for signs of disbelief but received only my absolute attention. Megan Kirkhope might have marvelled at the coincidence of two visitors on the same day, but there is no such thing when it comes to the stuff that stories are made of. Characters come and go, scenarios change, but everything is connected.

"A trunk." It wasn't a question. The elephant boy had a different name when I encountered him. When I distilled the story of his horrific childhood, a tale of dark solitude and silence. Of wanting, needing, someone – anyone – to communicate with. What a surprise to see him resurface like this when the very substance of *that* story was pooled in the glass by the old man's hand. A surprise, but not a coincidence.

Deluca's head bobbed shakily. "*Yes*, a proper elephant's trunk where his nose should be. With hairy pink nostrils dripping snot on the blanket before he pulls the blanket up to cover his face again.

"'Please don't stare.' Megan touches his shoulder. I think to reassure him. 'He doesn't like people to stare.'"

Deluca's laugh was arid. "Well, of course, I *try* not to, but I can't help myself, can I? He's just so fucking..."

"Weird?"

"No. *Pathetic.* I guess his whole freakish life must have been hell. He certainly seems incapable of looking after himself. Megan even has to wipe his nose for him.

"'When he arrived here we agreed to take care of him,' she says. 'My mother sends money for food, but he lives with me.'

"The elephant man chooses that moment to make a sound, like a *huff*, and inclines his head angling a large ear towards Megan.

"'He wants to hear my story,' she says. But she hesitates. Then she bends to him and she hesitates again. For the longest time."

"She really didn't want to tell him."

Deluca shook his sorry head.

"She knew what was going to happen. But she had to. She blamed Sandie, but it was *her* story. And all stories have to be told when the time comes. Did you hear it?"

"No. She whispered it. Into his ear."

"What happened, Vincent?"

Deluca took a shuddering breath. It became a dry rattle in his chest. He reached for the carafe but I moved it beyond his grasp. It was almost full. He emptied his whisky glass instead. Grimaced back the last drop.

"I watched a man cry himself to death."

I waited. Let him finish it in his own time.

"So, Megan's whispering to him, and right away those big wet eyes fill up. Tears brim along his eyelids. He blinks and they start to roll down his cheeks. Without dropping a word, Megan catches them in the washcloth. That's important. She's not wiping them away; she's *catching* them, gently, like each one is a pearl. At least to begin with. The longer Megan talks, the harder Manolo cries, and soon the tears are gushing from him. Great cartoon jets, rolling rivers over his cheeks and down his trunk. He huffs and snuffles until he's hoarse and

Megan's cloth is dripping. She fumbles for the bottle, wrings the cloth out into the funnel, into the bottle. This goes on. Megan whispers, Manolo cries. It's only after the third or fourth decanting that he subsides, slumps back to horizontal. Wheezing like a deflating balloon.

"Megan stops talking. She dabs the last of the tears with a mother's tenderness. Pulls the blanket up to Manolo's face, covers his trunk, covers the eyes. Then she twists the cloth to wring those last drops into the bottle. Her knuckles whiten on the rag she squeezes it so hard.

"'He's dead?' I don't know I'm going to say this before I already have. Megan flinches, but nods. 'How do you know?' I say.

"'Because I've come to the end of my story.' She takes the bottle, forces a cork into the neck. 'And so has he.' She thrusts the bottle into my hands. 'Tell her there's no more. It's dead.'"

Deluca stared at his hands.

"You didn't understand at the time, did you?"

If he shook his head it was imperceptibly.

"But now you do. Water attracts water. Stories beget stories. It's all connected."

Deluca didn't answer. Just stared at his hands. White as dry bones and sand. I placed a beer mat over the brimming neck of the carafe and walked out of the bar.

I had somewhere new to be. A delivery to make.

A story to tell.

Deep Draw *was written for an anthology in which each story was inspired by a sign of the zodiac. I chose Aquarius and, playing fast and loose with Roman mythology, made Ganymede, the cup bearer of the gods, the central character. In this interpretation, he doesn't just carry water, he carries stories too.*

The Secret Language

of Stamps

Mr Harman broke the news when she brought his sausages.

"I'm afraid I shall be leaving you next week, Mrs Geddes."

He folded his newspaper and looked up at her through his spectacles. A fan of lace-filtered light sparkled the silverware, illuminated the bowl of Seville marmalade and glossed her guest's lenses like the sea at sunrise. The moment unmoored her for an instant and she kept hold of the rim of his plate a fraction too long.

Mr Harman's brow wrinkled and that made Hilda's next coherent thought an uncharitable one: had her guest waited until this moment to relay this news for fear that she would not have brought his breakfast? Unlike most visitors to *Shangri La* who expected a plate mountained with fried food, he was not a man of huge appetite but he liked a pot of strong tea and appreciated a homemade preserve on his toast. And he *was* partial to his sausages.

She unfolded her neatly pressed landlady smile and released the plate.

"I'm sorry to hear that, Mister Harman. You have been the perfect guest." He had been the only guest for some weeks but her Navy widow's pension always saw her comfortably through the low season, so she was not worried about losing the custom. Only, perhaps, the company. "Business is it?"

He nodded, smiled his smile. "I have to take a lengthy sea voyage. I shall be leaving on Tuesday."

He didn't explain, and she didn't ask. He had never elaborated on the nature of his situation beyond the title, Commercial Agent, and she hadn't asked about that either. As long as his business was legal and he paid his rent money on time, such things were none of her business. She did know that he frequently travelled as far as London to attend appointments, that he made the occasional telephone call for which he left money, and that there was rather a lot of correspondence from abroad. Every day the postman brought envelopes from frightfully exotic parts and she stacked them neatly on the hall table. She did not pry, never that, but one could not fail to see those funny, foreign stamps; familiar, yet strange with their peculiar currencies and monarchs' heads in place of the king and good old pounds, shillings and pence. Funny, foreign stamps from God knew where. Sometimes she remarked on them, to make conversation, and Mr Harman told her a little about the funny, foreign places they came from.

Frank would have known them; the ones from around the Empire at least. He had been the postmaster at the local sub post office before his conscription. She imagined him, riffling the stack with brisk fingers, denouncing the stamps as too fancy, too colourful. In every way inferior to good, straightforward English stamps.

Still, that pile of long-travelled letters spoke highly of her lodger. That so many people should write to him was a mark of a successful man. Wherever they were from.

In the kitchen she lit the gas ring and put the kettle on to freshen up her guest's pot. A gust of wind shook the window. Outside, high puffs of cloud scurried like mice across the sky and below them, beyond the port's terraced rooftops, commercial ships waited in the harbour. Not so long since it had been frigates and destroyers awaiting orders, then slipping away into the Channel with the town's men aboard.

Hilda transferred three spoonsful from caddy to pot, filled the pot up from the shrilling kettle and then took it through. "It's a shame you have to be abroad for Christmas. I'm sure they don't do it quite like we do in England." She substituted the fresh pot for the cold one and slipped the cosy on.

"Can't be helped, I'm afraid, Mrs Geddes." He removed his glasses and polished them with the table cloth corner. Frank had used to do that and Hilda had scolded him for it. She did not scold Mr Harman.

"Well, it's a good job you told me today because I was going to order a larger fowl from the poulterer this morning."

"Then I'm glad not to have inconvenienced you. But I'm sure between your sister and yourself, you could have done the bird justice in any case."

Hilda's smile froze on her lips. How gossipy to have mentioned

Marion in their chit-chats. That really wasn't like her. "My sister will not be coming for Christmas, Mr Harman." She went on quickly to forestall any unpleasantness. "She moved away. To Cardiff."

"Please accept my apology for presumption."

"It's really quite all right."

"Still, it is a shame for a person to spend the festivities alone." Mr Harman replaced his glasses and his smile was a hesitant one. "And I have a confession."

"What would that be, Mr Harman?"

His smile steadied, widened. "I was rather looking forward to spending Christmas here myself."

Over the following days, Mr Harman arranged his affairs, and Hilda saw little of him. On the Monday before Christmas, however, he appeared late for breakfast and wearing casual clothes. When he took his seat at the table he draped a sports jacket over the back of the chair. He wore a sleeveless pullover the same sky blue as his eyes, and the shirt beneath was rolled up at the sleeves and open at the neck revealing that his arms and chest were pleasantly hirsute. She had never suspected that he owned such attire.

She placed his plate before him. "No work today, Mr Harman?"

"All my preparations are complete," he replied. "My affairs are in order, my packing done." He spread his hands. "And so I find myself with that rarest of things: a day of leisure."

Hilda raised her eyebrows. "How fortunate. And what do you intend doing with it?"

Mr Harman reached for the toast rack and began to butter a slice with noisy vigour. "Well, I rather thought I would walk down to the harbour later and take afternoon tea."

"A lovely idea," she said. And it was: she knew of few more appealing prospects than a cosy tea room on a midwinter afternoon. Frank hadn't abided tearooms, but after he was gone Hilda had haunted such establishments. Initially accompanied by her sister but latterly, after Marion's abscondment to Cardiff, on her own. Perched, often as not, at a window table, leaching warmth from the china cradled in her hands and staring out beyond the wide, grey Channel. "As fond a remembrance of the England you leave behind as you could find."

"Exactly so. I've already made a reservation." He spoke the words while chewing on his toast. Hilda was mildly horrified at his lapse in manners. "Mrs Geddes?"

"Yes?"

"It's tea for two."

"Is it, my goodness?" She gave his teapot a gentle shake and filled his cup. She could feel him watching her. "You're a terrible one for letting your tea stew. I hope you're more attentive with your companion this afternoon."

He laughed. "I shall certainly endeavour to be."

Hilda cleared her throat. "May I ask——?"

"Well, I rather hoped it would be yourself."

During previous visits, she always thought of the Continental as more of a café than a tea-room, but the Italian owners had clearly raised their standards since then. They provided as acceptable an array of sandwiches, scones and dainties as any Hilda had seen since rationing began. She felt full to bursting merely on setting eyes on the cake stand, let alone tasting the contents. But somehow, between them, they managed to devour it all. It helped that the tea was fresh, and was not permitted to stew.

Dusk descended in the afternoon, bringing a deep chill to the salty bluster that assailed them on leaving the tea-room, but instead of wending their back up the hill, Hilda found herself persuaded to stop off at the Anchor for a *winter warmer*. That was what Mr Harman – Ernest, *Ernie* – called the mugs of mulled wine he brought back to their corner of the noisy snug. They had another drink and they played a round of darts before shrugging on their coats and making their way back to *Shangri La* in the crystalline darkness.

Of that journey, she remembered nothing that was said, only that they never stopped talking and that the stars fizzed in the sky and that the air had cold teeth and that the pavement was glossed with ice so that she had to take his arm to steady herself, and that she could feel his warmth through both their coats.

Later, after they had said their goodnights, Hilda did not feel the need to bank the fire in her bedroom. The air was frigid enough for her breath to condense on the dresser mirror, but she retained the heat of Ernest's touch. It had kindled something inside her that made sweat bead even as she stood behind her door, skin pressed to cold oak. She listened to the soft scuff of his passage to the bathroom, the muffled domesticity of running water, an unselfconscious cough; and the return journey, the rhythmic flap of his slippers on the runner, a sound which she realised she was going to miss terribly. As his journey passed her door, he paused, and Hilda, naked and burning, held her breath. She held it until her chest ached, waited until she started to shiver, but she did not hear Mr Harman move on again. Not even the creak and latch of his own door along the hall.

Hilda shrugged into her dressing gown and softly opened the door. The hall was completely empty.

Mr Harman did not appear at breakfast. Instead, on the table, he left a flat parcel wrapped in jolly paper and an envelope containing a Christmas card and the balance of his rent money. The card had a message.

Dear Hilda,

How cruel to be parted just when we found more to talk about than the countries of the world. With your permission, I should very much like to continue our discourse – albeit in a one-sided fashion. Please, therefore, accept these small tokens of my esteem. I believe you will find them of interest.

Fond regards
Ernest M Harman

Well. *Fond Regards.*

Hilda placed the card on the mantle with the few others that had trickled in during the previous week. The watercolour of a snowy landscape was more tasteful than the jocular Saint Nicks that flanked it. On their own, the cards weren't sufficient to make the room feel festive, so she bolstered the display with a pair of holly sprigs and, in lieu of a tree, tied red ribbons to the aspidistra that sat on the Chinese stand in the corner of the room.

The postman brought a letter that day too. She knew without opening it that this was her pension cheque. She knew from the stationery, from the habitual typing mistake in her address and from the shoddy application of the postage stamps. In Frank's opinion, most people had needed to go back to school to learn how to address a letter properly. If it wasn't the stamps it was the handwriting, and if not that it was vague addressing. He'd have been fuming to see such laxness from a government department.

On Christmas Day she allowed herself a lie in, dozing in the embrace of the bed clothes and falling into an uneasy dream of the sea. She woke, remembering shifting shingle beneath her feet, the wide water stretching to the horizon, the dread of what lay across it. While she dressed, the telephone rang but she ignored it. It would only be her sister, and she had nothing to say to Marion.

Hilda's holy day routine was the same as it had been when Frank was alive. She had maintained the routine the Christmas she had received the telegram that his ship had gone missing and all of the years since. She prepared her modest lunch with a choir service on the wireless and stood for the King's message before tucking in. Only then did she allow herself to open her present.

The paper sloughed, revealing two slim books. The first was a rather scuffed atlas of the world. In fact she recalled owning one just like it for school, although her copy did not have a torn cover and the smiling, waving children of all nations had not been augmented with inked moustaches and eye patches. Indeed, her copy had been kept pristine. As a child she'd had no desire to learn about *abroad*. Abroad was where the war had happened, after all.

The second book was in even worse condition. The corners of the batters were worn, the gilded lettering sun-faded on account of its missing dust jacket, some of the pages inside spotted with mould, and in soft pencil on the corner of the first page was written: *1/-*. This was a volume, she was certain, that had done sterling service in the window of a second hand bookshop. She looked at the front again.

The Secret Language Of Stamps.

She thumbed through the volume with dwindling interest, disappointed that the book did not after all contain identifying descriptions of the philately of the countries that might be found in the atlas. Instead it appeared to be about some kind of secret signals used by Victorians to communicate with their paramours without their guardians' knowledge. Pages of illustrations of stamps on envelopes, the placement of each connoting a variation on: *I love you* or *Be mine*. In short, the sort of nonsense that would amuse the sort of fanciful schoolgirls who blew dandelion clocks and sent anonymous cards on Saint Valentine's Day. She was doubly disappointed that Ernest thought her *that type*.

Still, a book was a thoughtful gift at any time. She found a place for the pair on the top shelf of the bookcase.

Hilda had cause to fetch the books down several months later when she received a postcard from Ernest. Not the first card, which arrived postmarked New York City in early January; nor the second one which winged its way to her from California in March. It was the third one that made her fetch the forgotten gifts down from their eyrie. The cards themselves were plain, with her name and address filling the front in his large, spacious script. Much that she was delighted that Ernest had fulfilled his promise to keep in touch, she found room for disappointment in the lack of a picture. Now that she knew that he was in these foreign places, she confessed a surprising curiosity about what they looked like. The messages were more disappointing still, or so she thought at first. After the day they had spent together, after his giving her a Christmas gift, she might have hoped for something a little warmer than these perfunctory notes. But, no. In his first communication he had thanked her again for her hospitality and hoped that she'd had a pleasant Christmas. In the second he'd reasserted his intention to return and renew his tenancy later in the year. And in this latest missive, by the postmark from somewhere in Mexico called Campeche, he asked her to kindly hang on to the shirts he had left in the wardrobe. Anyone reading these would see nothing more in them than polite, professional communications from a tenant to his landlady.

So, it wasn't the cards themselves that piqued her interest now and it wasn't their puzzling contents either (there had been precisely *no* shirts left in the wardrobe of Mr Harman's room). What made her reach belatedly, stupidly, to the high bookshelf were the stamps themselves. Those on the cards posted from America were sky blue airmails, long like letterboxes and displaying a picture of an aeroplane. The one from Mexico was a drab green colour featuring native designs around the border, but that was unimportant. In every case, the stamps were placed in the centre of the top edge of the card.

Top right hand corner, Frank would have growled. *Top blasted right hand corner. How hard can it be? Perpendicular, if you please, and no more than an eighth of an inch in from the edge. We need to be able to postmark the thing without obscuring the bloody address.*

These stamps weren't slapped on, however. They had been deliberately placed. Hilda flipped through the pages of the green book until she found a picture of a stamp placed exactly so. The italicised script below the picture said: *You Are Constantly In My Thoughts.*

Well, the silly man.

Hilda would have been lying if she had claimed that her heart did not skip a little on making this discovery. She examined the cards again, handling them now with more care, as if she had just been told by a sale room valuer that they were of unexpected worth, which, in a way, was the truth. She still could not say she admired his handwriting, but now she appreciated the care he had taken to create these banal messages solely so that he, a man who appreciated discretion, could convey his true feelings in secret. Perhaps, she thought, she could be *that type* after all.

Brushing her thumb over the stamp on the latest card, she enjoyed the rough rill of the perforations and realised something new about it. The great black smudge of the postmark had initially made it hard to see, but on close inspection she now saw that the stamp was in fact upside down.

She found exactly that arrangement on the next page of the book. The legend read: *I Long For Your Touch.*

After that, Hilda anticipated Ernest's cards keenly, and the anticipation made the gap until the next arrival intolerably long.

Frank had never been an especially romantic man. His efforts during their early courtship had been so clumsy that Hilda had dissuaded him from persisting. She had not minded especially. In the Great War she had lost her father. She remembered him, like so many of men of the neighbourhood, smiling and waving as his ship eased out from the quay, had witnessed the devastation his failure return brought to her mother. The mockery the war made of such frivolous notions as *love* and *till death us do part* had given her, she liked to think, a sense of perspective.

She tried to bear this in mind in the mornings while she waited to see what the postman would bring, but she found herself unable to get on until the possibility that that day would bring another card, another message, had been quashed.

The next three cards arrived within a single week at the end of June. By this time she had bookmarked the section in the atlas that depicted the Americas and, on account of the fact that it appeared unlikely that Ernest could have travelled the length of Central America in so short a time, she assumed that she had the undoubted vagaries of various primitive postal systems to thank for this bonanza.

As each one arrived, Hilda barely glanced at the messages. All she had eyes for was the stamps.

On the first one, from Belize City, the rather dull stamp was in the upper left corner. The book interpreted its message as: *Though Our Bodies Be Parted, Our Hearts Are Entwined.* On the second, from a city called Managua which the atlas told her was in Nicaragua, the stamp was brutally perfunctory and had been rotated ninety degrees and placed midway down the left hand edge intimating that Ernest wished, to a degree that made her blush, that their bodies were not parted at all. And the third of the cards, from San Salvador, conveyed the message: *I Hope I Do Not Presume Too Much.*

If it was presumption, she found that she did not mind at all.

Frank had not been a presumer. His letters had been as rambling as two sheets, both sides, of Navy notepaper could possibly allow, wittering at length about the exploits of crew mates she had never met and only ever skirting on matters of intimacy. Frank would never have known how to say two things at one time. His stamp was always firmly in that right hand corner. Equally predictable, was that he signed every letter off saying that he would be home with her soon, usually squeezed in at the bottom as if that weren't as important as all the other nonsense he'd filled the pages with. And it had been a lie, of course. He had left England, grinning in his new Navy garb, and he hadn't come home again.

Hilda rolled up the top of the bureau and unlocked the private drawer tucked under the letter rack. His letters were still there. Of course they were: they'd been unlooked-at these last six years, with only the perishing of the pink rubber band evidence that time had passed. The only occasion that she'd opened this drawer since Frank's death had been to add the last letter, the one that had arrived like a lost dog more than a month after the official telegram. That letter lay loose on top of the bundle. It had become waterlogged during its route home to her and the paper was bloated stiff, the ink washed out so that only her name and part of her address were legible. Really, as the postman had remarked when he had delivered it, it was a miracle that it had got to her at all. It smelled tainted.

Hilda spread Ernest's cards on the blotter in the order she had received them. Touched each of the stamps in turn. Then, smiling, she gathered them and placed them on top of Frank's letters.

Hilda had never been the sort of person who cried at funerals. She believed that when a person has left you, they are gone and there's no point in dwelling on it. She had attended Frank's memorial service, but she had not cried. The other wives told her she was very brave. It was not bravery. Frank had been, in her way of thinking, already dead from the moment his boat left the harbour. Marion had called her a cold bitch.

She was continually surprised to find that she did not feel the same way about Ernest's departure. His cards maintained a connection in a way that Frank's letters from the war never had. Hilda took time to warn herself to be wary of fancy. Anything could happen. Ernest's business could fail, or succeed better then he hoped. He could be detained abroad indefinitely.

She received another card in the August. This time the message on the card and the one conveyed much more succinctly by the placement of the grim, smeary Chilean stamp amounted to the same thing: his business was concluded and he was returning to England. To her. *I Shall Be With You Soon*, the stamp said.

She placed that card in the pocket of her apron. Sometimes, she took it out to look at. Mostly, it was enough to simply be aware of its presence. A charm. A daily reminder that Mr Harman was coming home. Without the card, the message, the stamp, she would have found it difficult to believe that he would be *home soon*. Hilda didn't know how long *soon* might be. A month? Two months? More? Her imagination had him walking through the door on the anniversary of his departure. That would seem apt.

The first month passed without straining her expectation. The second also. It was only towards the end of October, when the bookings began to dry up and she had fewer and fewer guests, that she began to think about that ship, out there somewhere, tiny on the scale of the atlas, ploughing its way through ferocious foreign waters. She stopped looking at the atlas.

As the year slipped into dark November she removed Ernest's card so that she could wash her apron but, instead of transferring it to the pocket of the clean one as had become her habit, she placed it on the bureau. Some time after that she tidied it away with the rest in the secret drawer. A week later she locked the drawer and scrolled the bureau shut.

Without boarders to cater for, Hilda started visiting tearooms again. The Regent on the parade, The Albany. The Continental, of course. She went in the early afternoons when there was best chance of getting a table by the window and a view of the Channel. Once, as she entered The Excelsior, she thought she saw him, but before the bell had stopped jingling she realised her mistake. As ever, that day, she supped without company. She made no special plans for Christmas.

When the letter arrived in December, it was hardly a surprise. It was the black-bordered sort, which demonstrated that someone in his family – his sister it turned out – respected tradition, and its contents were brief and to the point. Ernest's ship – a Peruvian vessel named the *Valparaiso* and under the command of an apparently fool-hardy and reckless Uruguayan captain – had attempted to negotiate the Magellan Strait in a storm. The last reported position had been off southern Chile in late August. No wreckage was found. No bodies. Only now could the authorities declare Ernest Harman, along with the rest of the passengers and crew, legally dead. There was to be a memorial service in his home town up in Yorkshire and, as the proprietor of his last know British address, Hilda was invited to attend.

She threw the letter on the fire. When someone left you, they left you. And Mr Harman had left her all but a year since. After a moment's thought she retrieved the rest of his cards from the bureau and disposed of those too. And after a further moment she did the same with Frank's letters as well. The water-spoilt one sizzled as it caught alight, as if it contained grains of sea salt.

The next morning when she came down, she saw a postcard on the mat. She stared at the white rectangle from the foot of the stairs. She shut her eyes and, since when she opened them again it was still there, it could not be what it had at first appeared. It was just the similarity that had shocked her, after all plain postcards were hardly unusual. Approaching, she could see that this one didn't even look like his. Those broad pen strokes were conspicuously absent. In fact the card, she saw as she bent to pick it up, was entirely blank. She grimaced on discovering that the thing was also damp, as if it had been left outside in the rain. Possibly at the harbourside, judging from the kelpish odour.

The only feature of note was the stamp. A horrid scabrous thing that appeared to have been partially burnt and then left to mildew. The original colours were impossible to tell, but they had been badly inked and bled once wet into a black-green smear that obscured whatever the image had been and rendered the writing around the periphery into a strange and unpleasant alphabet.

Hilda immediately put the card in the dustbin, intent on forgetting about the thing. It could not, after all, be meant for her. Clearly, knowing that she had received similar in the past, the postman must have guessed that she might be the recipient for this unaddressed artefact. The fool.

It was just… *the stamp*. Its angle and placement at the base of the card. She held out for all of twenty minutes before finding it in the book and reading the words: *Do Not Forsake Me.*

Hilda went to The Continental and watched the harbour until the tearoom closed. The ships coming and going as always. By the time she returned home she had cleared her thoughts of fancies. She put the atlas and the stamp book in the dustbin and went to bed.

The next day was the anniversary of her last day with Ernest, but she spared it not a single thought. She rose early and scrubbed the house from top to bottom. She arrayed the Christmas cards on the mantle and hung the holly and put red ribbons on the aspidistra. She thought about telephoning Marion in Cardiff, but decided it would be a waste of tuppence.

The first post brought her no mail, but it was waiting when she returned from placing her order with poulterer. The card was as blank as before, and this time it bore two of those disgusting stamps. They said: *Do Not Forsake Me* and *I Long For Your Touch.*

Hilda stared at the thing, speechless with anger. She looked around, peered wildly into the front garden and the street beyond, expecting to see, what? Someone watching her, laughing at the effects of their cruel prank? There was no one there. Of course there wasn't.

No one knew.

She made a show of ripping the card up. It tore softly. The pieces clung to her fingers as she tried to toss them away.

That afternoon, Hilda sat in the parlour and grimly watched the front path. There would be words when the postman came with the second delivery. She sat there until dark but she did not see him. Eventually, she got up to start her dinner. She did not mean to look when she passed through the hall, but couldn't help herself. There on the little table where she had used to stack Ernest's letters was a small pile of white rectangles. Four, five six of them, she counted with her heart in her mouth. Soft and saltily damp and blighted by those cancerous stamps. They all said the same thing.

I Shall Be With You Soon

Hilda stared at the awful things. They were impossible. *He was gone.* And she dropped them with a small scream when she heard the noise at the door, saw the letter box creak open. The smell of something sea-rotten made her gag. The card, slowly pushing through the aperture made her scramble up the stairs and barricade herself in her bedroom.

In the darkness, she burned with fear behind the stout door. She pressed an ear to the oak and heard, at first, nothing. Then a soft, measured scuff, that was *so* like slippered feet on carpet, that *could* have sounded normally and wonderfully domestic, if only she hadn't known that it was absolutely impossible.

The sounds stopped at her door. There was nothing for an age. Long enough that she felt the first glimmer of hope that she had imagined the whole thing. Fancies never brought you any good. When someone leaves you, they are gone and do not reach out to contact you from wherever they are across the wide, grey sea, no matter how much you might want to hear all the things they have been saving up to say to you.

Then, slowly, it was slipped under her door. A card, with no writing, that would have been neat and white and safe, were every inch not covered with stamps.

Neil Williamson

One of the aspects of supernatural fiction I've always loved is when the spectre in the story attempts to communicate with the living. There's a terrible clarity to the messages of the dead and very few of us really want to hear what they have to say.

Sweeter Than

The music here is different. Even after twenty years Sheena still thinks so. The high-stepping tempo, the bright accents, the relentlessly jaunty beat, all aspirational flutes and brassy braggadocio. Back home, she is certain the music had an easier roll, a spark of rough wit, a playful meter. This is not nearly so demanding. Twenty years, though. She concedes the possibility that the memory may be romanticised, just a little. More than ever these days she thinks about going back to find out, but never has. Not since the travelling song came tripping along and pulled her parents and herself down the long road south.

Here, in this bar, the music ticks time. Like a metronome or a clock or a bomb, but with the cocktail-hour swing of shaker and cabasa. A veneer of good times stretched over the resolution of the day. A coda of good cheer, whether you've earned it or not. The sung-shouted orders and beep of the tills counterpoint the music. The television football commentary and the disharmonious squall of the skew-tied suits add another layer. Chris said this was supposed to be a quiet place. As if there's ever a quiet place in this city. Like the tempo ever drops.

Sheena checks her watch, straightens her houndstooth hem, and takes a long sip of a pinot the same damson shade as the lipstick she sketched on in the work loos after the account review overran. The wine is mellow, but sweet. Everything here is so sweet. *Sweet and neat and bang on the beat.* Nervously, she taps the pointed toes of the couture shoes that she squeezed into in the elevator. Still thinking of home, she remembers a song her gran used to sing about a quine and a loun. She tries to hum the melody now, but the music isn't having it. Self-conscious, she stops and watches the football instead. It's an international match, an anthemic to-and-fro of clashing harmonies and she knows the song of neither side.

"I'm *so* sorry." Chris's tenor voice stretches the vowels with real regret. His face is white from the cold, pink from running. The hem of his Crombie drips with gutter splash; his briefcase stuffed under one arm so that he can proffer the flowers he stopped to buy even though he was running late.

"Oh, don't worry." She smiles, completing the conciliatory couplet. Hears in her own voice those long vowels, those soft r's. Back home *sorry* and *worry* don't really rhyme. Twenty years of trying to fit in have rubbed the edges off her accent. Once, she struggled to make herself understood here. Now, she almost mistakes herself for a native.

She hears it again at the bar, buying him a pale ale – *to keep him hale*, the barmaid trills, winking as they make their transaction – and another glass of wine for herself. Is conscious of it at further random moments during the evening, first in the bar and then over dinner.

For a wooing shop, the restaurant is actually pretty tasteful. There are candles but they are not perfumed, the décor is romantic but not fussy, the *tables-pour-deux* are cosseted in booths, padded velvet affording the occupants privacy as they attempt to weave their courtship duets. That any song at any table on any given night is pretty much identical to the next is irrelevant. The job of the wooing shop is to make every customer believe their experience is special. Some people get addicted to romance. Treating each wooing as if it's the first time, trying to tease the music into that unmistakable swirl of violins that heralds a love song and brings the waiters around to *ahh* in syrupy harmony. But for most people the glamour only works when you're young and starry-eyed. After that, you know the pretext for what it is.

Wooing Shops. Back home they call them *Lumber Rooms*.

Matt brought her to a place like this, if perhaps a bit more up-market, before they married. It had been an…*awkward* evening. Not what she'd expected at all. Matt's burnished baritone was not a voice for duets. Its volume alone left little room for anyone else, let alone violins. Matt, of course, hadn't cared. Sheena already knew he was no romantic. She often thought he would not have bothered with marriage at all if his family and the firm, following his recent rise to partner, had not expected it. If the music had not demanded that this was the time for that particular cadence of his life to be neatly, sweetly resolved.

Sheena should have walked away, but she had been young. Starry-eyed. New in the office, her second job out of college, she had been pretty and she had been reserved. Exactly what Matt was looking for. At the time it had suited her to believe that he'd fallen head-over-heels in love with her. So she had gone along with it, even without violins.

The years following her family's relocation were difficult. Throughout her teens she struggled with the music, with the stuffy, four-square traditionalism of the southern suburbia she found herself growing up in. The orderly rows of square, redbrick houses. The happy, harmonious neighbouring families born to their metre. The neat, sweet, on the beat completeness of it all. Sheena's accent refused to let her voice blend, the rhythm of her northern words awkward and jarring. By the time she forced herself through college and succeeded in negotiating the employment market, she had made herself small and silent, reducing her engagement with the music to a bare minimum.

So what if she entered into a marriage where she was not her husband's harmony and counterpoint? She told herself instead that she was his grace notes, but deep down she did not believe that either. Deep down she said, *fuck it*. Why should she do what the music expected? If love did not matter to Matt, she saw no reason why it should matter to her.

Of course, the music had different ideas. There were dropped beats at important dinner parties. There was screeching disharmony with the in-laws whenever the inevitable subject of children arose. And in the bedroom, the music played her at her own game – its rhythms led only to Matt's pleasure.

On the afternoon that the music changed its tune, she realised she had been listening to the faint tinkling of disconsolate piano for several minutes before recognising it for what it was: their breakup song. The instant she acknowledged as much, the phone rang. Her so-called friend, Imogen, calling to tell her about Claire.

There was a long time between Matt and Chris. A time during which the music mostly left her alone to get on with her life. On the rare occasions that she met someone it mocked her with variations of the tinkly piano melody she'd heard that day. After a while she got the message and gave up trying.

Chris, then, was an accident. She met him queuing for pre-work coffees; shared raised eyebrows and wry smiles at the attempts of the barista chorus to find some sort of rhyme in the names written on the beverage cups. On a whim that day she had spelled her name out the way it is on her birth certificate rather than the version she had adopted at her first school after the move. The baristas predictably had faltered at the *io* and choked on the *gh*. Sheena had smiled as she took her coffee, but Chris had laughed aloud. The next day he changed his name too, tricked it out with K's and Z's. The day after that they were both at it. This became a thing. And once they tired of it, their thing became a few minutes of shared daily experience. A friendship. They talked and, in those exchanges, Chris contributed little, wanting to hear her voice, forcing her to sing. He was indulgent, attentive to her best attempts at those southern vowels and soft consonants. She liked that. When he admitted sheepishly that all this time his office was several blocks and several other coffee shops away, she liked that more.

The first date was a West End show. A musical. Sheena admired the way the composers fitted other music on top of *the* music, simple melodies that chimed resonances from the real thing. Tunes that were like the real music, but not. Only pretend. On the way to the tube she and Chris had walked arm in arm, and sung the finale song together. The music let them. Never once did she hear that sour piano and, after a while – because it was only pretend – she stopped listening for it.

Dinner is pleasant – more than *pleasant*: enjoyable, maybe even fun. Sheena has laughed more in the last two hours than in the previous ten years... but there are no violins to be heard in their corner of the wooing shop. Sheena's chief reaction to this is relief, which surprises her.

A Brylcreemed waiter clears their plates – Chris' scraped clean, hers puddled with the sticky plum sauce that all but overwhelmed otherwise savoury duck. Then, cued by a saucy trombone-slide in the music, the waiter sings: "Would you like the dessert menu? Or do you need to get along?" He winks cartoonishly at Chris. "Perhaps you've matters pressing, and something sweeter waits at home?"

Chris, bless him, blushes. "Oh, surely, no repast's complete." He stammers a little as he sings. "If the suppers must forego the sweet." He orders pie. Sheena would have been happy, regardless of the waiter's innuendo – the restaurant no doubt makes a lot of pudding sales that way – to have left, but she appreciates Chris's gallantry so she orders cheese. It is served with salty crackers and an apple that for once is almost tart.

When they leave the restaurant, she sings: "Let's go to the river.

Let's walk by the waterside." She realises that the idea might be considered romantic even though the rain, if anything, has worsened; but romance is not her motive. The river is where the music of the city meets the music of the sea. That music's concerns are deeper, slower and universal. The river, she has found, is one of the few places where she can relax. And, more than that, the river connects. She has heard that the water carries the melodies of every shore it touches and if you spend enough time at the riverside, its music will grant you a glimpse of home.

Sheena cannot say with any great certainty whether that is true. Sometimes while she sits here, she hears a snatch of a refrain that reminds her of home... but perhaps she only imagines she does.

They stroll along the embankment, listening to the music: the basso roll of water to their left and wash of traffic to their right, the castanets of their heels, the complex syncopation of the rain on Sheena's umbrella, all fitting easily into its ebb and flow. Sheena's pretty certain Chris is going to want to kiss her. This is their third date after all. And three is the music's magic number.

She hasn't been kissed for a long time. When Matt kissed her he used to make a lemon face.

Back home there was a game. Schoolgirls learned it the summer before they went up to the academy. The music brought them a new melody and sisters and older friends taught them the hand-me-down words that went with it. They sang the song while they roamed the precinct in giggling gangs, crowding the sweetshop and clamouring for paper pokes filled with confectionery. Every girl knew the words. Even the shy ones like Sheena, even the ones who would rather kiss each other than the boys.

I'm going to take that loun o'mine and winch him till the clock chimes nine. Kisses sweet as they can be. Kiss him once and he'll be mine if he kens the flavour o' me!

On the benches at the Post Office corner they'd opened their paper bags. The flighty, flirty girls had glossy red sweets, full and fruity. "Kisses sweeter than strawberries," they chanted. "Sweeter than raspberries. Sweeter than cherries." They each licked one and circled their mouths like lipstick. A challenge to the boys to make a song out of guessing the flavour and, if they were smart and wanted another, to declare that it paled in its sweetness compared to the kiss itself.

43

The self-assured girls could afford to be more subtle. The contents of their bags were spheres of spiralling black and white, tawny gold or deep brown. "Sweeter than mint. Sweeter than honey. Sweeter than cinnamon." They sucked, long and confident, until their mouths were full of the flavour.

Sheena, who never had much of a sweet tooth, didn't care what boys thought of her and had no immediate intention of kissing one to find out, chose the same sweets as the girls who were neither flagrant nor confident: yellow lemons fizzing with sherbet and sour nuggets of acid-green. If they were feeling mean the other girls sang: "Sweeter than lemons. Sweeter than vinegar. Sweeter than poison."

Sheena has a poke of sweeties in her coat pocket now. Green apples. She gets them from a stall at the Saturday market near the little flat she bought when the divorce settlement came through. It's become her ritual to peruse the colourful jars, contemplating what to buy, although invariably she chooses the same thing. There are little bags of green apples to be found in the pockets of coats and the bottoms of handbags. She sooks the sweets on the subway, crunches them to shards when she's working late. Sometimes, she'll drop a couple of them into neat vodka when she's watching movies at home, rattling them around the glass with the ice cubes. Green apples aren't nearly as sour as the soor plooms and acid drops she remembers, but they're the closest she can get here.

She wants one now. To pop it in her mouth and feel the comforting weight of it on her tongue, the tick of it against her teeth, to relish the sharp zing that punches through the sweetness.

She imagines Chris making a lemon face.

At least she has the song to hum. *Sweeter than, sweeter than.* By the water, the quiet phrase skites across the river's deep draw.

Chris squeezes her arm through her coat. "You sound happy."

"Happy?" She echoes his melody with raised eyebrows. It's been a long time since she would have described herself as happy.

"Happy." She sings it and when he choruses with her it sounds almost like a proper harmony.

There's a bench under a streetlamp. With the rain relenting, Chris tugs and they sit. The music flows past them, around them, like they are on an islet between the espresso-cranked metronome of the city and the sinuous meander of the river. Sheena surprises herself to discover how intently she is listening to the swish and swirl. She doesn't know what she's listening for. Piano perhaps, or violins?

There is a rose bed next to the bench. Large blooms nod and glitter with rain. Their perfume is sweet.

Taking her hand, Chris finds an eddy between the ticking and the draw. A few tentative notes, the beginnings of a refrain. "On a wonderful night like this." Rain trickles off his nose, and she doesn't know whether to laugh at the irony or wince at the old fashioned melody he has chosen. Either way, she wants to tell him to stop. There's no point to this. The music will spoil it because, when it comes down to it, she simply won't fit into his sweet, neat, precisely on the beat, life.

"On an evening of such perfect bliss," he continues, and there's a spark in his eyes that says he's perfectly aware of how hackneyed his words are. And corny or not, the words are working. The music stirs, folds around and lifts them. There are stirrings of violins.

Sheena's mouth is dry. Again, she wants him to stop, but now cellos join the violins, swelling beneath Chris's melody, layering it with significance, weight, truth like the layers of a cake. Flutes and bells glister his refrain like icing and decorations. Chris is grinning now, his eyes shining. His hand is locked with her own like jigsaw pieces. They feel *right*. Sheena wants to pull hers away.

A middle-aged couple passing while exercising a white Scottie dog with a tartan collar pause. They smile at each other. The dog cocks its head, smiles too. *Ahhh...* the couple harmonise with Chris's song.

"It would unforgivably remiss..." As he crescendos, Chris's voice takes on a warm tone Sheena hasn't heard before. Deep and soft, like toffee. The music swirls around him, smooth as cream.

Sheena's mouth is suddenly flooded and hungry. She can smell the mellow sweetness of his lips.

More passersby have gathered. A street sweeper in dayglo vest. A gang of chavs. A harassed businessman alights from a taxi, checks his watch, then, smiling, shrugs. The driver, leaving the engine running, joins him. The small crowd of strangers exchange grins and winks.

Ahhh.

"Not to ask you, miss..."

No...Yes.

"For one single kiss."

Sheena can't deny the love song. It bows her head, closes her eyes. The music tremolos. They kiss.

Chris's lips are soft and warm. He tastes of toffee and coffee and obviously, since it's what he ate for dessert, banoffee. He tastes of so much more. The kiss could last an hour and she wouldn't be done tasting him. A lifetime, even.

The kiss ends. That should be the signal for the music to swell and bloom and fanfare into the full-blown duet where the two of them would declare what's in their hearts and on their lips. But it doesn't.

Instead, the music stretches out its suspended chord. Turns the romantic pause into a palpable tension. Amid the straining strings, Sheena hears high, tinkling piano.

She opens her eyes. Chris's face is not *quite* a lemon face. He does his best to disguise it anyway. Squeezes her hand. Whets his lips, pretending to savour as if he'd just kissed homely, blonde, luscious Claire – a strawberry girl if ever there was one – and not this acrid, extrinsic husk of a woman that Sheena has become. Has always been.

Gamely – because his heart is a good one – Chris tries to rescue the situation. He changes his melody. "Your kisses are…" He falters quickly. "Are sweeter than…" *Sweeter than?* If only he knew the irony. "Sweeter than…"

The music stutters. The crowd have fallen silent.

"The word you are looking for." Sheena doesn't sing this. She declaims it flatly, ignores melody and meter entirely. "Is *wersh*."

The word resonates in the sudden silence. In the shocking *absence* of music. Someone coughs. One of the chavs laughs nervously. The businessman mutters to the taxi driver. They re-enter the vehicle and drive off.

Wersh is exactly the right word for what she is. And it has no place in this city.

Chris opens his mouth to try again, but Sheena hushes him. "You won't find a rhyme for me." She declaims again. "Not in your music."

The dog yips and strains as if embarrassed, and drags the couple away from the scene. The chavs disperse. The street sweeper shakes his head and wields his bristly brush again. Strong, even scuffs along the pavement that become a beat, that usher back the music.

Sheena can't look at Chris until he too is walking away. To the sound of tinkling piano.

She sits on the bench by the river in the rain for a while longer. She listens to the music of the river, thinks again about going back to her homeland. She wonders if everyone there is as sour as she is, or if it's only ever been her.

Rising, she walks home alone; her gait as always out of time with the music. From her pocket she extracts a sphere of green boiled candy. She pops it into her mouth.

It's not sour enough and about as sweet as she can take.

Sweeter Than was written for an anthology of stories that showcased words from the Scots language. I chose "wersh" which, roughly, means bitter or sour, but the story is really about having an innate sense of place — and of displacement — and drew on how I felt when I lived in grey, suburban Middlesex in the early 1990s.

Arrhythmia

– and the music floods in, sluicing away the dreams of silence. It's the percussive chink of dishes, the rustle and snap of Dad's newspaper, the excited kettle, the burbling wireless… and from the street outside the window, the muted, muttered march of the workforce heading out to the Factory.

Steve's eyes shutter open like aluminium blinds.

"Work, work, work," the workers drone. Their insistent rhythm heaves Steve out from the clingy embrace of the nylon sheets. "Work, work, work." He scratches the seam of his y-fronts, *scritch, scritch, scritch*, and hates that he did it in time with the song.

Fuck, fuck, fuck, he thinks.

"Fuck, fuck, fuck," he sings in the bathroom as he pisses, flushes, splashes his face with water.

"What's that, Son?" growls his dad from the kitchen. "Better get a shift on or you'll be late."

"Just humming a song," Steve mumbles as he dresses, wondering why his dad always says that. He's never late. He leaves half an hour earlier than his old dears for a start and, even if he didn't, no one's ever late for the Factory.

Mum beams at him through a cloud of ironing-board steam. "Sit down, Son," she trills. "It's on the plate."

Two eggs, a pair of frazzled rashers and a chubby sausage arranged in a greasy face smile up at him, the latest in the daily parade of fixed breakfast grins. He slices through one yolky eye, but any satisfaction it might have given him is nullified by the scrape of the unyielding crockery behind the façade.

Steve chews his food, punctuating with grunts his dad's judgement on the contents of the paper, which amounts to little more than parroting the Governor's pronouncements on everything from efficiency and productivity to popular culture. He eats slowly, not because he's savouring the taste but because when he swallows, everything – the music, the chatter – sort of equals out. He's almost able to pretend it's real silence.

From within the music, there's a squeal of electric guitar feedback, and a cup clatters. A spill of milky tea spreads across the formica.

"Who does she think she is?" Dad baritones. His face is redder than the tabloid masthead scrunched in his fist. "Jumped up little strumpet." He brandishes the paper. A grainy photograph of the miniskirted singer from last night's Top Of The Pops is the evident object of this outburst. "Thinks she's better than the rest of us? Tarty little crumpet."

Steve looks at the picture and remembers the spiky flaming hair, the pvc boots, the screaming, the attitude, and the mercifully brief snippet of something that bore scant resemblance to music.

Arrhythmia. Jimmy Jensen had called her that when he'd introduced the band, before the TV was occluded by Dad's fat arse and that 'music' was abrupted by the click of the dial.

"*Sub-vers-ive*, that's what they're calling it." Dad throws the newspaper down on the table. "It's not *subversive*, it's obscene!"

"Subversive?" Mum looks perplexed. "I don't follow. What does that word mean?"

"It means..." Dad's face goes even redder because he doesn't know, not really. "It means..." The old boy's voice wavers as he casts angrily around the kitchen for something to vent his anger on.

Recognising trouble, Steve pushes his plate away, downs his tea and stands. "God save the Queen!"

Jerked out of his aimless rage, his father also stumbles to his feet, and his mother at her ironing board straightens herself smartly. "God save the Queen!" they intone together.

Mum's habitual, "And God bless us, every one," follows Steve through to the hall where he throws his donkey jacket over his overalls and grabs his satchel. "Have a lovely day at work, Son." The front door clatters shut behind him.

There are eight paving slabs between the door and the gate. The path exactly bisects the lawn and is bordered by roses. The plants are budding, but will not blossom until the first of May, signalling the start of summer. Their garden, and their neighbours', and all the gardens in the street, in the town. An orchestrated unfolding of colour. Steve hates summer because that's when the music quickens pace, making the endless routine of *work, eat, play, sleep*, even harder to bear.

"Work, work, work." There are still workers filing past the gate, heading for the bus stop at the end of the street. As soon as Steve joins them, his feet fall into step. There is no escaping the compulsion to walk in time with the rest, to chant their morning mantra.

"Work, work, work," they all sing, but in Steve's mind the words are: *fuck, fuck, fuck.*

A gargantuan, multi-storied bus, red as a dragon in its Factory livery, lumbers away as he approaches the stop, but that doesn't matter because there will be another soon enough. There's always another bus for the Factory. A small crowd is already gathering and, while they wait, a portly man decides it's time for a song. He climbs up onto a low wall, sticks his thumbs under the bib of his overalls, and tenors: "Every morning at the count of eight, my friends and I all congregate, at our old street corner where we stand and wait for the daily ride to The Factory." It's an old music hall song, but it's eternally popular. People start to clap in time; a few hum along, encouraging the man to continue with the second verse.

"Well, we all pile in 'fore the toot at nine, and I takes my place on the production line, and consider it my fortune fine, to make my living at The Factory. But there's something on my mind all day. That I value more'n my penny's pay."

"I..." Some of the crowd join in, swelling the protracted note and beneath their voices the music too gathers for the chorus. "*Work, work, work* with all my might. So I can *munch, munch, munch* with my fork and knife. And then I'll *dance, dance, dance* to my heart's delight, before I *sleep, sleep, sleep* a peaceful night."

Since the bus has still not made an appearance, the man rolls on with the next verse and by the time the chorus comes around again most of the crowd appear to be in the singing mood.

"I'll *work, work, work* my natural life. So I can *munch, munch, munch* on gravy pie. And then I'll *dance, dance, dance* with my neighbour's wife, and only *sleep, sleep, sleep* when it gets light."

It's a song of optimistic fantasy whose many verses become progressively more ridiculous, developing from a hymn to duty and hard graft to claims of the kind of hedonism that none of these people have encountered outside of saucy postcards and the Lenny Harris show on TV. One reason that Steve leaves for work earlier than his parents is that he cringes at the gusto with which his father sings this song. And wants to die when his mum joins in with the actions.

"I *work, work, work* my blasted life. So I can *munch, munch, munch* till I split my sides. And then I'll *dance, dance, dance* throughout the night, before I *sleep, sleep, sleep* with my neighbour's wife."

The song continues as the bus jostles them through the city's ordered streets of identical red brick walls and postage stamp lawns, picking up more passengers, more singers of the song, until the enormous vehicle is full and it heads straight for the centre of town, for the towering stacks of The Factory.

"I'll *work, work, work* my neighbour's wife. And I'll *munch, munch, munch* on her gravy pie."

The last chorus resounds around Steve as the bus rumbles through the imposing gates.

"And then I'll *dance, dance, dance* till I'm berserk, and I'll *sleep, sleep, sleep* when it's time to... *work*."

The workers spill out of the bus in good humour, traipsing up the steps and following the colour coded corridors towards their assigned hall of the day. The music blends seamlessly with the pounding of the engines of production. Inside the Factory, the two are inextricable.

Steve is a blue, and today his route is a long meandering one that leads him down to a sublevel of the west wing that he is unfamiliar with. He half hopes that today will bring an interesting, even comprehensible assignment, but he's been at the Factory long enough to know how likely that is, so he contents himself with the fervent hope of agreeable companions for the day's toil.

His thoughts circle around one particularly agreeable companion. Half a hope, half a fear. He knows exactly what his mother's response would be if he told her that he'd been stationed next to Sandra McReady three times this month. *Governor's got his matchmaking hat on, Son,* she'd say. *Is she pretty? I bet she's pretty.* In Steve's view, Sandra is in fact very pretty, but he doesn't see what business it is of anyone else's. Especially not the Governor's.

People like Steve's mum believe that everything that happens in life from birth to death – how well you do at school, what grade you'll rise to in the Factory, who you'll marry, and all points in between – are decided by the Governor. Steve can't think of anything more horrible and tells himself that such notions are for the weak-willed, the sheep who have never had an original thought in their lives.

Today's manufactory is a long room. There are narrow windows high on one wall, their light striping the face of the huge clock that hangs from the ceiling, and falling on the spaghetti nest of rubberised conveyor belts below. When Steve finds his assigned place in the assembly line he can't believe his luck, because there she is, already at her station. The trim, blonde figure of Sandra McReady.

She's reading the day's instructions, hazel eyes flicking over the numbered pictures as she memorises the steps. Steve watches her for a few extra seconds as he hangs his jacket on the peg behind his stool, before climbing up beside her. Sandra, he notices, is smiling. A small private smile. A deep, glossy, red smile. The kind of smile you'd expect to see dazzling the boys at a Friday social. Although, that lipstick – There's an off-pitch squeal that might be some misalignment in the factory's machinery, but which really sounds like someone badly abusing a guitar. The sound lingers, fades only reluctantly.

Sandra glances up and catches him staring. Her smile gets wider.

Then the hands of the clock tick on to the hour and the whistles pierce the air. The pulse of the Factory intensifies and the conveyors jerk into life. Steve has barely enough time to adjust the height of his stool and glance at his own instructions before Sandra is placing the first of her finished pieces back on the belt and it's Steve's turn. The module is a lump of grey plastic with moulded apertures, a few already plugged by components, looking like the surviving teeth in a centenarian's mouth. Sandra's contribution is a cream-coloured bakelite plug, Steve's is to twist into place two smoky glass bulbs that resemble the valves that glow orange in the back of the television set. His other neighbour will add a further contribution, and so on. What happens to the module once it is completed is none of their concern.

It isn't difficult work. It requires speed and dexterity, but it is easy enough once you get into the rhythm. And in the Factory, the music is at its most compelling. On the huge booming *one* of the great engines, the squeaking conveyor delivers a new module and Steve grabs a handful of components. On the *two* and *three* and *four*, he *inserts-twists*, *inserts-twists* his bulbs, and then the belt rolls forward again carrying the finished module on, and delivering a new one on the down beat of the next bar. Around the manufactory hall bodies move in time: reaching, tooling, assembling with the beat; breathing on the off-beat. At some point a bell will chime, the belts will still and the workers will be permitted to drink water or visit the toilet, but absorbed as they are by their tasks, compelled as they are by the music, no-one thinks about that until it happens. For now they work, and while they work, they sing.

"We don't know what we're making. We don't know what it's for. If it's destined for a hospital or'll end up in a war. We only know we're working. From dawn till end of day. An honest day's effort for an honest day's pay."

The song carries them through their shift. When their arms tire it lends them strength. When their muscles ache, it soothes them. It moves the hands of the clock around in stealthy intervals so that the morning passes almost without notice. The song thickens with harmonies, complicates with counterpoints. The hall resounds with impromptu calls and responses, but the basic song remains the same. The beat remains constant. The work gets done.

"Did you?" Sandra's eyes are fixed on her work, but this contrapuntal aside is pitched to carry to Steve and no further. "Did you see? Last night on the TV?" She risks a second of eye contact to make sure that Steve has heard her. When she sees that she has his attention, those red lips breathe: "Arrhythmia..."

Steve almost misses a bulb.

Sandra smiles.

The break bell sounds, the conveyors grind to a standstill and the worksong dwindles out, leaving only the boom of the deep engines resounding in the air, vibrating through their feet.

Sandra retrieves her handbag and her pretty beige Macintosh. A nod of the head, a promise in her eyes. Steve stumbles after her. He follows her beyond the line for the water cooler, past the queue for the toilets. There is door, and a corridor, and then another door. And then stairs, stairs and more stairs. The astonishing silver-tipped heels of her ankle boots rimshot on the risers. Below the hem of her workdress, the pale flash of skin in the outrageously ripped stocking sizzles like a cymbal. The blue tail of a tattoo catches him off beat, makes him breathless by the time they reach the door at the top.

"We only have," Steve begins, but his voice comes out flat, atonal, in search of melody and scansion. "Fifteen minutes..." His words drift away over the flat roof, over the pipes and ducts and chimneys, up into the grey, silent air. Because here, by some quirk of architecture, some acoustic accident, there is silence. Or at least as close to it as Steve has ever experienced outside of his dreams. He can still *feel* the thud of the engines. It vibrates the tarmac beneath his feet, jumps through his fingers when he touches the brick chimney breast. But in his ears, there is nothing.

"Hey!"

"What?"

Sandra's red lips are a snarl. "You're the one," she accuses, her words spilling fast and angry. "You're the one! You're the one who's worried about time. Take this home." She's holding out a package. It's square, wrapped in a white polythene bag decorated with a poorly rendered skull and the words *Anarchy Records*. "Take it home. Take it home and listen to it tonight." Her eyes are blazing with something entirely alien to Steve. "And play it fuck-ing loud, all right?"

Steve takes the bag. Then Sandra smiles, stretches up on the toes of her wicked little boots and kisses him. The kiss is short and brutal, and Sandra's lipstick is smeared when it is over. Without another word she re-enters the Factory and disappears down the stairs.

Part of Steve already knows what is in the bag, and part of him doesn't want to confirm his suspicion. He just wants to stand here in the silence a little longer, but there, faintly, is the warning bell that signals the imminent resumption of the shift.

Steve sighs. He flaps open the bag, acknowledges the mini-skirted harridan, the bilious spatter of her name. He closes the bag quickly, slips it inside his coat and reluctantly goes back to the beat.

"Are you sure, Son, that you don't want to come?" Mum fastens the top button of her coat, pats her hair into place. It's the second Tuesday of the month and that means drinks with the Hendersons. Steve stares at his pork chop and colourless, diced vegetables, shakes his head.

Dad enters from the hall. "Come on, lad, it'll be fun." He winks and pats Mum's bottom, yolking the word *fun* with lurid potential.

"You can talk to..." Mum hefts a gift-wrapped box of Matchmakers.

"You can talk to..." Dad grabs the bottle of plonk.

"Jennifer."

"Veronica."

Steve's parents share a look of consternation. Of the Hendersons' two daughters, Jennifer is a year older than Steve and timid as a rabbit, while Veronica is a year younger and a precocious tease.

"No, thanks." Steve snaps his reply, forestalling his parents from saying any more.

When the front door snicks shut, Steve breathes out. One long, slow stream of air. He keeps on blowing out until he is empty, until his lungs ache, but he can still feel his heart. The music, reduced to its lowest volume. *Beat, beat, beat.*

Fuck, fuck, fuck.

Steve clears his dinner into the bin, rinses off the plate and cutlery, puts the things away. Then he goes into the living room and lifts the lid on the record player. To one side of the machine are Dad's records. Cheesy covers depicting men in dinner suits and bowties or women in lamé gowns and towering hair. Burt Goodman, Sylvia Hammond, and Dad's favourite, Charlie Montgomery. On the other side of the turntable, his mother's, much smaller collection of heartthrob chart-toppers. All hair oil, leather jackets with the collars turned up and 'dangerous' winks. To watch his parents listen to them you'd think this music was capable of transporting you, but how can it? There are four measured beats to every one of those bars. No matter how chirpy and bright, how croony and swoony. Four beats. *Work, Eat, Play, Sleep.* Transportation? You'd be as well putting your ear to the factory wall.

Steve slips Sandra's record from the polythene. Holds the garish cardboard square by the corners, by his fingertips. He stares at the sleeve, drinks in the clashing colours, the jagged lettering, the snarling girl frozen in the act of smashing her fist through a pane of glass, teeth bared and red lips parted in a yell. He flips it over, devours the other side too. The track listings: A/ Smash Your Way Out, B/ Tear It Up. The writing credits, the copyright notice, the logo and business address of the record company. Behind the text, a close-up photograph of a bluebottle sandwiched between two plates of glass.

Steve's fingers are shaking as he slides the vinyl out of the sleeve. He tilts it, and the light swims around its glossy grooves. He rotates the knurled switch with a satisfying clunk. The turntable begins to move, and the speaker issues that expectant noise that is part hum and part hiss. Steve turns the volume knob from 2 to 3. The expectation rises. He feels sick, but he doesn't know why. It's just a record. It can't possibly give him what he dreams of. This will be anything but silence.

He drops the record onto the machine. It shrugs reluctantly, rebelliously down the spindle. He watches it for one, five, ten revolutions before plucking up the courage to place the stylus onto the leader.

He realises he is holding his breath.

There's a percussive chunk, followed by a wire-thin whistle of feedback that sounds taut, like a restraint. Then, off microphone: "*onetwothreefour*", and then a crazed, enraged musical beast is released. Growls of guitar, slashing steel claws of cymbals, raging, inchoate screams, barely comprehensible. "Kick 'em down. Beat 'em up. To a pulp. Scream and shout. Smash it. Smash it. Smash it. Smash your way out. Out. Out. Out!"

Steve recognises the hook. On Top Of The Pops that two seconds had been two seconds too long, but now he can't get enough of it. "Smash it. Smash it. Smash it." The song goes on forever. The song lasts two minutes and nine seconds precisely. It finishes with a final foundering thrash, and that is followed by silence.

Steve starts the record again. Nudges the volume up one more notch.

Some time later he is lying on the floor, and shouting: "Smash it. Smash it. Smash it. Out. Out. Out." He's lost track of the number of times he has played the song. The record player's volume is at ten now, and even though the ducks are jouncing against the wallpaper and the crystal ornaments jumping on the mantelpiece, it still isn't loud enough.

Then the music cuts in with a soap-opera melodrama that easily drowns the record out. The room fills with a sickening swell of impending familial discord and framed in the doorway are his parents faces: Dad's red, Mum's ashen.

"Your old man? He actually broke it, man? Snapped the plastic. Like elastic?"

On the Factory roof the next day, Sandra's face is impossible to read. She's done something with her hair, it looks weirdly asymmetrical at the front, ragged at the back.

"I'm so sorry." Steve sings low and earnest, and is perplexed by the huge grin he receives.

"That's so... so... fuckin' cool! Your 'rents are cardboard cut-out cruel. What a pair of waa-aaa-aaankers."

Steve thinks that's going a bit far, but he's not about to admit that right now, so he imitates her melody. "Waa-aaa-aaankers!"

"Too right." She looks up at him through her lopsided fringe. "You know, you're all right. What you doing Friday night?"

"Nothing." Which is true. If Steve had friends that he regularly went out with, or had ever shown any interest in attending the weekend socials at the Factory, no doubt his parents would have added restriction of his movements to the punishment that banned his use of the television and the record player for the rest of the month. But since all Steve ever did was go to work then come home, it had clearly never occurred to them.

For the rest of the week Steve does what is expected of him. He goes to work at eight, he eats at six, he puts his light out and sleeps at eleven. His mother tries to interest him in conciliatory after-dinner board games, but the living room is radiant with Dad's constant glare, so he opts to retire early with a book whose pages he turns but doesn't remember. He doesn't see Sandra again that week, but that doesn't matter. She's written the details down for him on a scrap of paper that is pressed between the pages of his book. On Friday it is a simple matter to repeat the pattern of the previous evenings, then lie awake until the rest of the house has retired before stealing downstairs and slipping out.

The Makers Mark is located at the lower rent end of the Parade. It's a cold night, needles of rain prickling Steve's face and a ragged wind plucking at the tails of his workshirt. He's familiar with the Parade from helping Mum with the Saturday shopping, but that's during the day. These night time shuttered frontages are alien to him, like turned cheeks. The warmly lit windows above, blind eyes.

The segs of his workboots beat their ingrained, infuriating four on the pavement. Steve forces himself to break the rhythm, interspersing lopes and shuffles into his gait. Nothing calamitous happens, but the novelty quickly wears off. It's simply easier to go with the music.

Fuck, fuck, fuck. Steve's breath mists the air, becomes a song he hadn't known was there. "I feel." His melody is low, threaded with minor intervals. "Outside of everything. Outside of living and dying, and laughing and crying. And anything real." Near the grocer's there are some broken food crates. Steve scoops up a piece of wood, drags it along the wall as he continues to sing. "I feel... unreal. Brittle and paper thin. Fragile as butterfly wings, the most delicate things. Touch me..." As Steve rounds a corner he belts the stave satisfyingly against a lamppost. "...and I'll shatter." The upper third of the wood snaps and dangles by jagged splinters. He swings it around in circles as he advances down a side street. "I feel my own rhythm but I'm ruled by the beat. I'm light as a feather, yet chained by my feet."

Ahead he sees a pub. It must be the one he's looking for because there's nothing else out here.

"I know where I'm going from the first step to the last," he murmurs, "but the bus that I'm riding is going too fast." He comes to a halt, throws the broken stick away. He wishes he hadn't come, wants to go home. He wants to be anywhere but home. "I just want to make it stop. I just want to breathe. Jam the hands upon the clock. Hide between the beats." He hasn't a clue where he wants to be.

"I just want to be me," Steve whispers, and finds that he is moving again, closing step by step on the beery lights, the well of muted noise. "I just want to be me. Me. Me..."

Steve breaks off when he realises that there is someone leaning against the wall beneath the swinging pub sign. The corpulent man is wrapped in a woollen coat. He takes a puff of a chubby cigar and blows out exotic smoke. If he heard Steve's song, he gives no indication, but when Steve falters at the door, he glances at last his way. "And if you can't stop moving?" The melody apes Steve's down to the last note, but the clear tenor voice, unmistakeable from the television, is what is amazing. "If there's no such thing as silence? Why not indulge in a little noise and violence?"

"You're the –" Steve begins, but the Governor raises a fat finger to his lips. Then with a tap of glowing ash, he straightens up and saunters off down the Parade, apparently oblivious to the muffled blare that has been issuing from the building all this time.

There is perhaps a measure less of anticipation in Steve's heart as he eases open the pub door and walks into the buffeting cacophony, but it is quickly forgotten when he finds Sandra's hand and manages to lose himself completely in the all-consuming noise that, in the end, is almost as good as silence.

It is only many years later, when he and Sandra are married, that he will look back and feel cheated. Sandra and the others will remember a genuine moment of rebellion. Even if the only thing that gets *torn up* and *smashed out* are the walls of the old Factory, making way for a shinier, sleeker, more productive replacement. Even if people still spend their lives doing the same meaningless, incomprehensible jobs. Even if the changes to come that will feel so fundamental at the time are acknowledged in the end as merely superficial. They will remember Arrhythmia and claim a small part in what they'll call a revolution.

A revolution that began: *onetwothreefour.*

But Steve won't have that. Instead he'll remember the Governor's words. The way they lingered in the air like the cigar smoke, staining everything to come. The way they fell in perfect time with both the music and the pub's muffled chaos, equally bound by those four simple, inescapable, beats.

One, two, three, four.

Work, eat, play, sleep.

Live, marry, fuck, die.

It is only all those years later that he will acknowledge the truth that it seems he has always known. Sometimes, the music might change its tune, but it will never end.

I like to think of Arrhythmia *as my take on a period of UK history in the 70s when the generation gap suddenly widened into a cultural chasm. On one side we had cringe-inducing TV comedies like* On The Buses *and, on the other, the alienation of punk, epitomised in movies such as* Jubilee *and* Breaking Glass. *The story must have struck a nerve with a number of 40-somethings because it was shortlisted for the BSFA short story award.*

Pearl in the Shell

The Victaz crew bombs straight up the back of the bus but Paolo lingers at the top of the stairs, popping his pearls out, casting an ear around the other passengers, on the scope as always for a source of sounds. Over the road rumble and the motor's electric whine, the coughs and sniffs and murmured conversations, he zones in on the tapping of toes and tuneless sing-a-long; looking out for clues to what's cycling through their mixes, what might be hidden away in their shells. You can guess a lot from physical appearance, but a good sourcer uses their ears first and foremost. Paolo's crew haven't come across a shell they couldn't crack given enough time, but it helps to be certain it'll be worth the effort.

Best bet is usually students – wilfully obscure and ever resourceful – or old hipsters who've been around since the days of physical media. Anyone who might conceivably be hiding something a bit different in there. New popular music might have flatlined after ICoSP – the International Copyright Simplification Programme – but more people than the corporations would have you believe still value variety in their music.

Paolo is out of luck with this bunch of West End Wendies though. Exactly the sort that happily gobble down whatever the industry tarts up and slops out in the name of entertainment. Fools like that deserve what they get.

Moseying up to join the others, he passes a woman rattling her fingernails on her armrest with all the natural rhythm of a fibrillating pulse. He jostles her shoulder and is rewarded with a slow-focusing glower that chills right down when she checks him. The inked suit, the shirt with the stiletto-tip collar, the chessboard hair and the pearlescent array of shell-tech devices pierced around his face like a beachcomber's Christmas tree baubles. He grins. She snatches back into her shell and stays there. She's not the only one to notice the crew now. There are glances; distrustful, wary. Good. The crew expects that reaction, *covets* it. It's a proud tradition, rude kids sharing their music with the wider community whether the community likes it or not. Only difference nowadays is they don't know about it until a little present pops up in their mix with the tag: *Mashbombed by Victaz*.

Paolo topples into a seat, eases the pearls back into his ears. Nods approvingly. Swanny's got some beats rolling, ready in case Paolo turns up something of interest. Some mashers go about it full on, nailing a jumble of scraps and slices to a plank of Canto-dub and ending up with the musical equivalent of a horse chewing through a mains cable, but Swanny's subtler than that. His beats are aggressive but he's got a real feel for the dynamics of a good groove that spotlights each of those little snippets of song at the same time as binding them together. That's the secret of good mashing.

When Paolo lenses up a file list of recent finds in the crew's shell-share, Swanny lifts his head and grins.

"What's this?" He says it without moving his lips. Only the others can hear it, in the share. Older people look like bad ventriloquists when they do this, but it comes naturally to the crew. Cell phones were on their way out before they were born. They're the shell generation. Dinks laughs at Paolo when he says things like that. Usually follows it up with some tosh about making the most of every resource in a scarcity economy. *Bollocks*.

Swanny's used to Paolo's little finds but his eyes widen when he runs the first of the files. "Aw, come on, ya perv, that's no real."

"Classic 1970's porno. Lifted it off the lollipop man outside St Agnes's at lunchtime."

Swanny shakes his head. "Dirty old bastard."

"Who's a dirty old bastard?" Dinks drops her prized antique headphones around her neck, paying attention now. Girl's got a sixth sense for fanny. Even monster fanny like this. "Woah! What was it with the seventies man? They never heard of personal grooming?"

They share a round of lulz. Their toons roll around the share, giggling and clutching their sides.

"Sure, but check the music," Paolo says.

They both do. They both nod. "Ya perv," they both say.

This time their lulzing avatars hit Paolo's over the head with cartoon dildos.

"Aye, aye." Dinks is their cracker and, next to fanny and retro tech-chic, the one thing she's got an infallible instinct for is a poorly protected shell. A second or two later, a group of girls appears. Five of them, sixteen or seventeen, school blazers and full make-up, modest shell-tech jewellery: barnacle ear-studs and *chickering* winkle chain bangles. Absorbed in their shell-share, they don't even notice the crew and once Dinks gives Paolo the nod he makes quick work of skimming their files.

Strictly speaking at this time on a Wednesday morning, he and Dinks should be at college. There are exams coming up after all, but Paolo will ace them. Hell, he could write the questions.

Explain the effect that the International Copyright Simplification Programme had on the commercial music industry in the United Kingdom and The United States of America.

What that really boils down to is: *what's the magic number?* At the last count, the magic number was seventeen hundred and seventy eight. That's the exact number of individual and distinct songs recognised by the International Rights Authority. ICoSP came about because DRM didn't work and because the delivery platforms had moved to the automatic micropayment model and because corporate pop music had long been reduced to papping out variation after variation of the same old shit, eventually dispensing with the involvement of writers and performers entirely. So, now there are only so many unique *"combinations of melody, presentation and lyrical sense"*. Everything else is designated a copy.

It shouldn't have been a surprise: ignoring the mostly ignored and easily ripped off fringe artists, the history of commercial music was always more about flogging a formula than it ever was about invention and art. ICoSP was merely the acknowledgement of that fact. It only got really silly with the Universal Pact amendment, proposed by the multinationals who, naturally, were terrified. Once the uber-algorithms had worked out which songs were classed as being essentially *the same*, the amendment determined that the rights would be awarded to the earliest variant still under copyright at the time the statute was adopted as law by the signatory territories.

So now whoever holds the rights for "I Will Always Love You" also gets the cash from a thousand other compositions whose words cover the same general subject matter and have a roughly similar arrangement (and the operative words in that sentence are *general* and *roughly*). It came as a shock to the writers of the huge Euro-pop hit,

"Build You A Wall", that the bulk of their millions in royalties were suddenly diverted to the geniuses who came up with "Bob The Builder". It came as an even bigger shock to discover that the Sex Pistols owned the rights to much of the history of rock and roll. And with the duration limited to fifty years, irrespective of whether the creator was still alive or not, legal battles over the next inheritor of that particular golden chalice had been rumbling on for the best part of a decade.

There you go. Ignoring the looming monster next door represented by the Chinese industry who refused to touch ICoSP with the proverbial barge pole, that's the history of modern music. Sixty marks, please. If he has enough time at the end of the exam, Paolo might be tempted to add a caustic postscript to the effect that it completely sucks that music students actually spend the bulk of their education learning how not to get fined, sued or imprisoned. Hardly anyone writes new music. Some still try – *potentially*, if you managed to write a genuinely original song you'd have the rights brokers battering down your door – but if you attempt to release a composition that matches 51% or more of the 93 points of reference in an existing copyrighted song, the rights for your new effort are automatically awarded to the existing copyright holder and you have to pay them for the privilege of playing the song you thought you just wrote. You'd still get a performance royalty but, as the man said: *Fuck that.*

There is an exception, however. The preview clause. You're legally allowed to play up to two point seven seconds of any song before your app automatically identifies the rights holder and coughs up. And that's where mash comes in. Danceable patchworks stitched together by crews like Victaz – as in *Frankenstein*, yeah? – from slivers you don't have to pay for. It's a loophole they've been arguing about for years, even though mashes themselves are now also copyrightable. The whole thing is frowned upon of course, but the mash charts are one of the few growth areas in the industry.

The greyest area of the whole thing is that the only completely honest way of creating mash is from what you can preview on the net. There was a time when you could find almost anything online, but after ICoSP the former rights owners of tens of thousands of tracks removed them from sale rather than make someone else a little richer every time they were played.

That's why, if you're serious about the art of mashing, about conjuring some sort of originality from a rehash of existing work, you have to go that extra mile to make your source material different from everyone else's. Which means bending the rules a little to see what the world is hiding from you.

The girls are a surprise. One of them has a decent stash of obscure 50s soul, and another appears to have a fascination for the roaring twenties. Both are untapped areas for the crew so, invisibly, Paolo transfers a selection of files from their share to the crew's. Swanny drops them a mash bomb as a thank you. From the way he's smirking Paolo suspects that 1970s pornography will feature prominently.

In the Victaz's share, Dinks's avatar stomps a big boot and executes a shrill two fingered whistle. "Our stop, boyos."

Paolo's proud of the plan they're about to put into action. The problem with random public skimming is that the hit rate is low for the effort required, so they've been looking around for a higher yield potential scenario than the buses and the malls.

Then someone in the music business had conveniently died.

The crematorium is tucked away up on a hill on the city's eastern fringe, just green enough and distant enough from the traffic and general noise to give the illusion of peace. Trudging up the access road, all three find the silence unnerving, so Swanny pumps one of his latest mashes nice and loud and they kick into a swagger as they reach the rows of cars parked along the manicured verge.

Paolo pops open Heather Gilchrist's obituary for some last minute revision. The crew are posing as fans come to pay their respects so, should anyone ask, they have to know at least the names of the old band members, her grown up children, and a few of the songs that had made her famous.

The obit is more a sob story than a celebration. It spends too much time sentimentalising about how the rights crash ruined Heather's life; making the person secondary to the legal fight, the subsequent poverty and the final retreat into reclusiveness when the cancer was diagnosed. The bit that caught Paolo's interest though is tucked away at the bottom. A sentence of speculation about how it's believed that she kept writing, kept trying to make new music, just never released it to the public.

And that's bollocks. No one keeps their music to themselves.

Someone among her nearest and dearest must have copies.

They join the queue of mourners filing towards the door of the crematorium. Dinks is busy with something. Her avatar has changed to her gal-at-work one: swinging pick axe, hard hat and butt cleavage complementing the boots. In the corner of the share is a scrolling shell connection list. By the time they near the door she's cracked over half of them. Paolo wastes no time.

It's amazing what goes on in people's shells. While the mourners shuffle forward, respectful and solemn faced, exchanging murmurs of condolence and regret, they're watching news feeds, playing games, trolling creationist blogs for lulz. One fella is watching a clip of the deceased naked and grinning shyly, her fingers circling an erection, presumably the viewer's own. Paolo wonders if this is a remembrance of a sweet, private moment or simply a spectacular display of lack of respect.

Paolo skims over all this activity without much real interest. What he wants to know is whether she shared those new songs with anyone here. He starts with the porn star: finds his music stash and start shuffling through it. It's no bad selection, with a fair number of artists Paolo doesn't recognise. He instructs his shell to transfer the whole lot, and moves on to their next kind donor with relish.

Then, as he's about to delve into the shell of an older fella – neatly trimmed white beard and one of those old fringed suede country and western jackets that were all the rage a couple of years back – three things happen almost simultaneously. The queue shuffles forward, Dinks mutters, *"aw, baws!"* and a disconnection icon starts flashing above porno boy's transfer.

Paolo stares accusingly at the back of his neck but there's no sign that he's even aware of the crew's intrusion as he ducks under the lintel and nods seriously to someone inside.

"Bastard must have disconnected himself," Swanny says.

"Bit late for a show of respect," Paolo replies.

He's fervently hoping that this won't be a trend when the queue shuffles forward again and then Victaz are the ones under the lintel and their shell-share vanishes. Their faces are still stretched in cartoonish renderings of shock when the usher inside the door asks them: "Family, friends or fans?" The usher is a soft presence but his eyes are granite. They flick to the side and they all see the neatly printed sign on the wall. They all read the words.

"Fans are in the back three rows," the usher says. Meekly, they follow his indicating arm.

"This is no real. Bastards cannae dae that." Swanny thinks he's whispering, but that's not a skill any of them has ever had much practice at. Heads turn.

"Yes they can." Dinks is glowering. "They do it all the time during exams, don't they?" Swanny glowers back. Even at school he never had much reason to enter an exam hall.

As one the crew glare again at the usher, at the sign next to him.

Polite notice.

Out of respect for the deceased, the bereaved have requested that shell connectivity is suppressed in the chapel of rest.

Thank you.

"What are we going to do?" Swanny's not handling this well.

Paolo puts his hand on his arm, but the wee fella shakes it off. "We're going to see this through," he says. "Play our part here as we planned and then blag our way into the after party."

"Reception lunch," Dinks chips in.

"*Reception lunch*, whatever." Paolo takes an angry breath. "Plenty of time to do it then." But from the looks they're getting, the whispers exchanged, he's not at all sure they'll get that opportunity. "Let's just keep it together, eh? See what happens."

The other two nod, and they all sit down.

The assembly of mourners takes place to the accompaniment of sobs, sniffs and a piped acoustic guitar. It sounds familiar, maybe a diluted version of one of Heather's old hits. Then the big fella in the fringed coat steps around the coffin to get to the podium and makes a speech. Seems he was her friend and manager for thirty five years, and now he's assumed the mantle of being angry and bitter on her behalf. He batters on about her talent, how she could've, would've, should've been a global star if she hadn't been screwed sidewise by the system.

"And no one cared." He grips the edges of the lectern, cheeks and neck pink beneath his white beard, and casts an accusation around the room.

"Except for us." His voice loses its bellow, as if he's been punctured in the heart. "Her family, her friends, her fans. When she went underground and had to resort to shell hacks to retain control over her own songs, we kept faith. So we broke a few laws, but I know there's not one soul here who would have not done at least that for her."

While the assembly murmurs assent, Paolo sighs with frustration at the thought of years' worth of original music sitting in these people's shells. He's not used to what he wants being beyond his reach.

The manager hasn't finished. "But she never stopped writing right up until the end. And, my friends, the real scunner of this *fucking cancer* that first took away her voice, then her breath, was that she *did it*. She wrote a song that beat ICoSP, and we'd almost convinced her to go public with it." He slumps, diminished. "But then it didn't matter any more. It *doesn't* matter any more. Even if Heather had given her permission there'd be no point in releasing the song now she's not around to benefit from it. However, as final tribute to a musical genius and a true friend, my friends I think we ought to do her the honour today of listening to Heather Gilchrist's final song."

The big fella steps down and his place at the podium is taken by a skinny girl with a blotchy face. She stares glassily at the audience, turns her gaze to the panelled ceiling. Then, blinking away fresh tears, she starts to sing.

The girl's voice is soft and throaty, but the hushed space lends it body, a shiver of spiritual echoes. Not that you would recognise this as a song. Everything about it is off. The melody skitters around, continually promising to resolve into a tune but then sliding off again. The rhythm has a folky fluidity but that too strains expectations by dropping or adding beats at random intervals. Neither of these tricks is especially new; classical and jazz composers have being doing stuff like this since forever. It's a little like mash, but more organic. The girl's voice grows in confidence until it fills the room and, amid the continuing, soft sounds of grief, other voices pick up the melody and begin humming along.

But the music isn't what makes the song really special.

"What's she singing?" Swanny manages an actual whisper this time. "Is it Gaelic?"

Paolo shakes his head. The lyrics do sound familiar, but he can't actually distinguish them as words. Which is weird because he *knows* the song is a love song. He knows it, but he doesn't know *how* he knows.

"That's not Gaelic." Dinks's whisper is even more awed than Swanny's. "It's –"

"Just listen," Paolo says.

Afterwards, they emerge into sunshine. Stand off to one side as the rest of the funeral's attendees filter past: talking, smiling, their emotional tension discharged. The crew's shells reconnect almost instantly.

"We ready to roll again, Dinks?" In the share, Swanny's toon twangs his braces and hops impatiently from one brothel creeper to the other. Dinks's gal-at-work toon says she's busy on something. She's slid her cans up too, which is her signal for *really*, really, *do not fucking disturb me*. Paolo looks for the list of cracked shells reappearing. The targets are already climbing into cars and driving away.

"Dinks?"

"Forget them." Their girl slips her headphones down.

In the share, Swanny's toon turns bronto and tries to stomp her.

"That wasn't a real language, was it?" Paolo says.

Dinks shakes her head. She's pretty when she twists her smile like that, and she only does it when she's about to say something smart and is trying to find a way of saying it that the other two will understand. "According to the algorithms it's not a *recognised* language. But I think it is a real one."

"How did you manage to run the algorithms?" Bronto-Swanny pulls a face then shrinks back to normal. "Everyone was disconnected in there, man."

Dinks slides a scuffed digital recorder from the pocket of her blazer. A fan-shaped shell-tech dongle black-taped into a socket on the top. She's recorded the song inside, then uploaded it and run the algorithms while they've been talking. She always did like her retro gear.

Paolo grins. "You got it all?

She grins back.

"And the language?"

She grins even wider. "It's actually pretty neat. She invented one of her own. A collection of phonemes that don't in themselves form actual words, but still manage to convey the sense of the song." She looks from Swanny to me and back again. "C'mon, you understood it was a love song, right? You just didn't need lyrics to get it. We're so conditioned to the conventions of pop music that for the sentiments of most songs we no longer actually need the words, just their shapes. Corporate music hasn't cared about original lyrics for decades. Gilchrist went a step further and distilled it down to a musical language."

While she's been talking Paolo's done a bit of research and now pops up a Wikipedia citation on *Sigur Rós;* another on *The Cocteau Twins.* "It was a beautiful thing, but it's hardly a unique idea."

Swanny says. "Still passes the test. It could make someone a lot of money."

Dinks completes the collective chain of thought. "Whoever released it first would sure as hell cash in. Gilchrist's family are all about respecting her memory for now, but sooner or later they'll realise what they're sitting on."

"So, anyone with a copy of that music would have to work fast to stake their claim."

In the sunshine, outside the now empty crematorium, they all nod. In their shell-share, their toons do too.

On the bus back, there are a few other passengers that under normal circumstances might be worth cracking for a look-see, but the crew have other things on their minds.

"Fuck it." The crew look up, surprised that Paolo says this out loud. "Gilchrist's music is cool, but what is it really? A weird shit tune that drones on forever. Might have been her idea of art but it sure as hell isn't ours. Do we really want Victaz associated with something like that?"

Swanny grins like the bear who ate the baby. An instant later a track starts playing in their share. It's classic Victaz mash: Swanny's beats collaged with scraps of nineties R'n'B, sixties Northern Soul, the voice of Bob Wills, the king of Western Swing, calling out *howdy-ho!* And interspersed between these, threaded through them, snatches of Heather Gilchrist's last song. The meaning-laden but wordless vocal lilt is the only thing in the mash that repeats and, in doing so, it becomes something pretty old-fashioned: a hook. For mash this is revolutionary.

Swanny looks at the others in turn. "Yeah?"

Paolo and Dinks both say: "yeah."

He pushes it global.

By the time they get off the bus the track is getting download traffic and airplay in Edinburgh, Moscow, Rio. By the time they're home at Paolo's flat, it's made it onto night club playlists in Adelaide and Bangkok. Swanny prepares half a dozen variations, each of them mining a new facet of Gilchrist's song for its hook and ready to roll out to up the stakes when the first of the copycats appears.

The mass-shares go mental for it. This is Victaz's fifteen minutes global. Paolo charts their rocketing notoriety as the crew hops aboard the tube for that evening's sourcing. Because a mash crew's like a school of sharks. They have to keep predating or they grow old and cold. Always cracking, always sourcing, always looking for the next new thing.

There will be other songwriters' funerals – the city once had a lot of musicians, and they're all getting to that age – but until then who knows what else is waiting to be unearthed, cleaned up and cut into something glittering and abrasive and new.

The world tires of innovations faster than toys at Christmas. Anyone who thinks different doesn't know the music industry.

One of the things that Science Fiction allows you to do is explore the things that scare you without getting a reputation for being a fearmonger. For me, the uncertainty inherent in the current trends of online music provision and the constant re-examining of copyright law suggests dwindling returns for all creatives, but songwriters in particular.

Killing Me Softly

One thing that never changes in this city. The sound of the rain. Glasgow's eternal, percussive soundtrack. An even drumming on the concrete of this suburban driveway, a timpanic roll on the roof of the Renault Inspira parked up overnight, the occasional clear plink as drips from the porch find the milk bottles on the step, all threaded through with the almost melodic trickle of gutter-wash down the drain.

Where the rain hits the body splayed and broken across the Inspira's bonnet and windshield there are deadened notes.

My name is Doloreta Siwek. I'm CID. And I hate it when something spoils my listening pleasure.

The body belongs to Maggie Martin. She's not even cold yet but the facts are already accreting around her like an informatic old chalk line. She's forty four. A lecturer in languages at Caledonian. Mother of two distraught teenagers. Divorced, but aren't they all out in the Mearns?

Maggie's neck is broken from the fall. The rain is ruining the effect of a blonde streak job that must have cost her upward of a ton at the Rainbow Rooms. But that was some weeks ago; now her roots are showing. Her ends are split too, and turning pink from the blood pooling in the dent she's made in the car.

I look up into the rain. The house is a two storey Victorian villa. It's got those little attic dormers, like surprised eyes. One of them is ajar. That's how she got out onto the roof.

A stutter blast of actinic light freezes the image, and I take it all in: the fancy house, the slick slates, the open attic window. The rain like marbles.

No question what happened. The mystery is why.

The forensic photographer's flash whines. The various attending parties exchange professional mutters as they go about their business. Someone laughs; inside the house someone sobs.

And the rain is just rain. Not for the first time I think: *There is no music in life. Not any more.*

Back at the station, the chalk line is complete and Magnus has begun shading in the middle. "The gay divorcee. Literally so." Magnus dresses like a slob to fit in, but when he talks he gives away how ridiculously over-qualified he is for this job. "But according to the kids, there's been no recent paramours."

"Anything else?" I'd guessed that much from the roots. "I suppose a note would be too much to hope for?"

Magnus shakes his head. "No note. She was into karaoke, though." He forestalls my sigh. "I mean *seriously*. Competition level."

That's an interesting point at least. Setting aside my own personal feelings on the world's obsession with mimicry. Never mind the hollowing in my heart when I remember all the little venues that used to shake nightly to the sound of little bands performing their own little songs, that closed down one by one as the legacy of X-Factor really took hold and franchised 'star search' outfits opened up in their place. Forget the flame of rage that flares up inside me like the burn off from a Grangemouth chimney every time I see real talent wasted on trying to make it via those cut-throat contests. All of that is personal and I deal with it. I'm the only one that seems to care, after all. Suffice to say that at a certain level karaoke is a serious business, and more than a little blood has been shed in its name.

"Did she have a competition coming up by any chance?"

"Regional semis at the Crystal Palace on Friday. She was rehearsing hard. The kids appear to have been pretty supportive but I suppose anyone forced to listen to the wrong song played over and over for hours at volume might lose it." He gets nothing from me for that. "Well, anyway, they've both been spending a fair bit of time with friends lately."

I give him a belated, grudging nod that it wasn't impossible. "They certainly wouldn't be the first to get off on the grounds of domestic cruelty."

"So you *are* thinking murder?"

"This wasn't suicide, Magnus." It was true that the karaoke circuit attracted its fair share of the disillusioned, and on those occasions where they were forced to confront the gulf between their ambitions and their talent reactions could be unpredictable, but, as long as they had an audience, suicide was usually low on their list of options. Magnus' suggestion didn't sit right, though. "But, no. I doubt it was the kids."

"Which leaves?"

"An ex? A rival? A –" I don't complete that sentence. I've a feeling I don't like. "What was the song?"

Magnus grins. "You won't believe it. R Kelly's *I Believe I Can Fly*."

I believe it. My feeling has just coalesced into a punch in the guts from a cold and wet fist.

The Crystal Palace on Jamaica Street used to be furniture shop, then a chain pub. Now it's a hub for some of the more serious wannabes. There are a lot of competitions out there. The ones held in the swanky venues you see in the centre pages of the newspapers offer unbelievable rewards, but those competitions are for dreamers. They run Europe- or even World-wide, and are almost impossible to win. Circuit pros concentrate on the smaller contests. They're not only more winnable but also allegedly more about talent than image. That's about as close as our society gets these days to keeping it real. Back when, there were musical instrument shops on this street, famous venues on the corners. All of that is gone now and there's nothing between the city centre and the river worth a damn.

I drop in to talk to the manager just after they open up. We sit on the stage beneath the big projector screen. In his thin cardigan thrown over a buttoned up Fred Perry and skinny jeans, Graham Phillips dresses like an eternal indie kid with the permanent expression of worn surprise of someone wondering where his scene went. "I can't believe that," he says. "Maggie May's dead?"

"You called her that?"

"She called herself that. Sort of a *nom de plume* and a theme song rolled into one. It was one of her favourites."

"Was she popular? Among the crowd in here?"

He tells me about his crowd. There's a good handful of regulars and they consider themselves more of a community than the big nights at the ABC or the Garage. Sure there's competition, sure there are rivalries, but no dirty stuff. There hasn't even been so much as a salt-sabotaged Highland Spring in his time here. Generally his crowd are supportive. They appreciate a good chanter. When a singer brings authenticity to a song their applause is genuine, when they augment it with a little of themselves, it doubles. They coax, they cheer, they sing along.

"Maggie was one of the best for that," he says. "She acted the mother to the younger ones. She loved to find out their story. Help them achieve the next step in their journey. She found it inspirational."

"She believed she could fly," I remind him.

Phillips goes tight about the face. The way that makes it difficult to speak. I revert to the professional voice.

"So were there any new additions to your happy little family?"

"There are always new faces. Every week another one plucks up the courage to reach for their shot at fame," he says. "And Maggie knew them all."

The afternoon drags. The picture of Maggie stalls, incomplete, as information drifts in but adds nothing to what we know.

"We should get down there on Friday," Magnus says. "Check out Phillips's little family in action. Go on, you know you're ganting for some hot karaoke action."

"*Spadaj.*" I reserve speaking in Polish for when I want to convey contempt without disgracing myself. Magnus gets the gist, turns away with a wry smile.

After work I microwave a plastic meal, eating with the television on but staring out over the grey Clyde. When I bought this apartment I had grand ideas of sitting out on my thirty-inch-wide river view balcony on those stretched Scottish summer evenings, drinking cold wine and writing songs. I bought a chair and some potted plants from the garden centre, but the plants died, the chair is leprous with scum. My guitar is propped up in the corner of the room, mutely communicating its abandonment.

If my grandfather were here, he would have asked me: "Why, the river, Doloreta?" I'd have shrugged like the awkward teenager I always was with him. "Because I'm like you. I can't keep away from it. It scares me. It attracts me." The old sailor would shake his head, squeeze my shoulders. Nothing more to say.

My phone on the coffee table lights up limpidly as a call comes in. It's Magnus.

"Dolo, there's been another one."

I press my forehead to the cool glass. Below, the river chops up, unsettled. "Jumped?"

"Sort of."

"Where?"

"The Cinemax."

"Meet you there."

When it was built the Cinemax claimed to be Europe's tallest cinema so, obviously, it has lifts. The one in the glassed-over corner even affords you a view of the north east of the city (not its best side) as it speeds you to the popcorn troughing orgy of your choice. That's the one with the sag of incident tape across it, and Magnus waiting.

He nods towards the escalator. "We have to go up one to see it properly."

We have to walk up the escalator because, in a panic, someone turned the power off. "You know what used to be here, Magnus?"

He shakes his head, an indulgent, non-committal smile.

"Only the fucking Apollo."

He doesn't reply. He doesn't care.

On the floor above, forensics have propped the lift doors open. Torch beams swirl in the dark shaft like some kind of a caving expedition.

"Name's Gordon Middleton. He was a duty manager here," Magnus says. "He got in at the top, somehow, and waited till the lift was at the bottom."

I decide I don't need to see for myself. There will be photographs to pore over in good time. "And he was a singer at the Crystal Palace?"

"Yes, not one of the leading lights, but an enthusiastic clan member all the same."

"Bet you anything I know what song he was preparing for Friday." The tune has been in my head since we arrived.

It goes like this, the fourth, the fifth.

Magnus looks at me expectantly.

"The minor fall, the major lift?" I say, "although perhaps that should be the other way around. Given the circumstances."

He's still none the wiser, but he checks his note book. "Hallelujah by Alexandra Burke" His face couldn't be straighter if he tried.

"*Pierdol się*, Magnus." The invective is heartfelt, but it's not really directed at him. One song-related death could have been coincidence, but given that we are yards from the Clyde, I'm almost certain now.

My grandfather spent his life near water. He built ships for the soviets in Gdánsk. Before that, he spent World War II aboard the *ORP Piorun*, a destroyer built on exactly the same stretch of river overlooked by my apartment. And before that he patrolled the Vistula in the *Pinsk Flotilla*. He spent his life near water; he knew its music and he knew its dangers. If he were alive today he wouldn't be offering me a cuddle. He would warning me the hell away.

And it would be easy for me to walk away. There will be more deaths, but they will run their course. It's not as if there will be any kind of evidence. And it's certainly not as if I can explain my reasoning to my colleagues. It would be so simple to let it all sink and settle into coincidence and cold case.

Don't stir the waters, girl, unless you mean to fish.

"Guess we'll be going along on Friday after all," Magnus says cheerfully.

I manage a smile. "Okay, but I'm not singing."

He just grins knowingly.

Friday evening. I take the Clydeside walkway as far as Jamaica Street, walking close to the rail, listening to the insistent lapping of water on stone. Trying to hear something in it. Trying not to.

What's that?

A mermaid's purse?

And that?

A siren's comb?

Ew! What are those?

Poseidon's teabags. Well you can laugh, Doloreta, but how do you know they're not? The water holds more mystery than man will ever discover. Be wary of it. Always remember that.

When I get to the Crystal Palace there's a wee lassie on stage belting out Here Comes The Sun with well-intentioned gusto, but not the first idea of tenderness or finesse. No one's paying much attention and there's a genial buzz that leads me to suspect that the good Reverend Graham hasn't told his flock yet about why they're a couple of regulars down tonight. Wants to keep his scene together, give them the great night they expected. Tomorrow he'll email around with the terrible news, suggest they make next week a memorial. Give them time to practice.

Magnus takes an inch out of his Guinness as he peruses the song lists. "Jesus but there's a lot of choice."

"You think?" I'm scanning the faces. There's plenty of them. I estimate a hundred and fifty easily. They're grouped in table-based cliques, silos of contestants and their supporters, but they mix and mingle too. It's all smiles in here right enough. "How many of them would you actually choose to sing in public?"

"Yeah." He flips back to the start of the book. "I see what you mean. There's an awful lot of..." He searches for a word. "...earnestness."

I laugh then, because I would have said: *fake inspirational shit the lyrics of which, if they initially possessed any genuine feeling, have been overplayed to meaninglessness.* "Yeah, but down here earnestness wins prizes, Magnus. These people come here for empty inspiration because that's all that's left. Even the songs that were originally deep, affecting, real, have been laden with lush midi strings, choirs, dramatic change-up modulations going into the last chorus. *Hallelujah, Something, What A Wonderful World.* You should see what they did to *Love Will Tear Us Apart.*"

"That's a bit cynical isn't it? Even for you."

"All the good ones are gone, man. Ruined. Now, it's just words. At the end of the day, no matter how great the singer, it's only a song." I choke down a mouthful of acid lager. "If you're going to go up you should do it now. The professionals will be on soon."

He snaps the book shut with a grin that I instantly distrust, goes off to talk to Phillips who's operating the machine.

I survey the room again. Scanning the desperate hopefuls for the predator in their midst, the one who's come to prey on their neediness. But how do you spot a creature of legend in a crowd of humans? It'll be a woman, I think, but does it have to be? Images of rock-bound harpies and half-submerged mermaids are no practical use right now. I scan again, knowing only that the person we're looking for, somehow, won't fit.

Magnus gets up and starts crooning away to something with blaring brass and a swing tempo. Could be original brat pack, could be another new take. I don't recognise it either way. Magnus doesn't have a great voice, but he's giving it some anyway and the crowd are getting into it with him. Many of them are clapping along, a few join in with the last chorus.

I keep on scanning the crowd. When Magnus comes back I tell him to go up again. "Pick something really cheesy," I tell him.

"Cheesy?"

"Sorry, *uplifting*."

"Right. I'll see what I can find." He goes back to Phillips who first nods then shakes his head. *Later. The competition singers are on now.*

The competition is segregated into a complicated format that I don't even bother trying to understand, although it seems designed to ensure that as many people as possible have a chance of a prize. The singers themselves are fair to good. About the same standard as you'd expect to see in the latter stages of one of those TV competitions. A few really good voices. In need of pruning of those awful Mariahesque adornments, but solid. There is one girl, short blonde hair, pixie face. She has a voice like the side of a box of Swan Vestas, but she wastes it on Josh Groban's *You Raise Me Up*. In a different world I can see her sweating, red face contorted in a microphone-swallowing scream as she batters hell out of a beat-up Strat copy in a basement venue full of glorious noise.

"You should get yourself a nice girl like that." My interest must be more obvious than I realise. "Do you good."

"I don't think so."

He shrugs. "Everyone deserves to be happy, Dolo."

"What makes you think I'm not happy?"

Magnus doesn't answer that. I can't tell if I've offended him or if he thinks he's offended me and his best move is just to drop the conversation. The trouble is I really want to know.

The wasted blonde is the last competitor of the night. There's no delay before they start announcing the prizes. Blondie's table erupts in whoops and cheers when she is announced a winner. She's beaming, apparently content.

Why don't I find myself a girl like that? There's your answer right there.

There's another hour for the amateurs to strut their stuff before last orders, but I don't think we're going to discover anything more by hanging around than further levels of despair. "Let's go."

"Let me finish my pint first." And then, into the echo chamber of his glass. "Besides, you're up next."

He contrives to look innocent, but that's not going to save him from the tirade I'm preparing. And it's not going to be in Polish either. "You total fuck –" I begin, but then there's a radio microphone in my hand and the last word has echoed out through the PA. There's laughter over the opening strains of something that should be familiar.

"*Kawki?*".

I recognise the song as I take the stage. It's lushed up with strings and too even a swing, but there's no mistaking *Sea Of Love*. Never much a fan of the Pacino movie, but Waits' cover of the old song is as wistful a slice of melancholy as ever was committed to plastic. Magnus knows me better than I realise. In fact it's amazing that the karaoke machine has it at all. It's an awful arrangement, but I launch into it with growl and gusto.

Do you remember the night we met?

Waits' version was battered, downbeat, but fringed with wonder and hope that I don't feel. So I try to bring to the song an extra embitterment and disillusionment of my own. Not needing to see the lyrics, I squeeze my eyes shut and use the microphone as a conductor for my anger. My body is moving awkwardly, spit flies from my lips. God knows what the karaoke crowd think of my performance, and I don't care. This is not for them. Near the end I look and am gratified by the sea of glazed stupefaction. It might only be shock, but if the song has punctured a few milky cowls, that can only be good, right?

One face stands out. Rapt. More like *avid*. She's on the blonde girl's table, but doesn't really look part of the crowd. She's older. A lot older. Dark hair, wavy as the dark sea, but pulled back in a bunch. The denim jacket and Ramones t-shirt could have been from any of the last four decades. I've noticed her throughout the evening. Sipping water, clapping politely, murmuring some platitude at the end of every act, but never joining. Not once opening her mouth to sing. Until now.

Now she's mouthing along, like a lipsyncher on Top Of The Pops in the days when the artists weren't allowed to sing live for fear of giving the game away.

The song dwindles to a close.

I tear my gaze away from hers and hand the microphone back to Phillips, who says: "That was... well, intense." I savour the jealousy in his inarticulacy. There's a smattering of bemused applause as I pull on my coat.

I wonder what I've done. I have no idea what will happen next.

Outside, the cold air blows away some of my elation. But I'm fired up. I want to go out and rock.

"I'm getting a cab up west," Magnus says. "Want me to drop you?"

"No, I'm good."

I wait until he locates a taxi. The other punters from the Crystal Palace spill out and disperse around us. Magnus bids me good night, then a quick wave behind glass and he's gone.

I hang about for a few more minutes, wondering where I can get cigarettes from at this time of night. Then she is at my elbow, tapping out a matched pair of white Regals, offering me one.

"I loved hearing you sing." She lights me first, and I nod my thanks as I drag the smoke into my lungs. It makes me feel tight, wired. "Such emotion." Her voice has a Mediterranean stain. Ink in water. "Such yearning." I thought her eyes would be Aegean blue, but they're not, they're a silty brown. "It's a pity that they close these places so early. Back home we would just be getting started and we'd sing until the sun came up. She looks sideways out of those obscure eyes. They're set in shadowed sockets. "I have music at home if you want to continue to sing. It's not far."

"What about the neighbours?" I realise we're already walking. Curiously, our route is the same one I'd have taken to get home anyway. We've crossed the Broomielaw and are strolling along the quayside. I feel pissed, but out of practice as I am I've not had nearly enough to be drunk. It crosses my mind that someone could have slipped me a mickey, but I know it's not that either.

"I have no neighbours," she says, and when I see where she lives, I understand why. A lot of the buildings between the city centre and the Exhibition Centre were levelled to make way for chrome towers that were publicly touted as the new financial district but really were the city council's attempt to achieve the kind of night time riverscapes worthy of postcards. Nevertheless, some of the old buildings somehow managed to survive. We cross again in the shadow of the Kingston Bridge and head up Washington Street. There used to be recording studios here, and round the corner a notoriously dodgy venue. The kinds of places where bands that most people never heard of churned away, creating songs the public would never hear, that indie labels would set up back shop outfits to press singles and distribute them to only a handful of aficionados.

My guide has a miniature torch on her key ring. She switches it on, opens a door, slips inside. I know there is danger here, but I don't feel fear. I follow.

She is talking again as she leads me deep into the building. The paltry beam probes like the light of a diving bell. The words are swallowed by their own echoes. "Do you have a name?" I venture, and she laughs as if I've said something funny.

"In that song, the one you sang," she says. "Your use of the dorian mode. I liked that." Another door. She turns, shines the torch on her face. "I'm sorry. I don't want you to think I'm an expert in music. I'm —"

"Just old and Greek?"

She raises a perfect waveformed eyebrow at that. Smiles enigmatically. Pushes the door open. It scrapes heavily and I blink in the light from beyond it. It's only candles, but there are a lot of them, lit and burning low, pools of wax on the concrete floor like a frozen estuary rendered in a child's crayons. In the middle of the candles there is a mattress on the floor, a sleeping bag unrolled on top of that. Stacks of cardboard cartons along the walls. Some of them have split open, spilling their contents across the floor. Shiny black vinyl records, scattered like dragon scales. White in the centres. Like the staring eyes of the dead.

The room is part squat, part shrine, part lair. I have the urge to crash on the mattress, smoke some weed, laugh the night away playing every song we know on an acoustic guitar. I have the urge to worship. I have the urge to flee for my life. I can hear my grandfather's voice echoing in the last of these.

"You mentioned music?" It's not a large room and I can see immediately that despite all the records there is nothing to play them on. And there's no sign of an instrument either.

She smiles then, but it's not a kind gesture. "We are the music, Doloreta. Sing me your song again."

And now the urge to flee crawls up my spine. This is the crux. "You didn't bring the rest of them here, did you?" I say. "Why was that?"

Her *moue* of disappointment. "Because their songs did not belong here. Because yours does."

"You mean because two bodies on your doorstep would have led to your discovery? Are you planning on moving on after me?"

"Sing me your song." She's closed the distance between us. I feel her breath in my ear, like the sea in a shell. "How does it go? *Come with me to the sea.*" That one line echoes my original attempt back at the karaoke, but floods it with resonance and meaning that humble me.

I have to focus, block it out. "Or is it that you don't think anyone will find me here?"

"Sing the song, Doloreta," she commands. "*I want to tell you.* Like that, yes? *How much I love you.*" Her voice washes through me like surf, drags its tidal flotsam of meaning deep into me. What had I said to Magnus? *Words are just words. At the end of the day, no matter how great the singer, it's just a song.*

But it wasn't just a song for Maggie Martin or Gordon Templeton. And it's not just a song for me. Not now.

I'm drowning.

I'm curled up on the mattress, feeling like I've been dumped there like rubble off the back of a truck into a flooded quarry. I'm submerged, every syllable that comes from her mouth makes me heavier.

I'm drowning in a sea of love.

Soon the song will be over, and she'll have taken the life from me just like she did with the others. Soon she'll be gone, and the candles will gutter out leaving me in the dark, like something sunken.

Drowning.

They say that your life flashes past your eyes. Mine rushes like streams of bright bubbles. Leaked breath rising beyond reach.

A childhood growing up in a Scottish school system that had little time for a kid who would have been awkward enough being lumpy and punkily angry and gay without having a difficult name inherited from a Polish mother who had fled back to the old country before the daughter was ten. A string of teenage bands that were marginally more successful than her infrequent affairs. A dogged attempt to make some kind of career.

Occasional visits to Poland. Walks by the sea with the old man, who hadn't cared how I looked or who I loved or what kind of music I listened to. Being enthralled by his tales of the sea.

It takes effort to stretch out my hand, make a clumsy swipe that topples some of the candles. Splashing hot wax that burns my legs. A waft of heat, the smell of something catching alight. I'm dimly aware of a faltering in the song, but my siren continues.

Come with me to the sea.

Greek myths of travel and peril. Odysseus and Jason. I grasp around, my fingers encounter molten pain. My lips try to form words around my breath. I claw at the wax.

The siren redoubles her efforts and I feel the song drenching me, dissolving me. I murmur words, squeeze the hot wax into a ball. It runs through my fingers. Red, white, yellow. Streaked with oil-seam black from the melting vinyl.

And what did Jason do when he met the Sirens, Dolo? How did he save his men?

Plugged their ears with wax, Grandfather.

Using up the last of my will and energy, I cram liquid pain into my ears. Packing it in tight until it's caking my head, singeing my hair, searing my brain.

"Shut the fuck up!"

After the scream, I suck in a huge breath of the hot smoke that is billowing like time lapsed thunderclouds across the ceiling. And I'm coughing, although I feel it rather than hear it. I'm scrabbling to my feet. I'm in the corridor, blundering in the dark until I'm out in the cold and the dark and the rain, spewing saliva in ropey black threads onto jewelled tarmac.

The street is empty. At its end, the lights of the Broomielaw, the sculpted treescape of the walkway. The dark, waiting Clyde.

I try to call in the fire brigade, but I can't hear the voice on the other end of the line, and my own words are just a vibration in my larynx, a buzz in my skull.

My fingers touch my ears. Find smooth plates of wax. Still warm, but hardened by the few minutes I've spent in the cold. I wonder if I'll ever hear music properly again.

Even shit karaoke. Even the Glasgow rain.

Part of me dies at the thought. Part of me sighs.

Soft relief.

Neil Williamson

I'm very fortunate to live in a city with a wonderful live music scene. This nightmare scenario imagines live music being replaced by international competition karaoke. The Horror! I wrote this one after a trip to Poland where I learned some neat swear words and where I started thinking about the cultural and physical things that connect that part of the world and mine, about the bodies of water that lie between and who might traverse them.

The Bed

When you get home from work, there's a monster in your bedroom. It squats where the bed used to be, a brooding thing that swallows the light. It fills the room, leaving barely enough space to edge around to get to the wardrobe to put your football gear away. You're not even sure you could open the wardrobe. You decide not to try. You might wake the beast and be swallowed whole.

Feet on the stairs. You back out of the room to meet Eric. He's wearing an apron smeared with something brown. "Oh, well, I guess you've spoiled the surprise then," he says.

"What the fuck?" You gesture at the bedroom where the monster waits.

"Spoilsport." Eric kisses you, then taps your cheek. "You've not shaved today. And you're not meant to be up here. You *were* supposed to be lured through to the kitchen by the irresistible aroma of chocolate cake."

"There's cake?" The house smells of Airwick.

"There will be. I forgot to preheat the oven." Eric grins, and takes you by the hand and pulls you back into the bedroom. The monster looks bigger than ever. "Now you've seen it, what do you think of our new bed?"

You look at the thing again. You suppose it could be called a bed. It has the general shape of one, certainly. A headboard, a footboard, a mattress in between. Sheets and pillows. But...

"It's a monster," you say.

Eric tuts. "It's seventeenth century Freisian oak. With dairy motifs, look." You look. The wood is so dark that you didn't notice at first, but sure enough in between the four-inch posts, carved like stout trees and begging for a toe to stub, there are reliefs of cows at pasture, being herded, milked. The headboard is topped with a carving, two boys reclining back to back, each of them holding a curved horn to their lips.

"You only said you were going to buy a new duvet set."

"I did," Eric sits, pats the creamy cotton, "but it didn't go with the old bed."

Reluctantly, you join him. "So you got carried away?" He grins sheepishly. "How the hell did you get it in here?"

"The boys from the shop were very accommodating." Eric arches his eyebrows, never able to resist an innuendo. "Well? What do you think then?"

"It's a monster," you repeat.

"It is not. It's *our* bed." Eric takes your hand again. "We've been together over a year. It's a milestone."

"It's a millstone…"

Eric's expression turns like November weather. Without another word he gets up and goes back downstairs, and you realise, too late, how that sounded. You'd been thinking practically. Of having to take a window out to shift the thing if you ever decided to move on from this tidy suburban semi. You didn't mean…

Thing is, it's not *your* bed. Your bed has always been simple. Barely more than mattress, sheet, a single pillow. You've slept that way since you were a child, throwing unnecessary blankets onto the floor, even in winter. For a couple of years in your teens your parents had despaired at your insistence on sleeping on the floor.

What this really is, of course, is having to give up the things you think of as *mine*. The digital clock on the living room wall is gone, a walnut long case that never tells the actual time in its place. The leather sofa that Eric bought is equally fancy, though that at least is comfortable. You take a deep breath and force yourself to let the bed thing go. And it's not that difficult after all.

Later, you'll get your own back by telling him the bed looks like the sort of beast that the unwary would purchase from a creepy old junk shop in one of his Hammer Horror films, and see how well he likes it after that. But first, you go downstairs and apologise.

Eric likes to spoon when you sleep. A full contact embrace: legs folded into yours, chest pressed to your back, arm thrown around you like a steel brace. His body is often uncomfortably warm. His breathing feathers your neck. If you're lying awkwardly when the arm comes over you have a couple of minutes at most before he plunges into sleep and locks you in for a night of discomfort.

Not that you sleep much. Your nights are a stitchery of time passing, every surfacing from unconsciousness a small jolt of relief. You're not sleeping when Eric thrashes, grasps your teeshirt, shouts out something unintelligible.

"Hey, love, it's okay." In the dark, his eyes are like deep sea fish, glistening and luminous. "*Eric.*"

"Whuh?" His words are tangled in cotton. "Uhuh, sorry. Just a..." He groans softly. "Just a dream."

"Not about the bed turning cannibal? That was meant to be a joke..."

"No, it wasn't that." Eric breathes out, relaxes. Then he touches your arm. "You're still warm."

You laugh, to make light of it. "What?"

When he speaks next, he's more lucid. "Fucking dream." He shivers, then: "Matt? What scares you?"

"What do you mean?"

"You're always so placid, so in control, you know?"

"Do I have to be scared of something?"

"Isn't everyone?"

"Well. I *used* to be afraid of not waking up when I went to sleep."

"You did? Because of your heart thing?"

They diagnosed a stenosis when you were a baby and your parents, in their wisdom, chose to tell you when you were six years old that there was a problem. That you had to be careful and not run around too much, not to play sports, not to... There was a *list*.

Up until that point, bed had been a lovely, swaddled oblivion. Afterwards, a trap, that one random night, sooner or later, would *snick* shut, squeezing the breath from you as you slept. As you grew up, you defeated the fear with the simple evidence of continuing to wake up every morning and getting on with life. The knowledge that the trap wasn't a trap after all. Just a bed.

"Yes, because of that."

Eric touches your arm again. Then he says: "For most of my adult life I've been terrified of dying in bed alone. Lying there for... I don't know, days, maybe weeks because... because there would be no one to find me."

"Well, you've got me now," you say.

"I know."

"So what was the dream about?"

"Oh, don't ask me. It's so morbid."

"No, go on."

"Well..." You can hear the shudder in his breath. "Now, I'm scared I'll wake up and *you'll* be..."

"Dead?"

"You don't have to say it like that?"

"How else would you say it? One of us has to go before the other one day. Like I say, I used to think about that all the time. Not waking up."

"But it doesn't worry you any more?"

You shake your head. "I'm still here, aren't I?"

Eric's voice is muzzy again when he says: "Our bed is so old. How many people must have died in it? Tens? Hundreds?"

You don't answer for a moment, then: "I'm sure they did a lot of living first." And you're grateful when he reaches for you again, pulls you to him.

Eric goes back to sleep, holding you tighter than ever. You lie there, counting your constricted breaths, feeling your lungs work against his embrace. In one of the moments of wakefulness that you thread through the oblivion as you wait for morning, you think: *there are worse things to be afraid of than not waking up.*

At first you think Eric's got up and you panic that you're late for work, but his arm is still in lockdown position. It's just that you can't feel his weight, his heat, his presence. The bedhead looms above you, solid like the side of a hole. Likewise, the black oak at your feet. You lie still, waiting for the panic to set in but, when it doesn't come, you finally acknowledge that, after all this time, *it* has happened. You realise that you never stopped expecting. It feels like an anticlimax.

You squirm around. Moving in place like an eel buried in sand. Look into his sleeping face. And wonder: what will wake him? Another nightmare? The coldness of your skin? And, you wonder, what then? Once his hysteria has ebbed and he's made the calls he has to make. Once he's stripped the beast. Once time has stitched on. How long will you lie here in the belly of this bed, with all the other people that died in it? The tens, hundreds. For that matter, where are they, these multitudes of the dead? You listen for voices from below you in the pressing pit. Maybe a minute passes, or a series of minutes, stitched into an eternity.

There are no others. Just you. Just Eric. This is your bed. The one you have made, and now lie in.

Time stitches. The rusty old ratchet of the trap ticks one notch tighter.

Soon is the same as forever.

I'm intrigued with the dynamics of couples. The things they share, the things they never divulge. Sharing a bed every night is one of the most intimate things we do, and yet we still manage to feel utterly alone with our thoughts, and our secrets. The things that keep us awake while our loved ones slumber.

Fish on Friday

Hello, Ms MacArthur? Hi, there. This is a courtesy call from ASDaTESCo. My name is –

ASDaTESCo. The Agency for Sport, Diet and Technology Empowering Scotland's Citizens. My name is Aiden –

You *know* who we are, Ms MacArthur. Our representatives have had cause to contact you several times already this year. Well, that's not very nice. We're *not* Nazis. The ASDaTESCo initiative has been instrumental in transforming this nation from the Sick Men and Women of Europe into a horde of happy, healthy Hamishes. Yes. Yes, *Hamishes.* It's from our advertising campaign. You must have seen it. Oh, you don't watch telly? Having to go the bike to power it is too much of a palaver? Well I'm sorry to hear that; have you tried adjusting the – no, no. I see. That's a shame. You're missing out on a whole lot of entertaining and informative programming. Yes, true, much of it is sport-based, but studies have proved that competitive sport is far more inspirational than all those reality shows and soaps and nasty, fattening cookery programmes they used to show. Especially since the ASDaTESCo Sport-in-Schools initiative saw Scotland shoot to the top in so many fields of international competition. Our happy, healthy Hamishes are sport-mad. What, you didn't even watch the World Cup Final? It was a classic. We were *very* unlucky. If it hadn't been for that pen – no, okay, fine. Not everyone's a sports fan.

Anyway, the reason for my call, Ms MacArthur, is not regarding your entertainment habits. It's about your dietary ones. Our system has flagged that your refrigerator seems to have forgotten to order your fish for this coming Friday. Well, yes, it *should* be impossible. And it only happens in one household in the whole city: yours. Look, Ms MacArthur, we know all about your history in *hacktivism…* Don't say that. We're *not* spying on you. We're *not* totalitarian oppressors. No, you're *not* living in a jackbooted Orwellian nightmare state. Ms MacArthur, please let's try and keep this conversation civil. We don't want to have to impose sanctions on you again. Just accept that we're aware of your history. Well, because you have a police record... and because you put *hacktivist (retired)* on your Social Housing application form. We know you can hack into our system, Ms MacArthur. A child could hack into our system. But they don't, and do you know why? Because everybody likes the system. Everybody likes being happy and healthy.

Look, fish has many excellent health benefits – to be fair, it's not entirely relevant that you don't *like* it. It's part of your Social Housing agreement that you consume foodstuffs from the approved list. Just like topping up your calorie bank using the bike so that you can watch TV, use the internet and, ha ha, obviously, open the fridge. No, I'm afraid the fish is non-negotiable. And look at what you're missing! That haddock is reared right here in the River Clyde... It's *not* a cesspit. The Clyde may have had a, ahem, *murky* past... That was a joke. Yes it *was*. Well, I thought it was funny. Anyway, nowadays the river is a paragon of sustainable aquatic ecosystems. It's won awards. And the haddock are instrumental in...Don't call them *Frankenfish*. It's a simple and perfectly safe genetic modification that helps them grow big and tasty. Yes, big and – no, I hadn't heard that. A child? Oh, that's awful. I can't believe I didn't hear about that in the news... Just a minute, there's no record of a haddock eating a little – Miss MacArthur, are you pulling my leg? No, it *couldn't* happen. They're *not* monsters, they're just big fish. Believe me the river is perfectly safe and clean. That *scummy* stuff? Ms MacArthur, the Glasgow Green algae farms are central to the city's sustainability. The algae purifies the water, increases O_2 levels in the city centre and is a vital component of those mealworm burgers that you enjoy so much. Well, you eat enough of them. Yes, I know you *have* to. Yes, indeed, the approved list.

Oh, wouldn't you just? Yes, we noticed the *fillet steak* on your fridge's order in place of the fish, of course. What, *in place*? No *that* wasn't a joke. And neither is ordering *steak* of all things! You *know* that red meat is most definitely not on the approved list. Why? Because it's one of the most harmful, environmentally unsound, and ideologically objectionable sources of protein in human history, that's why. Look, I know you're an educated woman, Ms MacArthur. You can't deny that the ban on farming large herds of costly mammals that did little more than transform perfectly tasty and nutritious vegetables and grains into health-toxic meat and environmentally disastrous quantities of methane gas is beneficial not only to our own nation, but to the planet. Hmm? What do you say to that?

Tasty? *Ugh!* I can't believe – I wouldn't *want* to try it. It's barbaric…

Ms MacArthur, I have to apologise. That was an unkind and unprofessional thing to say, and reflects badly on me as a government-partner representative, a member of the Institute of Professional Customer Advisors and a happy, healthy Hamish. We understand that older citizens such as yourself still have difficulties adjusting to the new Scotland. The changes that swept through our society after independence were more extensive than anyone could have forecast. For younger generations, the way we live now – as a fit, healthy, caring, sharing, socialistic society where everyone gets not what they *want* but what they need – seems natural, but for people like your good self who remember the bad old days of apathy, obesity and dietary catastrophe, it must have come as a terrible shock. Scotland is the envy of Europe now – I'm sorry? I'm giving you the what? The *boak*? I'm sorry, I don't understand.

Yes. Yes, that's perfectly true. Technically, my organisation, in its previous incarnations as leading chain supermarkets *did* largely dictate the national diet on a for-profit basis. And their aggressive monopolisation strategies *were* a factor in ridding the high street of its beloved independent traders. Yes, the butchers and the grocers and the fishmongers and, that's right, the corner shops and the… Sorry? What was a *chip shop* again? Why are you laughing? But that was the old Scotland, Ms MacArthur. The old way of doing things. There was too much choice, and that allowed people to make *poor* choices. Yes, the Scottish Government knew that the ASDaTESCo name might retain negative connotations, but at the time they bought out the stores and supply chains from their owners it was deemed advantageous to ease the transition by retaining the branding. And not only that: redefining the names of those two old monsters provides a symbol of how we have redefined the attitudes to health and nutrition across the whole country. With the ASDaTESCo initiative, every Scottish man, woman and child gets cheap, healthy, varied and one hundred per cent locally-sourced food delivered to their home automatically as part of their citizenship contract, which also includes their home, appliances and, guaranteed, the minimum amount of exercise required to keep them healthy and happy. Yes, those letters used to represent many bad things, but not any more.

So, can we agree there'll be no more hacking your fridge's ordering script, Ms MacArthur. Hmm, please? We really don't want to put you on a week of double exercise again. No you didn't *almost starve* last time. You had all the krillcakes you could possibly eat, and you had unlimited access to the contents of your fridge. All you needed to do was pedal a little. Oh, Ms MacArthur, that's simply not true. You're not a frail old woman. Your health report says there's plenty of pedalling in those legs of yours yet, and you've three years until you qualify for a visiting old-person's calorie donor. No, I'm sorry I don't know if they wear tight shorts. What a question to ask. Look, if you're not keen on pedalling the bike do you know that there are other ways you can add to your calorie bank? Many of your neighbours, for example, put in a few hours a week tending the locust farm on the roof of your building. The work's not too taxing and you get the added bonus of doing your bit for the city's food bank.

Ms MacArthur, are you all right? Are you crying? Oh, look, I'm sorry if I've been a little stern with you, but it really is for your own good – I know, it's difficult. I know, you just want things to be how they used to be. But really, I promise you it's better this way. Look at yourself! How many ninety seven year olds were as fit and able as you are now back in the bad old days? There you are, see? I told you it makes sense. We're fortunate to be living in these times, Ms MacArthur, very fortunate indeed.

So. Please. No more steaks? Or, any of the other things that have mysteriously crept in there over the months, let me see... mutton pies, beef olives... *traditional haggis*, you scallywag. Even if the system let these things through to the ordering script, I don't know where on Earth it would get them from, I really don't.

Okay, thank you. Good. So your next delivery will include the haddock, as originally intended. Just try it. I'm sure it's not as bad as you think. Will you? For me? Good! I'm proud of you. We'll make you a happy, healthy Hamish yet.

Oh, before I go, I've just noticed that there seems to be an error of, goodness me, a factor of ten in your cooking oil. I'll just amend... No? Oh, you use it for lubricating the bike? And that works, does it? Well, that's very of resourceful of you. Waste not, want not.

Absolutely. To be honest, the approved gear oil *is* rather expensive. Well, in that case I'll leave it be. It's not as if you're going to *cook* anything with it, after all. Ha, ha. Well, I'm glad we managed to see eye to eye at last. Have a happy, healthy day, Ms MacArthur.

Goodbye.

There can't be a single author in Scotland that wasn't angered, amused and inspired during the months leading up to the 2014 Scottish Independence Referendum. All sorts of outlandish and dire warnings were issued about the future of the country and it got me wondering whether it might actually be possible, if not desirable, to end up with a genuinely benevolent dictatorship.

The Posset Pot

The day I found the posset pot was the last time I got myself into serious bubble trouble. Scared me shitless at the time, letting my guard slip like that and I admit it put me on the downer that, ultimately, sealed poor Ettrick's fate. I'm not writing this as a confession, but he deserves a record. I miss the old bastard more than I would have thought possible. Every day I wish he'd not been so stupid, but even I can't shoulder the responsibility for what happened to him. Some things just happen.

Ettrick always maintained that it was *me* who had a death wish. Said it was understandable, given my circumstances. But Ettrick didn't live in the real world. He didn't understand that, since the bubbles, survival had become a matter of pushing your luck. If you wanted to eat, if you wanted heat – let's not even mention the occasional luxuries he was quite happy for me to bring home from my expeditions – you had to be out there, where the bubbles were.

I was picking my way down the embankment from the University tower towards the River Kelvin. My thoughts had strayed into memory, thinking about how it used to look. That smooth slope of greensward, the trees, the southern aspect of the city stretching out beyond; not the weird moonscape it's become, precisely cratered as if God had been at it with his ice-cream scoop. Like a scene out of some... no, see that's the thing: Hollywood never imagined an apocalypse as bizarre as this.

Dwelling on the past like that, even for a handful of seconds, was deadly, and I missed the tell-tale wink of microturbulence, the rainbow shimmer that presaged the incursion. The bubble was suddenly just *there*, hanging above the ground a yard to my left and growing fast. I scrambled up the slope, watched it carefully from a safer distance. As always, it was exactly as thin and beautiful as the ones we blew from detergent solution when we were kids. It expanded quickly, but stopped at beach ball size. I spun around, looking for multiples, but there were none. Only then did I let out my breath. While I was fucking lucky that it had stopped at this size, I wondered what I'd have done if it had grown larger. Large enough. I wondered if I'd have risked it.

"Jesus Christ, Aird. You've got to pay attention." Enunciating my self-admonishment righted my priorities, reoriented me towards survival and away from recrimination, but I kept the words to a mutter. Even if you are one of the last people left, it's still not right to talk to yourself in public.

I watched the bubble run its course. Despite the havoc they've wrought, they remain fascinating. They're so perfectly, delicately constructed. Like actual soap bubbles in so many ways, except they don't drift in the air currents. They hardly even distort the light. This one hovered a foot above the weeds, rotating slowly. As always, I jotted down the details – l0cation, size, height, spin – before the tell-tale darkening of the sphere's surface began. I call it *steeling* for the way a bubble's appearance changes to resemble a huge ball bearing in the last few moments before its integrity collapses. I backed away a little further. You never know what can come through in an exchange.

When the bubble popped, a rush of air ruffled my hair and set some newly decapitated dandelion stalks nodding like proverbial headless chickens. A rush of air, but nothing else. *Sky again*, I wrote, then breathed deeply, catching the exotic lemongrass and pepper aroma of the air of Elsewhere. I felt the prickle of tears.

The sky was deepening behind the remains of the University. The building's lovely, overworked symmetry has been sliced through so often now, sphere after sphere intersecting with the remains of the masonry, that those once ornate neo-gothic spires have been turned into a forest of precarious, delicate peaks; imagine African termite mounds modelled by rudimentary algorithm, but too slender, too sharp. Sometimes, unable to support themselves, bits fall off. I don't think I'll ever accept Glasgow's new topography. It changed so fast. It's barely recognizable as a city any more.

There was little else of note on the trek home. In Kelvingrove, the last tree had toppled. The crown lay on the ground like a head of broccoli, but the entire trunk was missing and, with it, a sizeable bowl of roadway. The bubble that took it must have been huge. Before our world began to be swapped piece by piece for another universe, trees wouldn't have been high on my list of things I'd miss. But the place looks so empty without them.

And I saw a foam in Yorkhill. It appeared along the side of a bisected Vauxhall Vectra, spilling along the car's flank like shaken up lemonade. It effervesced, sizzled and left a trail of acne-like scarring across the door and roof.

The streets around here are always the worst for me. Not because of how much they've changed, rather the extent to which they haven't. Within the length of a street the signs of bubble activity decrease so dramatically that it is only too easy to remember the days when the city was whole.

I always try to avoid glancing along Yorkhill Street. I always fail. Karen and I viewed a flat there only a week before the first bubbles appeared. The Estate Agent's board is still there, planted hopefully beside the door of the tenement close. As if the housing market's suffering a temporary blip and will soon recover. Ironically, it's in an infinitely more desirable area now. Ettrick calls this the *golden circle*. Two or three blocks of tenements that have inexplicably retained their full complement of roofs, walls and floors. They'd go for a bomb if there was anyone left here to put an offer in.

But there isn't. There was just me and Ettrick. And now there's just me.

Ettrick's flat is at the very centre of the circle. The tenement is in the middle of the block, and the flat is on the middle floor. Insulated. We never worked out how or why. It was this miraculous intactness that drew me here after the evacuation. We'd both had different motives for staying behind. Ettrick was agoraphobic, or so he claimed anyway, and I'd sworn not to leave without Karen. Stupidly, some would say, but I couldn't help that. Anyway, once we'd discovered each other it made sense to stay together. To try and help each other. That's what humans are supposed to do, isn't it?

Inside the flat, I let the shutting door announce my return while I shrugged off my pack and hung my duffel coat on the antique coat stand. The hall smelled of Mr Sheen.

"Who is it?" Ettrick was fearful even when he had no Earthly reason to be.

I used to make smart-arsed replies, each of them equally impossible – '*the postman, the tax inspector, Julian Fucking Clary* – but the humour wore out fast. "Just me," I said.

Ettrick appeared at the kitchen door. "We're out of polish." He was wearing marigolds. "I don't suppose...?"

I sighed inwardly, but Ettrick's constant cleaning was the least of his faults. "Get the kettle on," I said. "And let's have a look."

I put my pack on the table.

"Where did you get to today?" Ettrick said, as he slid up the window sash and retrieved a jam jar from the row brimming with the previous night's rain. Early speculation wondered whether the bubbles might affect the weather, but Glasgow's always been a rain town. If there was one thing we aren't short of, it's fresh water. He poured the collected water into a saucepan and lit the camping stove.

While he did that, I took a marker pen and hatched a series of lines on the city map tacked to the wall. "St George's Cross," I said. "Some of Maryhill too." I fished out my notebook next, and began to mark my bubble observations on the map as well. The foam instance was right on the edge of our protected zone. In contrast to the red scrawls and black crosshatching, the circle of yellowing streetmap really did look golden.

"That's too far away."

"Not if we're going to get through the winter." I lined up my booty on the table. Two invaluable camping gas cylinders. Assorted cleaning products. A catering sized bag of Tetley tea bags. Two pigeon carcasses wrapped in newspaper.

The pan on the stove began to bubble. "Are those fresh?" Ettrick patted nervously at his wispy hair. He was kind of freaky about disease.

"Killed them with my own hands." It hadn't been much of a feat. The birds had been tottering around a garage forecourt blinded by foam.

"Good. Been a while since we had some decent protein."

I smiled at that. He was always like a pernickity househusband criticising the weekly shopping. Next came my own personal triumph. The Asda bag rattled as I extracted it.

Ettrick fell on the package then curled his lip. "Cruet?"

Cruet. Philistine.

"Trust me, you'd not be looking forward to this pigeon half us much without a bit of salt and pepper. And look." I held up a fistful of jars. "Tarragon, basil, coriander. Chilli flakes, man! And they said civilisation was dead." I had no intention of telling Ettrick that I'd almost broken a leg liberating these little inconsequentials. Getting up towards Maryhill Road, underground bubble activity had caused subsidence. A winding close staircase had given way and I'd narrowly saved myself from a fall. The homes themselves were not as intact as they had appeared from the street either. It's hard to tell sometimes. You can view a building from all angles and your hopes rise, only to find that it's little more than a shell when you get inside. This one wasn't that bad, but there wasn't a great deal to salvage either.

There were bodies, though. At least, parts of bodies. Back at the beginning, when bubbles were popping up everywhere and the city, the country, the world were rife with panic, fleeing once and fleeing again, there were a lot of bodies. From the catastrophically dismembered to the apparently intact whose injuries had been wholly internal, but no less agonizing, to the ones who had escaped the bubbles but nevertheless fallen victim to the dissolution of society that had followed.

I never got used to the bodies. It might have helped to talk about them but Ettrick forbade any mention of the subject. Even by that time, when most of the carnage had been scooped off to Elsewhere along with everything else, I still stumbled across them on a regular basis. Here I found a man's decayed head and abdomen, face down in a crawling position, a child's arm in one green tee-shirt sleeve nearby, both severed and sealed by the spherical section that passed through the laminate flooring, the ash deadening, the joists and the downstairs ceiling. I was quick about jumping across and performing a ruthless excavation of the kitchen's cabinets.

If we were forbidden from mentioning the bodies, we talked about the bubbles constantly. We agreed on some things, disagreed on others. The reason for it all we laid confidently at the door of CERN, or some similar and perhaps less public enterprise. A next-generation LHC somewhere malfunctioning, causing unpredictable and uncontrollable localised spot irruptions of other universes into our own. That much we borrowed from the theorists on TV before we lost the media, and presumably the theorists as well.

Beyond that it was all down to speculation. How many universes? One? A million? *Overlapping Earths*, Ettrick said once before dismissing the idea in favour of the one he would stick with: that the bubbles were wormholes briefly connecting our Earth to random points in its own history. *Not Elsewheres, but Elsewhens.* He produced a dense stream of logic to support his theory that was hard to find a chink in, and grew more robust every time we returned to the subject, but being out there every day, I knew he was wrong. Instead, I favoured his comment about overlapping Earths, and constructed my own body of evidence to support that theory. I imagined two versions of the same planet, similar apart from some fundamental differences, somehow passing each other in space-time. Points of contact happening in different places, at different times. Maybe even different planetary inclinations. Here we mostly got their air, while on the other side of the Earth we'd heard reports of the opposite, rains of rubble. If that was true, though, this period of conjunction was limited. The planets were already passing, and beginning to drift apart again. The frequency of the bubbles was dropping off.

Time was running out.

"What else did you find?"

There were some books. Some paperback, but also a few of the showy hardcovers that Ettrick preferred for his Library. I hadn't even looked at the titles, but the old man seemed happy enough.

"There's something more."

He looked up from riffling the pages of a Lonely Planet guide to Nova Scotia. "Something came back?"

I nodded. "In the kitchen where I got the spices. A bubble had taken out part of the work surface, a slice of turf wedged into the hole in its place. Flowers and everything." Trying not to remember the astringent scent of those flowers, the weird olive colour and silken texture of the grass. I reached into the pack one last time and extracted what I'd found.

"Oh, my." Ettrick peered at the object. "This is quite wonderful."

It was rare that anything but atmosphere came through from Elsewhere. Rarer still that it survived intact. Especially something this fragile.

The object was like an odd combination of a tea pot and a large mug. It had a spout, and perpendicular to that jutted two handles. There was a lid too that reminded me of a cookie jar lid. The pot was constructed from glazed earthenware, yellow with a pattern of detailed but unfamiliar red flowers.

Ettrick lifted the lid, sniffed cautiously. "Incredible," he said, scraping at the inside and examining his fingernail. "I believe someone's actually *used* this recently."

"Used it for what?"

"For drinking out of. It's a posset pot, of course."

He pounced on my mystification. "A *posset pot*," Ettrick repeated, almost slow enough for sarcasm. "For the preparation and consummation of possets. Don't you know what a posset is?"

I was going to reply that I hadn't a clue – Ettrick's petty general knowledge oneupmanship had got tired months ago – but surprisingly the word rang a dull bell. Something I'd learned during my time at catering college. "It's a kind of old fashioned drink, isn't it?"

Ettrick nodded. "It was used as a cure for colds and the like, but it had no actual medicinal properties. The 18th century equivalent of comfort food. Hot milk curdled with booze, sometimes made into a custard with eggs, and flavoured with cinnamon, nutmeg, that sort of thing. You ate the gloop with a spoon, and drank the alcohol through the spout."

"But you said 18th century?"

Ettrick nodded.

"So what was anyone doing eating out of a 300 year old antique?

Ettrick twinkled. "This is no antique," he said.

"No," I said.

"It's more likely than –"

"You don't know," I cut across him. "If you smelled the air when a bubble pops..." I waved any further discussion away, pointed at the little pan rattling away on the stove. "Kettle's boiling."

He scurried to turn it off. We might have had a surfeit of water, but we couldn't waste fuel. Even so, a good cuppa was the one luxury neither of us had been willing to relinquish just yet.

We drank in silence. I stared at the map and the activity chart, aware that Ettrick was watching but really not in the mood. Conversation between us was limited at the best of times. It wasn't as if we had much in common. One of us was an IT guy whose skills were so obsolete it wasn't even funny. The other, a retired academic. One had a restlessness born of technology withdrawal. Even now, I still feel the phantom umbilical of the wired world. Ache for a Facebook update, a tweet, a minute of Grand Theft Auto. Ettrick just got happier the more books he could add to his shelves.

One of us had been a virtual shut-in for years. The only thing he missed about the world was that Tesco didn't deliver any more.

The other missed his friends. His family.

Karen went right at the start of it all. She'd dawdled to look in the window of a Byres Road estate agent. I'd turned, laughing at her dogged determination to find something we could afford, walked back towards her. And then she was in a bubble, surprised, astonished, beautiful in the sun-shimmered construct like Glinda, the Good Witch of the Fucking North. She'd started to come out, an arm, a shoulder emerging, but she was too slow. The bubble steeled fast. I hadn't a clue then. If I'd kept my head there might have been time to pull her all the way out, but I panicked, pushed her back in. Surrendered her to Elsewhere.

"The bubbles are definitely getting less frequent," I said at length.

"Are you sure?"

I shrugged. "The ones I see, anyway. There are more singletons, not so many clusters." I took a breath. "And the majority bring high air."

"You don't know that."

I did, though, whatever Ettrick might say. It seemed entirely logical to me that when the air was frigid and odourless, it came from higher in the atmosphere. Much too high. When the air was warm and spiced, it came from close to the ground, to trees and grass and earth, but those occasions, like the bubbles themselves, were getting rarer.

"Dinner, then?" I said, and the worry eased from the corners of Ettrick's mouth.

"I dug up a shaw of tatties," he said proudly.

"Better get scrubbing then." I grabbed a carver from the knife block and the pigeons from the table. "And I mean scrubbing, not peeling. We can't afford to waste the nutrition."

The sun was pinking and peaching the high freckles of cirrus, the evening air cool by the time I finished with the birds. I stretched stiffly and looked along the backs of the tenements, the reflecting windows afire. A peaceful apocalypse.

In the kitchen, I pan fried the pigeons with thyme and garlic, a dribble of precious oil. The potatoes I dusted with dried rosemary. It tasted about as good as anything we'd eaten in months.

Afterwards, Ettrick made himself scarce. I heard books being slipped from shelves, riffled through, pushed emphatically back in place. I let out a deep sigh, begrudging for the thousandth time that that archaic medium had survived while the endless versatility of electronic communication that had all but replaced it had vanished overnight.

I got the wind-up radio down. The decals of the inane afternoon show for which it must once have been a phone-in prize were decoloured, the goofy leers of the presenters almost faded to white, as if their owners were vanishing from history like Marty McFly's family, and like the movie they were in too. The red plastic winked in the candlelight like kola kubes. I wound the handle twenty, thirty, forty rotations to get the clockwork running and extended the aerial. The soft static sounded like the sea. Distant and disheartening. Nevertheless, I bent my ear to the speaker and inched the tuning dial up through the bands. Up and back down. The sound of nothing.

"Any luck"? Ettrick reappeared holding a couple of books. The cover of the topmost one showed a picture of Michael Aspel standing in front of some stately home.

"Bloody hell," I said. "The Antiques Roadshow? How old is that?"

Ettrick flipped to the front. "Nineteen Eighty Four," he said. "But it hardly invalidates the contents..."

"I know." I held my hands up. "It's just brings back memories. So, what about it?"

Ettrick showed me a glossy picture of a piece of pottery that bore some resemblance to the pot the bubble had left.

"I found a recipe too," Ettrick, opened the other, much older, book. *The Household Companion.* "Look. Cinnamon, eggs. The alcohol they used was *sack*. Do you know what sack was?"

I ignored the invitation to ramble along this particular sidetrack of Ettrick's esoteric knowledge. "My grandmother used to make us hot milk with a drop of whisky in it," I said, and immediately my mouth remembered the warm comforting milk, the aromatic alcohol making me drowsy as I nestled in front of the fire and the mantle clock ticked and the TV murmured. Wanting to fight the drowse of my eyelids so I could tell the kids at school that I'd stayed up to watch Kojak. "Oh, God, what I'd give right now..."

"For what?"

I didn't know how to answer him. For a taste of that milk, for certain, but also for the simplicity of childhood, when there was nothing greater to worry about than peer acceptance. Or if not that, for the time when milk was in the fridge, the 12 year old Caol Ila was in the booze cupboard, and Kojak could be torrented on a whim.

"Fuck," I said. "It's all gone."

Ettrick's face fell, and I knew he suspected a dark wave ready to break over me. "You need a drink," he said. "We don't have whisky, but a drop of port perhaps."

We had three partial bottles that I'd looted from a Threshers. The glass had been fused to a razor sharp plane across what would have been the necks, so we tried to drill through the bases. A lot of effort and a considerable amount of mess later, I said, "Well, that's it. We might as well just kill ourselves now."

Ettrick froze with anxiety.

"I was joking." I sighed. "I've got plenty of reasons to keep going." I tried a reassuring smile. "Well, one anyway." I couldn't help the way it sounded. He knew I wasn't referring to him.

"Karen's not coming back, Jim," he said. "No one ever comes back."

"I know." He still didn't understand. I wasn't waiting for Karen to come back.

"Hardly anything of use or value comes through on this side of the exchange."

"I know, Ettrick." I was waiting for a bubble – the *right* bubble – and to have the guts to take the chance, but how could I ever tell him that?

"Which is why –"

"I know, man. You don't have to spell it out."

"*Which is why* we have to treat everything that does as a gift."

"A gift?" I got up and retrieved the china pot from the table. "How incredibly useful." I was almost shouting now, but had to get it out. "How fucking *generous* our universe is, don't you think? It takes everything we had, and everyone we knew and loved, and what do we get in return? A lovely antique fucking *chamber pot*." I'd had no intention to do so but suddenly the pot was raised above my head and all I could think of was the satisfying crash it would make. Then Ettrick was holding my arms and for a moment it was as if I was the old man, him the younger. I lost the strength to hold the thing, my legs folded beneath me, but Ettrick was strong, kept both of us up. He eased the pot from my hands and lowered me into a chair.

"Fuck," I said.

He hovered, uncertain. "Jim..."

I got up so fast that the chair unbalanced. He caught that too.

"Fuck off, Ettrick."

I went to bed.

I never lost the fear of waking up to discover that a bubble had manifested around my bed and transported some portion of me to Elsewhere.

After Karen went, that fear had become half a hope.

There was no bubble in the night. Grey dawn shimmered the bookshelves in Ettrick's spare room with an otherworldly sheen, but there was no mistaking this for Elsewhere.

With a rain jar I drowned the grogginess and the lingering tatters of dark thought. I didn't bother with breakfast, wanting to be out before Ettrick stirred, but in the hall I found discarded scrap of paper that stopped me. Ettrick's handwriting was predictably neat. His shopping list unambiguous.

Eggs – powdered? Milk – UHT/condensed? Sack – good sherry, not the cooking stuff.

The rain became a downpour as I reached the edge of the golden circle. I forced myself to stop and work out which direction Ettrick had taken. He was a smart man, but he was thinking irrationally. Whether he was trying to prove that he was able to pull his weight after all or thought he could make me *feel better* with a warm drink, he was off his head. Ettrick may even have listened attentively when I related my daily experiences of the bubbles, but apart from a couple of encounters right back at the beginning he didn't *know* what it was like out here. He didn't know the signs, wouldn't have a clue what to do if he got himself in trouble.

All the same, if he'd gone to the bother of making a shopping list, wasn't it possible that he'd also taken a moment to check the map? What would he see? The area I'd not attempted to scavenge yet. The place I'd been leaving until we were completely out of alternatives. The city centre.

I headed east. Slowly, searching and calling his name. There was no response and I saw no activity, but that didn't mean there hadn't been any. I skirted between the crater fields and pinnacle forests that had been the Kelvin Hall and the art galleries, but saw no sign. By the time I traversed the length of western Sauchiehall Street I was soaked through and cursing the old bastard's name even as I yelled it out.

At Charing Cross, the Victorian tenements of the West End and the city centre had been permanently separated in the 1970s by the deep cut of the motorway. After the bubbles, it became a precipitous trench that I'd hoped might be safely circumvented by a mile or more's detour to the north in search of a place where the collapsed roadway might be crossed. The same would be true to the south, even if I was brave enough to attempt a river crossing downstream from the shifting, cracking, rubble weir that was what remained of the Kingston Bridge.

If Ettrick had made it this far, he would have discovered that this was the reason that I'd left the area untouched.

But there was another way in.

I wouldn't have chanced the pedestrian footbridge unless I was absolutely desperate. The concrete arch had been almost nibbled completely away, the iron railings all but missing. If it was still just about possible to cross, only a madman would try. As I mounted the ramp, I saw something that both reassured and chilled me. A beacon-bright red tube of flimsy polyester, caught on a stanchion and flapping in the breeze like a wind sock. It was a sleeve from a red cagoul that I had last seen neatly on a shelf in Ettrick's hall. I had often sneered internally that a man who never went out should own something so outlandish as a pac-a-mac. Now I forced myself to examine it: the crimped cuff at the narrow end, the melt-blackened plastic at the other. No blood though, either on the sleeve or on the ground. Which meant chances were good that Ettrick hadn't been wearing the thing when the bubble appeared. I imagined the rain coming on, the hapless old man unpacking the thing, shaking it out and getting in a fankle even as a bubble formed and steeled inches from the back of his head. Jumping, surprised by the *pop* and the fact he was holding on to this suddenly useless, incongruous piece of material and actually breathing the air of Elsewhere into his own lungs.

Well, that would shut the fucking know-all up on that subject at least.

The crossing was worse than I feared. With every step I felt the concrete span move, as if unsure of the earth that anchored it. The moorings were exposed and crumbling into the pit below. The rain swirled around me, my feet stumbling as I navigated the edges of holes and, once, a pile of deposited sod. The Elsewhere grass had been a velvety olive colour and sported tiny star-shaped flowers. Both were long since withered and faded but I couldn't help kneeling, breathing deep. The aroma of the other place was barely detectable.

I bellowed into the wind. Cried and cursed until my throat was raw and my fists turned white.

I found Ettrick in a glass-fronted shopping centre. The windows were peppered with circular holes like someone had used it for golf practice. He was in a whisky shop. Standing, soaked, in his cardigan, with a wire basket filled with liquor and peering at a bottle of *Oloroso* like a connoisseur on a spree.

"What the *fuck* are you doing?"

It was hard to tell if I'd given him a fright or if the stretching 'O' of his lips as he turned to face me was the beginning of a smile or a word of welcome. It was hard to tell because, in the second it took for him to react to my challenge, Ettrick was enveloped by the shimmering skin of a bubble. It grew that fast. One moment, a wink in the air, a point disturbance in front of his chest; then a rush of expanding air and there it was. It cleared his head easily and encompassed the shopping basket with room to spare.

It was close to being the *perfect* bubble.

The only problem was that its lowest extremity stopped some eight inches from the floor. I walked towards him, palms calming, mouth opening to tell him everything was going to be all right. I *did*. The words were right there on the tip of my tongue. There was no question that I was going to save him. It was only the question of whether I would be close enough to exchange places that gave me an instant's pause. I took two more strides, and took the breath needed to give my petrified neighbour the instructions for his safety. In a matter of seconds he would be safe and I'd have at least a chance of being with Karen again.

That was what was going to happen.

But universes do not operate according to our preferred order of things. They are not serendipitous; not kind or just or fair.

The bubble steeled rapidly. Ettrick's terror as the skin opaqued to a thunderous, oily silver, leaving only trouser cuffs and sorry shoes emerging from its base, was apparent.

"*Jump.*"

I thought he wasn't going to make it. I'd never seen him do more than shuffle around the flat. Then one foot rose into the bubble, and after a brief wobble, the other followed it. I imagined him, inside, off balance and realising that he wasn't going to just *hang* there. Even as his feet started to return to earth, his hands must have flown outwards, the corner of his basket escaping the sphere just at the moment that the structure, and all inside it, vanished to Elsewhere.

The pop was a thunderclap that shocked the breath from me and caused the already perforated window to come crashing down. A sudden wind. A belt of coldness.

The sheared corner of the basket spun on the floor. Its edges were melted.

Nothing else came through. Not even the faintest aroma of the air of Elsewhere. I was sure the bubble had exchanged with near-vacuum. I thought of two planets in two universes passing, exchanging earth and air for a time before moving apart. For ever.

The bubbles are rare now, and those that do appear bring nothing but cold. The idea that I might be jumping into space has dampened my enthusiasm, but it has not killed the urge completely. Perhaps, when circumstances are right again.

And perhaps it won't be necessary after all.

The posset pot, if that's what it was, saw me through the winter. I found an untapped off-licence closer to home and brewed up a variety of warming cocktails during the dark months. In my head, Ettrick and I went over and over the theories. I even read some of his books.

I went out at dawn this morning for the first time in ages. I don't know why, it just felt right. Kelvingrove, in the spring was always beautiful. Now, it is again. Beautiful, and strange. The craters are filled with grasses and flowers; the spider-spindle ruins of the buildings are cloaked with encroaching vines.

It's like a different world.

Earlier, I stood in the middle of what I can barely now recognise as

Kelvin Way. The air is warming, and it carries a scent. Something familiar. Sharp lemongrass, hot pepper.

I think of Elsewhere – and *Elsewhen*.

And I'm starting to hope. That all I have to do is wait until the bubbles return.

The West End of Glasgow, especially the areas around Glasgow University and Kelvingrove, is both old and beautiful, so obviously I wondered what it would be like to destroy it all. This is one of those stories that just comes to you. It literally popped, fully formed, into my head.

Lost Sheep

Hope To Die fizzed into coherence. The cabin-bubble, frantic with the ghostlight of tactical displays, reverberated with noise: the scream of a klaxon, the imperative twitter of warning systems, the groan of superstructure under stress and the laughter of the man who occupied the gimballed chair suspended in the centre of the sphere. Daniel Gibbs, youngest child and official black sheep of the Gibbs Galactic Cultures dynasty was scarlet, shaking and sweat-soaked with excitement.

The scrawling displays slowed and, one by one, the warning noises diminished until only the blaring klaxon remained. "We'll be havin' the siren off now, Danny, yeah?" Hope sounded a little annoyed. "You complete cock."

Gibbs relaxed, spun lazily in the chair. His laughter dwindled to a sigh.

The klaxon cut out. "All that noise, mate." Hope's vocal pattern was still the abrasive baritone she'd picked up from her most recent scrap of Earthwave. It made everything she said sound peeved, but in this instance there was even more than the usual amount of – what had she called it? – *nark*. "It is really not fucking necessary."

"All right." Danny pouted. What wasn't *necessary* was his ship, however human it might pretend to be, complaining about noise. He'd been warned about her attitude when he bought her. For the price he'd paid for her, though, he could put up with it most of the time. If nothing else, her abrasiveness kept things from getting boring. "You have to admit it adds to the drama, though," he said.

The ship approximated the sound of breath drawn in through teeth. "Don't you start with me about fucking drama, you nonce. I fried my quantum racks to a crisp there finding a safe spot of space for us to pop into. You just had to sit back and enjoy the ride."

Now she was really killing the buzz. "Aw, come on, Hope. We're safe, aren't we?"

"Of course we're safe. No thanks to you. They're getting closer, you know. Your family the Hegemony, the representatives of who knows how many law enforcement and security agencies... and let's not even mention the bounty hunters? Bunch of fuckers. Do you know how many fucking spins that took us?"

Danny shrugged. As far as he was concerned the occasional need for a speedy exit was an occupational hazard. It went hand in hand with the notoriety and the rewards; at least, when there *were* rewards. Their riotous escape had been a distraction from the plunging disappointment experienced on arriving at the planet whose cultural rights he'd been planning to claim-jump. A newly discovered planetary system was rare, and a virgin culture an order of magnitude more so. He'd had the rights deals secured and the money spent long before Hope slipped them into the system, but as soon as they arrived he knew they were too late. The cultural claim notice broadcast across the system's media spectra had made it all too clear that the Hegemony had got there first by some margin. The euonymists had already begun their naming work on the inhabited planet, and the Hegemony-wide broadcast and trade rights too were neatly parcelled up among various divisions of the Gibbs Corporation.

Disappointment, in fact, was barely sufficient to describe how he had felt. He had been raging. The whisper from the Grüber Brothers was supposed to have been exclusive. In the tantrum that followed the realization that it was anything but, Danny had vowed expressively and in several languages to make sure that they were repaid for their mistake. It might still have been possible to sneak close enough to the new world to grab some footage that he could flog quickly before the sanctioned cultural tsunami rolled across the Hegemony worlds, but in his prolonged incandescence he'd lost the opportunity for even that consolation.

When the sudden swarm of antagonistic ships bore down on them, Hope took over and their escape became a rush of coherence and decoherence that Danny had no chance of following. The displays had swum with snapshot ghosts, lingering images of threats that were already a subspace spin away: everything from Hegemony hulks to diamond-glitter drone arrays, all of them hunting for him with the same cut-throat avidity with which he sought unsanctioned cultural novelty to titillate the jaded palates of the populated galaxy. All attempting to outmanoeuvre Hope's tactical strategies. Pieces moved, bets spread; a game of risk and reaction. Even as they cohered, Hope had sent them spinning off again to some other point in space, the ship juddering with imposed seizure imperatives, jerking under weapons fire, but every time they'd managed to slip away, try again. It had been a wild ride.

"Over *seventeen fousand* spins" Hope said. "This malarky is getting too risky by half. Remind me why I do this again?"

"Because we're a team?" Hope usually went along with that *shtick*, but on this occasion her only response was a snort of derision, so he followed it up with: "And because I own you."

After a beat, Hope said: "Well, you'll be hearing from my brief on that score, wontcha?"

Danny didn't know what a *brief* was. Hope picked up the most unlikely phrases from the old Earth broadcasts, the strung-out signals that had leaked across the light years during that short period of the planet's history when high-powered, modulated EM had been the primary method of media broadcast. Commercially speaking, Earthwave material never went out of fashion, and dedicated collectors could make a modest living. Danny's sister, Imelda, headed Gibbs Old World. It was a minor division but it provided a steady contribution to the family fortunes. That was Mel all over, though. No ambition. She'd always been perfectly content with her allotted role, seeking out those vanishingly faint signals, collating humanity's old stories.

Old stories, though. Who cared? Next to the corporate soaps and the melo-historicals, where the ratings were really at was discovering how weird other people – on other planets, in other systems – could be.

The galaxy was immense, and in a couple of thousand years of human colonization still only a fraction of its treasures had been uncovered. The thought of what else might be out there waiting to be found, and exploited, constantly thrilled him. Planets, civilizations, hilarious sexual practices: when it came to entertaining the masses, novelty was everything.

He'd never understood how or why his ship had become a stodgy old Earthwave nut.

"Where are we, anyway?" Danny said.

"Don't know, do I?" He heard the sulk in her sigh.

"Yes you do."

"All right, keep them on," she muttered. One, two, three displays blossomed on the curve of the bubble. A galactic limb. The details of the nearest star clusters. Proximity estimates to the nearest Hegemony worlds, to the nearest habitable world, to anything. All, literally, astronomical.

Hope didn't need to say it, but she did anyway. "We're way out there, mister."

"Take us somewhere else then."

"No can do, buster. Seventeen thousand jumps takes it out of a girl. I'm going to put my feet up and take it easy."

"What?"

"Didn't ya hear me? Ya got cloth in your ears? We need to recharge, and there ain't a whole amount of energy out here. It's gonna take a while."

Danny groaned. "How long?"

"One hundred and sixty three hours. Give or take a smidgen."

"A *smidgen*...?" It was then that he cottoned on that Hope's voice had changed. The blunt baritone had been replaced by a brassy, rapid-fire patter. At least this time it was female. "So let me get this straight," he said. "There's no energy out here, but you've managed to find Earthwave?"

"Give the boy a doughnut!" The cheerfulness was already grating. "But that's just about all there is. So for the foreseeable, you'll find me tucked up with a new, old movie. Want to watch?"

"No." *Movie* was one of her favourite Earthwave words. A movie was like a melo-historical, but not as good.

"Your funeral, mac. See ya in the funny papers."

Privately, Hope agreed that the escape had been exhilarating. She relished the excitement of her role in Danny's story. Just like in a movie: she was the loyal companion, the wisecracking sidekick, the grumpy getaway driver. She even put on voices so she could play the parts properly.

Dramatic thrills like this were why she had agreed to Danny's ownership. She loved her Earthwave movies but there just weren't enough of them, so she'd sought out her own adventure. It had been a proper rollercoaster right from the start, full of intrigue and escapes and brushes with the law. Lately, though, the excitement had worn thin. If this had been an Earthwave drama it would have come to its conclusion by now, but Danny was never quite clever enough or daring enough to pull off the great coup that he dreamed of and Hope always managed to extract them from the inevitable pursuit. All in all, it was becoming tiresome. On balance, she was coming to the conclusion that she preferred her movies after all.

To be truthful, she was only sticking around with Danny now to see what happened at the end.

It took only a fraction of the estimated downtime for Danny to go crazy with boredom. While Hope drifted in space, scooping up atoms, he ate, slept, played his interactives. When he grew tired of those, he scoured the most recent feeds for leads, recatalogued his finds, even attempted to reconcile his financial affairs.

"All right," he shouted. "Show me a movie."

Without comment, Hope displayed the moving image on the bubble: a grainy office scene with a man and a woman talking over each other so rapidly as to be incomprehensible. From what little he could follow he gleaned that they worked for a media organization, but they were using methods of securing their stories that seemed, bizarrely, to be considered illegal at the time and their endless arguments on the subject formed the bulk of the story. They might have been in love too, but that seemed coincidental. Beyond that, the experience was a mystery. He kept watching in hope that something might explode; it often did when things got tedious in Earthwave dramas. On this occasion, however, he was disappointed.

"Why did the police arrest that man?" Danny moaned, more to have something to say than because he cared.

"Just follow the story, bozo. It ain't *War And Peace*."

"It'd help if there *was* a story. Although I still fail to see why that's always so important to you."

"Buster, if you can't watch a movie without complaining, so help me I'll..." She broke off.

"You'll?"

Shh.

The imperative was not uttered aloud, but directly via his C-link. Danny's blood cooled. If they had been tracked down already, they'd be unable to spin their way out of trouble.

What is it? he replied.

There's another ship out here.

There was a pause while she assembled whatever data she was

receiving from the grey market multiband sensor arrays that he'd installed specifically for the purposes of knowing what was out there before anyone else did. In the business of cultural claims you needed every advantage you could get.

"What kind of ship?" Danny said aloud.

"An old one. I *think* it's an original Sol system generation rock."

"Don't be stupid. It can't be."

"If you're calling me a liar, Mac, you can take it up with my sweet old grey-haired mother."

"All right, all right." Anything to keep the peace. She was still wrong though. It really couldn't be an original gen-ship from the time of the first diaspora. Not all the way out here. Although, now he thought about it… it wasn't *inconceivable* for a ship to drift this far out into the darkness. If the guidance systems had been damaged or if its crew had succumbed to attack or contagion, transforming their vessel into a drifting tomb, awaiting discovery. It wasn't *impossible*.

"What else?" he said.

"Hold your horses. There's only so much you can tell from external scans."

If this ship was what Hope claimed… it'd be a *goldmine*. Danny was already thinking of the deals he could make. Legitimate ones for a change. He might even be able to *sell* something to GOW instead of sneaking footage from under their noses all the time. He pondered over whether it would be better to sell off the contents individually or hold out for passing them off as a single lot – a living museum. Mel would piss her pants over that.

"Well?" His voice quavered with impatience. "How do we get aboard?"

Hope laughed. "We ask the occupants, obviously."

The rock was occupied? "You're seriously telling me that some fluky tomb-raiding bastard stumbled on this before us?"

"Not exactly, bub. This ain't no mausoleum. Someone on it just hailed us, and they're *very* friendly." She effected a low whistle. "And you're not going to believe this. They claim to be the descendants of the original crew. Ship's called the *Saint Rachel Of The Further Fields*, a privately funded resettlement venture that left the Sol system on June 18th 2189 OEC. The original heading was one of the Vela worlds, but they never completed their journey."

Danny juggled some figures. "2189 by the Old Earth calendar – that was before subspace spin was discovered. They can't have been travelling linear all that time. That's hundreds of years."

"*Thousands.*"

When Danny had absorbed this information, his spirits soared again: not only was the ship a relic but, if it had been travelling the dark reaches between systems all that time, whoever inhabited it was a living link to Old Earth.

"What are you waiting for?" he yelled. "Get us over there!"

"No need," Hope said. "They're coming to us."

This was how it always was. Just when Hope thought Danny Gibbs's story had run its course and was lumbering towards the inevitable buffers of ignominy and incarceration, something new cropped up. A glimmer of hope. She had been with Danny long enough that she needed no persuasion that her owner was an incorrigible and unrepentant bastard. He sought out novelty not for its own intrinsic value, but for financial gain and for how much it would add to his own notoriety. Just by following his orders she was legally complicit in most of his less savoury activities. But, if there was anything she had learned from her Earthwave dramas, it was that no one was beyond redemption. And if there was one thing she couldn't resist, it was the possibility, no matter how slim, of a happy ending.

Danny was examining the unrefined exterior of the asteroid and marvelling that it had once been easier to build a deep-space worthy vessel by modifying a lump of rock rather than simply fabbing it. Wherever the vessel's travels had taken it, they had not been without incident. The lumpy surface sported craters of various ages as well as black scorch marks, glittering silicate growths, and a field of weird conical structures that scans indicated had once been quasi-organic. This ship had been about. He stared hard, as if the ancient object might vanish the second he took his eyes off it. He hardly dared blink.

"The *Saint Rachel* has agreed to provide us with an energy feed," said Hope. "But they want something in exchange."

Aha, there it was. He'd known this was falling too easily into his lap. "Go on, tell me."

"They want to meet you."

"They *want* me to come aboard? Straight off, without coercion or anything? What's the catch?"

Hope's reply was pensive. "Why does there always have to be a catch? Apparently you're the first human they've had direct contact with for several generations. Naturally they're interested in meeting you and hearing your story. Everyone's got one, ya know. And there are precious few of them out here in dead space." Her sigh was pitched somewhere between exasperation and disappointment. "Of course, you can always make up a lie. That's what you're good at, right? They'll never know the difference anyway."

Danny brayed. He could certainly lie.

The welcoming committee wasn't up to much.

During docking, Danny had spent time concocting a tall tale to impress his hosts with; hopefully enough that they'd be open to the idea of negotiations. He'd even gone to the trouble of getting the look right, dragging out his old uniform and cleaning the boots for the first time since his disastrous visit to that colossal ball of sucking mud known as Banou. That affair had been the last in the string of shitty down-the-pecking-order assignments that had persuaded to leave the family service and go freelance. He'd got himself a ship, some decent clothes and sworn never to don the familial straitjacket again. Ah, well. Screw principles. His story wouldn't be mentioning any of that. As far as his audience knew, this uniform was that of a military officer, not a corporate lackey. The ribbons spanning the serge told of a much-lauded career in service; the crumples and stains betraying the hard times that had befallen him after being heroically injured and honourably discharged. As far as his story went, he would be making exactly the right impression.

His hosts could at least have made a similar effort. When he exited the docking chamber he was met by a cluster of crones, peering from behind each other like timid children. On second glance, though, they were not perhaps as old as they seemed. Certainly, they wore unflattering woollen robes, their curly, greasy hair came in various shades of grey or white, and the teeth revealed in their off-putting smiles of welcome were yellowing pegs, but many of their faces were incongruously youthful. If they had been citizens of the Hegemony he would have been surprised only at their aesthetic choice, but he had been expecting people as isolated as this lot to be much more primitive.

The woman at the front of the cluster stepped forward. "Master Daniel Gibbs. You are welcome aboard the *Saint Rachel Of The Further Fields.*" Her voice had a soft vibrato to it. "We are simple travellers across God's far country, but the sisterhood would be honoured if, while we attend to your needs, you would share a meal with us, and perhaps tell us a little of yourself."

Sisterhood: collective name for a female-only religious order, Hope supplied over the C-link, helpfully, filling in the gaps in Danny's knowledge. *Saint Rachel: character from prime Christian text known as The Bible. A keeper of sheep who became the wife of someone called Jacob. God: character from The Bible around whom Christianity was –*

I'm aware of who God was, thank you.

Danny grinned. This was going to be a piece of cake. He stepped forwards but was halted by a polite shake of the spokeswoman's head.

"It is our custom to remove our footwear while aboard the *Saint Rachel.*"

He looked at his boots. It had taken hours to get anything approaching a shine out of them.

Just do it, Hope whispered.

Grumbling, Danny complied. He paired his boots neatly before joining the women in the corridor beyond.

"Oh..." He looked down, wriggled his toes in the sudden, soft warmth.

"Carpet making is one of the textile crafts to which our order has dedicated itself." The leader flexed her own toes. The nails were exceptionally thick. "You may address me as Bell," she said, walking on.

Danny lingered, mesmerised by the carpet's pattern, a race of mathematical and organic geometries that intermingled in beguiling fashion. The other women had to crowd him to drive him on in the wake of their spokeswoman.

"Bell?" He trotted reluctantly after her. "Captain Bell?"

The woman's chocolate eyes regarded him with something like humour. "Simply Bell."

The carpeted corridor led to a huge internal space. It was ringed and criss-crossed by gantries, stairs and walkways on many levels both above and below the one on which they entered. Peering over the rail, Danny had a dizzying view of the floors below him falling away towards a flat, green expanse. Looking upwards, he was almost blinded. The interior lighting in here was brighter than the suns on many worlds he had visited. There was warmth too, though not quite enough to take the edge off the circulating air.

"We will be delighted to conduct a tour later." Bell had noticed that he was staring. "But the dinner hour is upon us. This way please."

The group filtered along the carpeted gantry and down a nearby stair. On the balcony below was an expansive commons. Here the design on the carpet spread out, complexifying to an impressive scale. Danny's eyes, constantly drawn to the pattern, felt on the verge of making sense out the abstract designs, but there was too much in the way. The floor was obscured by tables, a serving counter, and a sizeable complement of rough-robed crew, ready for their meal. Danny's group descended the stair and a murmur of expectation rose to greet them.

When they approached the servery, he realized that one of the women was trying to get his attention. "I'm sorry? What's happening?"

The woman's grey hair stuck out in long tufts. Her close-lipped smile bordered on obsequious, her voice tremulous. "The Bell is selecting what she wishes for her evening meal."

Danny watched as the spokeswoman lifted lids on each of a selection of tureens and platters, nodding and conversing with the servers. He couldn't quite make out what was in the dishes, although there was a worrying amount of greenery on display and the steam that drifted over was only vaguely aromatic. He preferred his food meaty, spicy and mildly hallucinogenic, but he was well practised at gritting his teeth and smiling in the name of a business opportunity.

Bell finally pointed at a deep pot, and was briskly served from it with a bowlful of stewed vegetable matter. Immediately, the other women lined up and selected the same choice. Danny must have allowed his confusion to show. The sister who had spoken to him before gave him an understanding smile. "We follow the Bell's lead," she said. "She's never wrong."

Danny, reminding himself that religious communities could be prone to strangely slavish behaviour, nodded as if he understood, accepted his own bowl of steaming roots and sat with his hosts.

"All of our food on board the *Saint Rachel* is grown naturally." Bell speared a chunk of something fibrous. The fingers that manipulated the fork were tipped by horny nails and when she bit into her forkful Danny got a good look at those teeth. He had thought they were badly kept, but in fact what he saw were strong yellow pegs. They mashed efficiently on the vegetable.

Danny took a mouthful of his own meal. The taste was actually not too bad, but the vegetables were barely cooked. On his first attempt to crunch into them he feared he might actually have broken his own teeth.

"Delicious." He choked, sluiced the mouthful down with a sip of water. When he had recovered he said: "If you don't mind, me asking, What happened?"

Took your time, Sherlock.

Danny ignored Hope. His focus was on Bell. It wasn't just the teeth, the nails, the hair: it was in those big, placid eyes, that flattened nose; all ubiquitous features among the crew.

"What happened, Mister Gibbs?"

"To your people." He arranged his expression into one that he hoped conveyed compassion. "To your humanity."

The steadiness of her gaze was unnerving. "The *Saint Rachel Of The Further Fields* has been travelling a long time. She set off from Earth with a complement of three thousand, six hundred, backed up by a full genetic database of human, livestock and food crop genomes. The mission, as you would perhaps expect of an order like ours, was a simple one: to find somewhere to settle where the grass was greener – both literally and ideologically – than it had become on Earth."

"The grass...?"

It's a metaphor. Just go with it, okay?

Bell ignored his interjection. "The *Saint Rachel* journeyed successfully for many generations."

"How many generations?"

"Hundreds." Bell's dark eyes were unreadable. "And therein lay the problem. Over time our mission was... *reinterpreted.* Instead of settling, our people chose to continue travelling. We had encounters. They were not always without incident or consequence. At some point on her travels the *Saint Rachel's* databases became corrupted and, not long after that, we are told, a contagion was contracted that affected the DNA and threatened to kill off the crew."

"You are *told?*" It was just a hint in the wording.

Bell did not appear to be insulted that he picked up on it. "It was many generations ago, and records have not always been maintained."

"So, what happened?"

"To save the sisterhood it was decided to introduce genetic material from another species."

From the livestock, Hope said on the C-link.

"Which species?"

Now Bell smiled, showed her peggy teeth. "The one sacred to *Saint Rachel,* of course," she said.

"The sheep," he said aloud. To Hope he said, *You're recording all this, right?* Even if they got nothing else from this venture this interview would syndicate far and wide.

Bell smiled. "It proves that we are beloved of *Saint Rachel.* Had it not been for the sheep our people would not have survived."

"Do you still consider yourselves to be human?" Danny asked the question because it would be on the lips of every Hegemony viewer when they saw this. And because he relished the flicker of reaction that, finally, he managed to elicit from the woman's imperturbable features.

"We are all God's creatures," she replied.

Danny searched his bowl for edible bits of vegetable. *Is she saying what I think she's saying?*

Hope was guarded. *That somewhere along the line their community deliberated decided it would be preferable to make themselves more* flock-like? *I don't know, fella, religion's a funny thing. Especially when left to its own devices for a long time. She might not even know for sure. Doubt you'll get her to come out and actually say it, though.*

Danny chewed thoughtfully. *Doesn't matter. The melo-historical they make of this will make it pretty obvious...*

Noticing that the sounds of mastication had stilled, he looked up from his bowl. Everyone was staring. Dark eyes, patient gazes, all trained on him. For a second he was seized with an irrational fear that these unnerving people were capable of eavesdropping on the C-link.

Hope allayed his fears. *They've told their story. I think they're waiting for yours.*

Danny was no stranger to having to bluff and brazen – in fact he relished any opportunity to grandstand – but for some reason now the moment had come to deliver his fabricated history he dried up. He scanned the sisters' flat faces. Their anticipation was palpable, and suddenly the tall tale he had intended to palm off on them seemed silly and obvious. Very little knocked his self-confidence, but this did. It uncapped a well of self-doubt that had been sealed-off since the last time his mother had appraised his commercial performance.

The Honourable Captain? He was glad to be on the C-link. He feared that if he'd had to speak aloud at that moment, nothing would have come out. *They'll see right through that.*

Hope hesitated before answering, and when she did she had dropped most of the artifice from her tone. *Why not tell them your real story then?*

Don't be ridiculous. I'm trying to get them to trust me. Danny took a deep breath, felt his confidence ebb back. *No, the Honourable Captain will work. I'll make it work. It's only a story after all. I just need a minute.*

The moment stretched, then Bell pushed aside her bowl. "Perhaps you would enjoy that tour now."

When she stood, a loose gaggle of the crew did likewise. They were fewer in number than the welcoming party had been. The rest of the women went back to eating, their stewed roots clearly a bigger attraction than Danny had proved to be. He cursed himself for allowing himself to be so easily thrown. He'd seize the next opportunity, and dazzle them.

Bell led them a short distance to a bank of elevators. He and the woman who had spoken to him at the servery followed but no one else joined them, the remainder of the women drifting away. It didn't matter, he told himself. He only needed to impress their leader.

"The fields please, Floss," Bell said, and the remaining acolyte jabbed her thumb at the control button.

As the elevator descended, Danny's eyes wandered to the floor. Even here there was a square of carpet. This sample was a little worn but the design was clear enough, and here at last it formed a recognisable picture. The geometries resolved into angular silver shapes, whorls of actinic white and lines of cerulean energy, all against the unmistakable curving sweep of a planetary ring system. Noticing his scrutiny his companions pressed against the walls so he could see the complete picture. Yes, it *was* a space battle, and the craftsmanship involved in its depiction was exquisite.

Hey, Hope whispered. *That looks like –*

"You might know this scene as the Battle of Harmony's Shelf," Bell said.

Danny's eyes widened. *Harmony's Shelf*, of course. It was an iconic image from the early times of the Hegemony, when cultural rights had been contested by violence instead of bureaucracy. He'd seen it represented in the media hundreds of times. Only never quite like this. It was as if it were drawn from a different perspective, the other side of the battle than the traditional views. He admired the skill and the imagination, but it didn't change what the image implied.

"You've not been so isolated after all," he said. "This is a Hegemony classic."

Bell shook her head. "We have had no contact with your Hegemony," she said. "Not directly. We do stumble across your communication broadcasts from time to time, but we prefer real experience to *dramas*."

"I don't understand you."

"This scene was woven as it happened. The *Saint Rachel* was there."

Danny gaped at her. Harmony's Shelf had been discovered tucked away in a hazardous corner of the galaxy. The landmark conflict over who brought its unlikely cultural riches to the eager eyes of the Hegemony worlds had been titanic and brief. The odds upon randomly stumbling upon that event would have been astronomical. Bell was clearly talking nonsense, but her expression was completely free of guile.

"You're telling me that this primitive rock, which has spent most of its travels in empty space, just happened to wander through the Ostermann zone during one of the most famous battles in Hegemony history?"

She beamed at him as a teacher might at a bright pupil. "That is correct." The elevator opened. "Come and see our sheep."

They stepped out of the lift onto what could have been the surface of a temperate planet. The effect was so startling that it wiped Danny's next thought from his head. The fields he'd thought to be flat from above in fact rolled like a natural landscape, replete with hills and streams. A zephyr riffled the grass, and the light that had all but blinded him above bathed the scene with a radiance that was, this far down, rather pleasant.

And then there were the sheep. Danny was familiar with such

animals, of course. They were among the standard livestock that humans had exported from Earth, although their genetic make-up had usually been altered to suit whatever environment they were imported into, leading to substantial variations between the specimens he had encountered. While the animals grazing here were comparatively modest beasts, there was something quintessentially *sheepish* about them. There was little doubt that these animals came from old stock. And old stock was a very valuable commodity.

"They're all white?" Danny said. "That's traditional, I believe."

"We spin and dye our wool by hand." One of the animals had meandered towards them and Bell buried her hand in its fleece. "That's the way it has been done since our order was founded. We see no reason to change. And besides, we now believe that God prefers his creatures... unaltered."

She met the sheep's gaze instead of Danny's, underlining with obvious regret the close kinship between her and the animal. If her ancestors had once thought that the intention of their holy scripture was to be more like their sacred animals, it seemed that in more recent times the tide of interpretation had flowed back the other way again. This was pretty tragic. It was going to make fantastic melodrama.

"So that's why you never settled?" he said. "Because the promised land was promised to humans, not to... whatever you believe you have become?"

Now she did look at him. "One of the reasons, perhaps." Instead of elaborating, however, she turned abruptly and strode back towards the elevators.

"Where are you going now?" When Bell ignored him, he readdressed the question to Floss. "Where's she going?"

The older crew member simpered. "We do not question the Bell's whim." She lifted the hem of her robe so that she could hurry after her leader. "We only follow."

What the hell? Left alone, Danny vented his frustration to Hope as he watched the women disappear behind the elevator shaft.

She's still waiting for your story, McGrory. Hope had resumed her chatty persona. *You've gotta tell them something. C'mon it'll just be like confessional with Father O'Reilly.*

The reference, as usual, was lost on him.

What's got into you, Hope? he said. *Whose side are you on? Can't you see the opportunity we've got here?*

Yes, I can. Hope's voice was suddenly serious. *I really can. And I really want you to take it.*

Her tone mystified him, but she was right about one thing: he was losing them. He could feel their cooperation evaporating. Danny hurried to catch up with his hosts. Behind the elevator he found a staircase, where the carpet resumed. He followed the engrossing design from tread to tread. At the top, the pattern resolved into a second image; this time depicting tall, twisting crystalline spires. No one in planet-hunting circles in the Hegemony could have failed to recognise it.

Cowrie's World, Hope supplied unnecessarily.

Wrenching himself away from the beautiful rendition of that planet, he found Bell and Floss in conversation with the tenders of some raised vegetable beds.

"Well." He beamed. "This is very impressive."

The women paused in their conversation and blinked at him. Once again their unwavering expectation rattled his confidence. This time, however, he threw off the doubt, rallied his determination not to miss out on his prize. That was until he spotted yet another picture in the carpet at the women's feet. He dropped to his knees to examine the circle of suns. "The *Kori-kori Configuration*," he whispered. When he looked up, the women had moved off again. He managed only a few steps of pursuit before the pattern gave up another familiar wonder. *Wilson's Duality,* in all of its vapour-bound glory. His hosts had begun to ascend to the next level.

"Wait," he called.

Between the leafy beds and the stairs he stumbled over the *Awakening Of The Mechanitrona,* the *Butterflies Of Dhelve,* and, if he wasn't mistaken, the *War Of The Three Worlds.* All of these were key events in galactic history, household names. But, again, each of the scenes was subtly different from its clichéd Hegemony representation. And that was just the ones he recognized. He followed the pattern as it raced and resolved into image after image, and discovered that the really startling thing was that the unfamiliar scenes outnumbered the familiar ones by an order of magnitude.

If Bell could be believed, the carpet wasn't just a work of exceptional artisanship, it was a comprehensive historical record of the significant places and events of the last few thousand years. But that really was impossible. The galaxy was too large, their ship too slow and ancient.

On the next level, a cohort of crew was tackling various processes involved in turning fleece into fibres. Bell stopped to pass a word and a smile with them before walking on again.

"Wait," Danny shouted again, and when that had no effect. "My story..."

This time she deigned to wait for him. "We would love to hear it," she said. Her gaze drilled into him.

"Well..." Danny was out of breath and had a pain in his side from the chase. He swept an arm in a semi-circle, indicating the carpet on which even now he was spotting scene after amazing scene. "But first... it was a lie, wasn't it? Or a joke, a joke at least? When you said that your ship was at Harmony's Shelf, and that was how its image got into your extraordinary carpet." Neither woman responded. "Because if it's true, and all of the other images are true, were woven from *actual experience*... well it's not possible, is it?" Neither woman offered even an ounce of refutation, and so he was forced to complete the chain of thought himself. "Because, no one gets that damned lucky!"

Bell looked crestfallen. "It was neither a lie nor a joke," she said. "Every image you see in our carpet was, exactly as you say, woven because the *Saint Rachel* happened to be at each place at the right time. It is not coincidence, Mr Gibbs. Nor is it luck. It is the Bellwether's gift. We call it divine guidance. If you prefer a secular explanation, you might call it *instinct*, perhaps something we inherited from our ovine cousins. And that is the other reason that our ship never settled. We are a wandering flock now. It is our role to cross the endless spans of the cosmos and witness as many of God's great works as we can. We trust *Saint Rachel* to guide us, and she always does so. We have seen such wonders."

Danny still found it impossible to believe her. And yet, if what these women said *was* true, this carpet was potentially a map to a thousand wonders unknown to the Hegemony. The *Saint Rachel's* story itself would be a flash in the pan, and even a broker's fee on the sheep's genetic property rights would be of little consequence compared to the riches awaiting him via the combination of these images and the ship's log.

He had to have this carpet. More than ever now, he needed to get these women on his side.

"Thank you, for humouring my curiosity," he said at last, a combination of avarice and excitement quashing the last of the nerves. "And for that I owe you my own tale." He sighed, and inflected his voice with an appropriate degree of weary fragility. "You must forgive my reticence. Once you've heard what I have to say, I think you'll understand how difficult it is for me to relate. I was born into a military family on a tiny world of so little significance that I won't trouble you with its name. Our family was not a high-ranking one, but our people were involved in a long war and it was expected that we would do our duty, so I enlisted in the orbital patrols."

Danny had closed his eyes to convey how emotional this all was for him. When he opened them, Bell had wandered away again. The woman called Floss smiled encouragingly, however. "Go on," she said.

"Well, I..."

"Continue, we're listening."

Edging after Bell, who had now reached the base of the next flight of stairs, Danny went on. "It wasn't just I who enlisted. My brothers and sisters all joined the same unit, and we forged a crack force whose reputation soon spread beyond our little planet."

"Oh dear." Floss's face crumpled, then she turned and followed her leader up the stairs.

"Wait," Danny protested. "I'm telling you the story."

"Well, yes," Floss slogged up the carpeted steps. "But we were hoping for the other one."

"What other one?"

"The one about you and *Hope To Die*." The hem of the woman's woollen robe danced in front of him. "That one seemed quite funny. There was lots of running away."

"How do you know about that?" Of course the answer to that question at least was obvious. And Hope's subsequent silence as much as declared her guilt.

Floss's answer drifted down to him. "*Hope To Die* told it to the rest of the sisters. It sounds very exciting, although apparently you can be a bit of a scallywag at times. I do hope you get your just desserts at the end."

What exactly have you been telling them? Danny whispered to Hope, but his ship chose not to reply.

At the top of the stairs, Danny followed Floss over to a corner where Bell was attending an industrious group of crew members. When he joined them he realized with horror that they were ripping the carpet up. They used tools to unpick the weave and main strength to yank the threads free. He arrived in time to see a picture being pulled apart. A beautiful, emerald green world whose images he would now never be able to sell to the Hegemony.

"What are you doing?"

"We only have a finite amount of floor, Mister Gibbs," Bell said. "When new events occur, we have to make room for new pictures."

"But it's *priceless.*" The pile of threads was growing, as was the exposed section of blank decking.

Bell shrugged. "It's just a record. The experience for the crew members who visited that place was priceless." As she spoke, a further influx of crew members arrived and doubled the level of industry. Boxes were opened revealing skeins of bright wool. A complicated apparatus was also erected. It was only when they started applying the yarn to it that Danny recognised it as a loom. The third item that was brought to the scene was an ancient viewing screen.

"Thank you for your visit, Mister Gibbs," Bell said. At her feet the crew had worked fast to create a perfect blank square fringed with threads. "Your ship's energy has been replenished. You're no doubt eager to be on your way."

"Wait, no. I wanted to do a deal. I can make you rich."

The soft snuffling sound that Bell produced sounded quite unlike laughter, but her bared yellow teeth did suggest that she found his last statement humorous. "You've seen how simply we live. What could you possibly offer us? Now we'd like you to leave because we have work to do."

That was when the penny dropped. The realization of it flushed through Danny in a hot rush. "Something's going to happen, isn't it? That's why you're out here. Your *instinct* led you here." Immediately after the realization came the full blown panic. "Please. I want to see it. I *need* to see it. To be a witness – like *you.*" On the C-link he muttered. *Hope, get on this. Record everything.* "Please, this is vital..." *Hope?*

The ship still didn't answer, and Bell turned her back on him, saying only: "Goodbye, Mister Gibbs."

The crew members that bore down on him were stronger than they looked. They crowded him, buffeted him, drove him away from the scene. The last thing he saw as they herded him into the elevator car was the screen flickering to life, displaying a swathe of dark, pregnant space.

"What about my story?" he yelled in desperation.

This time, the snuffling laughter came from the sisters who crowded the rising elevator car with him. When they reached the docking level they wasted no time in bullying him back aboard *Hope To Die*.

Danny felt the mechanisms of disengagement beginning but he remained sprawled on the floor, attempting simultaneously to master his fury and regain his dignity, all the while ignoring the pain in his temple caused by the impact of the shiny boots which had been tossed after him.

"Thanks for your help there," he muttered to Hope as he heaved himself into his chair. "Now perhaps if you wouldn't mind, can we fire a beacon into that forsaken relic? There's no way I'm giving that carpet up." Silently, the command bubble displayed a three-sixty view of the space around them. The ancient rock was already drifting to a respectable distance, but from his own ship there was no other sign of activity. "Hope, don't piss me about. I'm telling you to tag that ship."

The new voice was flat and devoid of character. "I'm sorry, Dave. I can't do that."

"Oh, don't start on me now with that stupid Earthwave shit. I'm seriously not in the mood. In fact, forget the tag. Send in a crawler colony laden with nerve toxin."

"I'm sorry, Dave. I can't do that."

"Oh, go *fuck yourself*."

"I'm sorry, Dave. I can't do that either." Then in her normal voice she said, "I am sorry, Danny, I'm not playing along any more. The story's over."

When Danny finally understood, he felt both sickened and thrilled.

"Who did you call?" he whispered.

"Does it matter?"

He'd never seriously considered that he might one day actually be caught, but the knowledge that – according to the sisters at least – his demise was going to be an event of galactic significance almost made it worthwhile.

He checked the view. For a while there was just the *Saint Rachel*; then, just as a wave of doubt began to lap at his certainty, the first Hegemony ship spun into view. Danny swung in his chair and began to laugh. He could imagine it now, the sector crowded with ships: the forces of law and security and corporate malfeasance from a host of systems, a clutch of independent bounty hunters too. He was on a lot of lists. He wondered how many there would be in the end. *The Thousand Ship Capture Of The Outlaw Daniel Gibbs* had a nice ring to it. As dramas went, his story would be prime time for sure.

Danny waited, laughing with excitement.

In the end, one ship was all that was required. Hope allowed them access without fuss or comment and when Danny left her, meekly and hardly noticed by anyone, he wasn't laughing any more. It wasn't a particularly satisfying ending, she admitted, but at least it was an ending.

Hope was not entirely happy either with her own part in bringing events about. It wasn't at all like being a character in a movie. There were repercussions. Guilt, she discovered, was not an especially pleasant feeling.

In future she would be quite content in the role of observer.

When the Hegemony security ship had gone, she observed that the Saint Rachel Of The Further Fields remained. She watched the gen-ship for a time. It just sat there, waiting patiently. They were good at patience, she noted, and they had seen so much.

Hope decided to wait with them out there beyond the galactic fringe. Yes, she'd had enough involvement; it was time to try patience. In time, she had the feeling she would be rewarded.

Later. Something winked in the deep darkness. Something bright blossomed.
Something amazing happened.

I don't often delve into the farther reaches of Science Fiction, but when I was asked to contribute a story to an anthology with the theme of 'dark currents' the idea that came to mind was to wonder what happens to all of the electromagnetic waves that

Neil Williamson

propagate outwards from Earth, all of our radio and TV broadcasts inching out into space. Ultimately it's a story about choosing the story you want to be part of. And it has a spaceship full of ruminant nuns!

Silk Bones

First Forgetting

It was snowing when Ria arrived in Carrmore, and didn't look as if it would ever stop. Taking time out from unpacking the boxes and bags that she had crammed into her little green Skoda for the drive north, she went to the bedroom window and watched the flakes descend with universal patience out of the black sky. Then she rested her forehead on the glass and exhaled a breath she'd held so long that her body was sore with it.

The house was not a big house but neither was the Skoda a big car, and her possessions – mostly clothes and toiletries, her tablet and phone and, for some reason, the small TV from the spare bedroom where she'd spent more nights than not in recent months – looked paltry spread out on the floor. Once she'd scattered these few tokens of herself throughout the rented house, the place felt a little more homely. When she started to think about the things she had left behind, she went back to the window. Back to the snow.

Ria had known the Highlands would be wintry, but had not expected this much white. The garden, buried several feet deep, was featureless and flat and the boundary hedges between the two-storey, stone-built property and its neighbours were rounded like rolled cotton gym towels. It was perfect.

The next morning eased her slow and soft out of her deepest sleep in months, unexpected sunshine illuminating the paisley curtains like whorled stained glass. Then a knock reverberated up through the house and made Ria's heart skitter like a panicked mouse. When it sounded again she relaxed a little, realising that it was an impersonal rap, not an impatient fist. Risking a peek from the window, she saw a neat line of crimp-soled prints in the snow leading to the gate to next door's equally pristine garden. A porch, guttering fringed with icicles, obscured of the visitor all but a swish of skirt, a booted ankle, but those were enough to calm the mouse. No one she knew dressed like that. She threw on a jumper and jeans and went down.

The visitor had a smile that out-dazzled the scintillations of the garden snow. *Ashlin Duff*. Ria thought the woman was singing to her, but she was merely introducing herself as she stepped with care into the tiny porch and then entered the kitchen itself. "Kent you got in late, so I brought you some bits and pieces." The cardboard box she hefted contained an entire week's groceries.

"I can't accept this." Ria's mouth was musty. She had not spoken to another person since calling in sick to work. Not to the petrol station attendant on the M6, not to her family. Certainly not to Richard. "Thank you, but really…"

"It's no bother." Ashlin Duff smiled again, shifted her grip on the box. "Do you mind if I put this down?"

Ria stepped out of the way. "Sorry. Of course." She'd come here for solitude and wasn't ready for this intrusion, but she allowed it to happen. This was just a friendly stranger, and it's easy to lie to strangers. She forced a smile. "If there's coffee in there, would you like a cup?"

With her North Face jacket, wellingtons and old fashioned skirt, sky blue tartan with pale green and orange checks, Ashlin looked like a country doctor or a geography teacher. Though a startlingly pretty one. "I'd love to, but I've messages to run." She scribbled something in a notebook, ripped the page out and left it on the table. "Another time though, eh? Give me a shout if you want anything."

And with that Ashlin Duff was gone and Ria had her solitude back. *Aisling*, she read from the note next to the neatly printed number. It looked even more musical that way.

Ria put the food away, quickly filling the cupboards and fridge. Aisling's kindness was embarrassing. There was too much here to qualify as *a few things*. She'd gone to the trouble of cooking as well and there were tubs with neatly written freezer labels, even a casserole dish containing a huge piece of pork shoulder that had been rubbed with spices and slowly roasted. Even cold, the aroma was unbelievable but it would take a week to eat the thing on her own. The lack of surprise in Aisling Duff's voice when she answered the phone and accepted the dinner invitation made Ria suspect that this had been the plan all along.

The mouse wakened again as she put the phone down, unsettled by her boldness. Ria had come here to get away from people after all.

To pacify the panic, she made tea. Proper loose leaves, steeping in a pot under a knitted tea cosy until it was black as tar. Milk that she decanted into a kitsch jug shaped like a cow. She took her mug outside to look at the snow, and almost immediately spilled her drink as her foot skidded on the lower step. It was iced over with stalactite drips. Little wonder that Aisling had been so cautious when she entered earlier. Making a mental note to salt it later, Ria bypassed the step and went out to stand at the edge of the snow. It came up to her mid-thigh. Outside, it wasn't as cold as she expected. More as if temperature was absent. Sound too. The garden had a temple stillness that the unceasing snowflakes only accentuated. Aisling's footprints along the path were partly covered already. The perfection almost restored.

Ria went back in and explored the house. When she'd rented the place she'd done so in a frantic rush from the public library, caring only that it was somewhere quiet, somewhere far away. She had no actual knowledge about the property or its owners. Now she browsed the bookcases, opened all the drawers and doors, rummaged through the tools and paint pots and rolls of off-cut carpet in the cupboard under the narrow stairs, and discovered that the smaller bedroom on the upper floor was not a bedroom after all. It was a sewing room.

She found that odd. When you entered the rental market, you made your property serviceable and comfortable, but kept it impersonal. Perhaps a few generic books or DVDs at most; otherwise you risked preventing a tenant from settling, making the place their own. And who would retain a sewing room when a second bedroom opened up the property to the family market?

The room's only light was cloaked in a velvet shade that pooled secretive illumination over a work table on which sat a treadle-cranked Singer sewing machine. Shelves contained a library of pattern books, spectra of thread bobbins and Tupperware boxes that held assorted zips and buttons, poppers and hooks and eyes. Along the back wall were stacked bolts of cloth like a forest, boles furred with multihued moss. Cotton and chintz, satin, velour.

Silk. There was a lot of silk.

Ria was drawn to a bolt so buttercup yellow that it glowed, so soft it was like cream slipping through her fingers. Cool and gentle on her skin as snow.

She thought about the sewing room while she prepared dinner. An odd revelation of the owner's personality, as if it were a memory that the house were unwilling to relinquish. As the pork warmed through, the kitchen filled with luscious spices that awoke an appetite in her more intense than she'd experienced in months of anxious sparrow-picking. There were potatoes among the groceries but she couldn't face the effort so she opened a packet of wraps instead. She chopped a wizened red chilli, then shredded half an iceberg lettuce. The knife felt strange and heavy and she found the act of slicing through the crisp leaves addictive, chopping until the bowl overflowed. She put it on the table with the other things.

What else? Wine. Aisling had taken the liberty of buying half a dozen bottles, all white. *Pinot grigio, chenin blanc.* The sort of thing Ria habitually helped herself to large glasses of at home. She poured herself one now. It was cold as icemelt.

"How did you guess I preferred white wine?" She asked this as she poured the last drops of the bottle into Aisling's glass. They had consumed virtually all of the pork, shredded with forks, dolloped with crème fresh. There wasn't even much lettuce left.

Her visitor's smile was a secretive thing. Shy, like she needed permission. "Lucky guess." Aisling stretched over. She was wearing a lovely ribbed sweater the colour of a January sky. There were pills in the wool, a strand flying from one of the cuffs, but it was obviously a beloved garment. Something she knew she looked good in. The turtleneck roll accentuated her pointed chin, the pale blue worked with her dark lipstick and the smoked haze of her eye shadow. The fingernails hadn't been shaped for a while, but were freshly lacquered to the same glossy colour as the glaze that she now wiped from the denuded shoulder bone. That she curled her tongue around and sucked clean. "No one with any sense really drinks red wine, do they? It takes *far* too long to drink."

Ria's turn to smile. It was something she could have said herself.

Aisling took another scoop of the sauce, then sat back, savouring it. "So, what brings you to Carrmore?"

The question came in such a relaxed fashion that it took Ria aback. As if Aisling and she were old friends instead of new acquaintances. Her guard shot up. "I... suppose I just wanted to get –"

"Away from it all?" Now Aisling's smile was a mix of impatience and sadness. "Sorry," she said, evidently realising the presumption of her interruption. "It's just that everyone comes here to *get away from it all*. I meant, what specifically?" The presumption again, as if it was perfectly natural that Ria should open up to a complete stranger about the awfulness of her life, the thing she had done. Aisling gave a small sigh, and when she spoke next her voice was buttered with patience. "You don't have to tell me, but do you know about the silkbones?"

Ria shook her head.

"Carrmore is a place where people come to forget. It's not just the peace, the gentleness of life here. It's the snow. Do you... *understand?*" The hitch implied she had been about to say something else. Ria had a weird certainty it was going to be *remember.* She didn't reply. Aisling pointed at the remains of the pork. "When I'm gone, take this bone and clean it up. It should be large enough unless you've got a real catastrophe on your hands. Once it's spotless, whisper your troubles to it. Be specific, tell it the things that made you come here. All of them."

Ria stared, not quite sure how to respond. "And then?"

"And then parcel it in cloth. Nice and tight. Silk works best. Swaddle it as if this is a most valuable possession, something that you have no choice but to let go of: grave goods, a dead child. Make it beautiful." Ria was still puzzling over the question of how her visitor knew that she had silk in the house, and almost missed the last thing. "Then take the parcel out into the garden and bury it in the snow."

"And what will all that rigmarole achieve?"

"Just do it, and you'll see."

When Aisling Duff left a little later, the parting was embarrassed and rushed. As if her neighbour had hoped for the course of the evening to go a different way. Maybe there had been a motive behind her generosity after all. Ria watched her pass through the slatted gate. Felt something akin to guilt, something like shame as she returned the woman's wave. When the gate closed it dislodged a rill of soft snow that pattered to the ground, and when Ria looked through the slats again, Aisling had vanished into the darkness. Ria felt bound to wait until her neighbour was safely inside, but though she waited a full minute the lights of the house did not come on.

Ria did the dishes first. Enjoying the scald of her skin in the soapy water while, through the window, she watched the unhurried flurry of the snow tumbling out of the darkness. Only once the kitchen was spotless did she realise that she hadn't binned the shoulder bone with the rest of the scraps. She stared at it, knowing that what Aisling had suggested was ridiculous, but… she had to do *something*. Using the flat of a cook's knife, she scraped away the rags of meat and fat; scoured until only bone was left, smooth and cool. Then she ran fresh water, frothed it up with suds and dunked the thing into the basin. She broke out a new scourer and gently washed the bone in long shriver's strokes, and when it was clean she patted it with a towel.

Upstairs, she pondered the bales of cloth. The yellow one still stood out, so she chose that. The big scissors slid through the material with a hiss, leaving a thready edge that made her feel she'd spoiled its perfection. She spread the golden swathe on the kitchen table, folded the cloth once, matching the edges and pressing down on the seam, and then once again. Only then did she place the bone in the centre, and as soon as she saw it there – a thing itself of internality, a thing that should never be seen, its secrets exposed; the joint knob flaring into a plane that was both flat and curved and that bore fascinating ridges, that was smooth at first glance but, on closer inspection, was pocked with pores like an ancient cave structure – did she realise quite how much she needed to speak the thing that had been on her mind these many months.

So she told the bone. A dry whisper at first that became a babble, that became a torrent of words. She told the bone about the… Well, to begin with it was *boredom*, she supposed. A restlessness disaffection. About the online bingo, and then the slots which drained away her cash as effortlessly as the bone was absorbing all of these words. About maxing out first one new credit card then another. About Richard continually asking why she'd become quiet and evasive. The look on his face as he asked all the questions she'd been fearing since the thing had got a hold of her. And, worst of all, when he said the thing she didn't understand: *"Why do you do these things?"* As if this wasn't the first, the one and only time. Even him knowing that there *were* things that she was keeping from him formed a chasm between them. She hadn't volunteered any further information, and he hadn't pried. They had a good life together, a good love. Neither wanted to be the one to test its strength, its fragility.

Now she did say all the things, told them to the bone and, as the words blizzarded out of her, she began to feel warm. It built first in her vacated chest, kindled around her mouse's heartbeat. It rose to her throat, a lapping wave of heat that quickened, then surged up her neck and tightly over her scalp. A boiling skin of pressure. On the very last word it released with a hot, pained *pop* that left her dizzy and breathless and afraid. She stared down at the bone and the yellow silk, and then hurriedly wrapped the one in the other, tucking the corners tight and securing the bundle with safety pins. Then she blundered out into the garden, wading into the undisturbed snow. It soaked her jeans, wet though still not cold.

After a dozen laboured paces she stopped and slipped the package into her cardigan so that she could use both hands to break the surface of the snowfield in front of her, which resisted her fingers like the crust on a *brulée* before it gave. It took her maybe a minute to dig a hole wide enough, deep enough. By the end, her hands were red and raw, and then at last she felt the cold. It burned her skin, leached fire into her bones, but Ria wasted no more time in planting her package, wanting to be shot of it, repulsed by the shame. She scooped the snow over the top and then stumbled back into the house without once looking back.

That night she had difficulty sleeping because of the cold. The heating must have been broken and there were not enough blankets in the place. She got up when dawn crept like a stalker behind the paisley curtains, and looked out to see that, with the snow continuing to fall at its unhurried pace, the garden was once again featureless.

Her memory of why she had expected it to be otherwise was gone.

By lunch time, so was she.

Second Forgetting

Ria couldn't believe she was doing it, but she played Richard's message to a complete stranger. Her husband's voice, compressed by the speaker of her old, spare phone, sounded artificial, invented. In the twenty four hours since she'd arrived in Carrbridge, with its silence and snow, he'd begun to feel less and less real. His questions, the confused anger that she knew lived under his skin.

"I don't know how much more of this I can take," Richard said. "These things you do."

She and the woman who called herself Aisling Duff, had had a wonderfully companionable evening. Great food, a lot of booze, easy chat and much needed laughter. There might even have been a twinkle in Aisling's eye; a spark, an offer. Had the circumstances been different… Well, but they weren't. And, now that they were talking about *this*, the moment was most definitely lost.

Aisling listened without interrupting. "He sounds worried," she said at the end, serious now.

"I don't know what he means. *These things*." Coming to Carrbridge had been a heartswallowing leap, a pin jabbed in a map. "This is the first time I've ever done anything like…" She swallowed. "And he doesn't even know what it is."

Aisling nodded, but her smoke-shadowed eyes were troubled. After a moment she said. "No, it's not." She took Ria's hand. Not in an impersonal manner, the way you might comfort a colleague who'd learned of a bereavement, though not in an intimate way either. This was a gentle, familiar clasp. As Aisling told Ria about Carrbridge, her fingers sought out the pulse in her wrist, soothed it. As she told her that she had been here on several previous occasions, the candles sizzled. As she told her about something called *silkbones*, Ria's eyes tracked from the remains of their lamb shank to the unrelenting tumbling of snow outside the window. Then back to Aisling's earnest face.

"Why are you telling me this?"

"Because…" Her visitor drew a breath. "The silkbones, are meant to relieve you of the big things, hen. Things that have got too heavy to carry around in your head. Always there. Obstructing your thoughts, your ability to function. The things that sink you. But, Ria, your visits here are getting more and more frequent, and believe me…" for some reason, she was crying a bit now, "there are only so many secrets the snow can take."

"What do you mean by frequent? How many times?"

"More than is good. Because when the thaw comes… and it always does… you'll get your bones back. All of them."

Aisling's words churned Ria's deepest memories. She had known nothing about any of this, only now it felt as if she sort of did. "The thaw?"

Aisling looked pained. "Every now and then the thaw comes and anyone's bones that are still buried become exposed for the world to see. All your secrets. You can only lay them down for a little while.

You can't lose them forever."

For some reason this knowledge woke a trickle-melt fear in Ria. "What can I do?"

Aisling's cool fingers squeezed her hand. "This time don't use the bone. Tell me instead. Face to face. A problem shared…"

Ria stared into Aisling's open face. Made herself think about the thing: the money she spent on adult dating profiles; the two feverish yet sterile encounters that she'd arranged in a city hotel when Richard was out of town; his baffled anger when she'd *accidentally* lost her new phone because she didn't know how to erase its call and data history. *Why do you do these things?* She couldn't answer him. She was not in the habit of revealing her secrets to others. Not ever.

"But if I tell you…"

Aisling nodded, murmured, "It's what I'm here for, I think."

Ria hardly heard her. "If I tell you then I won't forget it, will I? It won't wipe it out and go back to normal."

Aisling paled. "Ria, you can never wipe it out, not really. The silkbones…"

"But you said that's what they're for. Forgetting."

"Until the thaw."

"That's long enough."

Aisling nodded quietly, squeezed Ria's hand. Soon afterwards she made her excuses to leave and, as Ria watched her negotiate the icy step, she felt only the tiniest twinge of guilt at not asking her kind neighbour what had been so clearly troubling her own thoughts. She was too eager to try the thing with the huge lamb bone and the silk from the odd little room upstairs. Anything to be rid of the knowledge of what she had done. Clean slate, go back home and resume the good life she and Richard had built together.

She felt like an idiot doing this thing, with the pillow of folded silk, the clean bone resting on it – and could there be anything more bare than a bone? Could there be anything more bizarre than treating it like a confessional? – but once she spoken her frets she no longer felt stupid. Once it had absorbed all of her worry she felt calmer. And once she had planted the bone out in the snow, watching until the descending flakes covered it up and she had begun to shiver, she felt at peace.

The next morning she woke in the bedroom of her little getaway place, rested and relaxed, and smiled with anticipation of going home. The only thing that marred what had been an entirely uneventful stay was the odd note that she found among the milk bottles. She hadn't noticed it on her arrival though it must have been there for weeks. A note left by the property owners for the gardener perhaps in times before the snow had set in. In a neat female hand, it said:

Dig them up. All of them.

Third Forgetting

It had seemed like the ideal spot to get away to – quiet, remote, and far enough north that it sometimes still snowed in June – but now that she was here in Carrmore, Ria couldn't settle, couldn't relax. The temperature fluctuated uncertainly; when she wore her sweater she felt stifled, when she took it off she got goosebumps. Outside, the garden was too still. Not a breath of air, not a flake of falling snow to top up the even spread that had covered the lawn and beds to a tremendous depth some time ago, that now glistened with an icy slickness in the grey afternoon. Not a sound – no birds or distant cars, no children, no neighbours' too-loud TV. She had come here for peace, but this degree of isolation was alarming. It left her with nothing but her own thoughts. The things she'd done.

There was a gate at the end of the path. It led into the garden of the house next door. She wondered if maybe someone would be in. She'd interacted so little recently that she thought maybe exchanging a few words with a stranger might be a relief. Stepping out from the kitchen, Ria almost lost her footing on the step directly below the row of quietly dripping icicles. She would need to salt that later. Gingerly, she made her way along the path and when she pushed the gate to next door's garden, a rim of ice fell off in a solid block. It shattered on the snow crust, the pieces skittering away.

The house next door was similar to hers. A fine construction of grey sandstone, mossy lintels, neatly painted windows, the roof and chimney breast capped with white so evenly it was like a Christmas card. The garden was entirely hidden by snow. She could tell before she peered through the window that she would see a tidy, comfortable home, but one that had not been lived in for a while. Another rental house. She didn't knock. Suddenly, she had no inclination to shatter this stillness.

Back inside and with the daylight already starting to fade, she put on the TV but the shows were all full of people and the things that people did. Crimes, betrayals, infidelities. Realising that she was hungry, she investigated the fridge and found it bare apart from a tub of chicken wings left by the last tenant. She opened the tub and examined the contents expecting the worst, but they could have been placed there that morning, the meat orange with spices.

Rather than brood, Ria heated the food and ate. She gorged herself, fingers and mouth getting messy as she stripped and savoured every last morsel of the delicious flesh, discarding what could not be consumed into a bowl. A growing pile of bones, grey-white bows and pins like ancient jewellery unearthed from a Neolithic burial site. Exposed things.

Rather than think, Ria took the bones to the sink and washed them, concentrated on making them beautiful. She found some offcut squares of green silk in the odd little sewing room upstairs and pretended she was a museum curator, setting each of these precious things to the best advantage. And then to each of them she told its provenance. Discarded in a railway station hotel in Bracknell. Crumpled on a bookie's floor. A carpark off the A4. The spare room floor after a Skype session with a stranger, the shivering light of thrill and shame. Each, an inconsequential event, a one-off, never to be repeated. Each best buried. As she told each story she flushed with heat and pressure, groaned with the relief that came of knotting each parcel of silk. But it wasn't enough. She had to be rid of them, get them out of the house. Rushing outside she slipped on that damned step and pitched forward, scattering her bundles across the snow. She scrabbled after them punched holes through the ice to bury them, and by the time she was finished her clothes were soaking and her hands bleeding. But it was done, and she was too exhausted when she went back in to do anything but sleep.

Ria wakes with a wail that catches behind her clenched teeth. Lies panting in sweat-damp sheets as the rags of whatever she was dreaming about flutter at the corners of her mind. It's not morning, she's not even sure where she is. She wonders why Richard isn't here, and then she remembers.

Ria gets up and draws back the curtain. The cloud cover has teased apart like tissue and the moon is partly visible. In its paltry light, the garden is glowing, glittering. Such a strange thing after the perfection that looked as if it had been untouched forever. There is a sickly wrongness to the scene.

She goes down and opens the door and, in the silence, it is the tiniest of sounds that tell her what is happening. The brittle ticking of ice, the music of drips, the trickle of running water. And sure enough, now that she hears the sounds, she sees it too. The porch icicles are splashing rapidly onto the step. The snowfield surface is pitted and slumped in a dozen places, as if hot stones lay beneath the surface. As she watches, a portion of the crust caves in with a sigh. The path along the side of the house is already exposed and meltwater gurgles through the exposed iron grid below the drainpipe.

Every drip, every unhurried crack and shift, contributes to the dread growing in her belly. A thing for which she can see no reason other than the spoiling of the perfect winter picture that has, it seems, not brought her the peace she was looking for.

She tries to scoop snow into the nearest rapidly expanding hole but where her hands touch, it melts still faster. She tries to crawl up onto the surface, but her hands and knees simply plunge through the crust, hastening its disintegration still more.

There's nothing she can do.

Dawn is fringing the clouds when she spots the first tatter of sodden silk, a scrap of emerald that flaps open as the snow recedes to reveal something pale inside. And the instant Ria recognises what it is the memory hits: the anticipation of the hotel bar, the starched sheets, the rough, impersonal sex, the electric excitement of betrayal and the crawling guilt that came immediately after it was over. The second one is closer, tumbling to her feet as a section of the packed snow calves off. The sodden material unpeeling around the animal bone, the memory of yet another betrayal. They come thick and fast after that. They flurry. The coloured cloth, the bones within. Sex, money, often both. Nights, days, lunch times that she would have sworn in a court of law to have had no knowledge of, but now are undeniable.

The ruined silks come in all colours, the bones in all sizes and shapes. Odd, awful things. As the snow melts, Ria takes all the memories into her, pictures Richard's face, hears the disbelief in his voice: *Why do you do these things?* And knows the honest reason: *Because I wanted to, because I needed to. Just one time. What harm can just one time do?*

It's not long until Ria can see what is under the snow. Flattened grass, a border of twiggy shrubs, a dirty plastic football. Soon the snow has shrunk to one remaining mound beneath the shade of the trees along the back hedge. She approaches it, bare feet on the real earth, toes in the dead grass. She should be cold but she is burning with the shame from all the bones she'd buried here. And this, she knows, is the first one, the worst one. The one that started it all.

Ria sits on the grass and waits until eventually it comes to light. The wrapping had been a sensual sky blue. Now it is water-shot and scabrous, shaped not unlike a woman lying on a couch. You could imagine that. Perhaps after a wonderful meal and too much wine. You could imagine stroking her hair as she slept, head on your lap. Wondering what that night meant. The kiss that had gone on forever, that you'd wanted, bone deep, to lead to more. And, as you wondered, your thoughts would turn as they always did to Richard, to the good, simple love that you shared and cherished, but that could never be called *passion*. Then it would be you shaking her awake, asking, demanding, shouting at her to leave. Pushing her out of the door so that she slipped, and fell. And there was blood on the step and on her face and in her hair, and through it the white gleam of cracked bone. And you know that is something that should never, *ever* be seen.

What could she have done, Ria thinks, but bury it deep?

What can she do now, with all of these things under the warming sun of a springtime morning but sit here alone, and pray for snow.

Snow is the ultimate secret-keeper. When you look at a pristine snowfield there is no way of telling what lies beneath, and you never want to be the one to break that perfection to find out. This is a story about how we deal with the big secrets in our lives. What if, by burying them, we could forget them?

Messianic Con Brio

That first rainy Wednesday in October was not a day to be lonely. While couples huddled close, laughing, under the first real onslaught of the final winter of the twentieth century, single figures scurried, isolated hunchbacks, gazes downcast, made pariahs by steely curtains of rain. The day-long downpour had been incessant and spitefully cold, washing out the city to a smeary grey background. Looking out at it all from her refuge in Kumar's laundrette, dreading the return journey, Gillian was thankful she'd have someone waiting for her with a fluffy dry towel and a mug of sweet tea. Well that was the theory. In practice, George would let her find her own towel, and if she was making tea, he'd have one too thanks. But at least he would be there.

Her thoughts were interrupted as a bedraggled figure clattered in through the laundrette door, dragging a bulging bin bag. It took her a second or two to recognise the woman, petite under bulky and rain-darkened clothes with hair plastered thickly across her face, as her friend Martha. This was a surprise. She hadn't seen Martha in weeks.

Gillian watched Martha deposit the bag and carefully drape her dripping coat over the back of a plastic chair. Only then, and when she had brushed the ropes of wet hair out of her face, did she look around and clock Gillian's presence.

"Hi," Gillian said, helpfully. She had known Martha a long time; way long enough to know that you sometimes had to bludgeon your way into her awareness. Her friend's finchy features went totally owl just for a moment, then settled into her characteristic wavy-line half smile.

"Gillian, hi," she said, removing her glasses to wipe them with a grey tissue summoned from the recesses of a sodden jumper sleeve. "What's up, doll?" Replacing the glasses and wiping the drips from her nose with the same tissue.

"Oh you know... same old bananas. I'm working full time now at the theatre, so mustn't grumble, generally – although what I'd give on days like this for a washing machine. And George is... well, George."

Martha's, "Hmm," may have been one of distraction since she had turned her attention to loading armfuls of stale clothes into the drum of a vacant machine. Gillian took it as a sign of Martha's long held contempt for the main man in her life.

Martha finished her loading and fed the machine detergent. Gillian allowed herself to be hypnotised by the spin cycle. Small talk with Martha always tended to dry up quickly. She'd never been the kind you could just *chat* with: not when she'd been a hanger-on to Gillian's group of friends at school, not even when the two of them had, for the sake of a familiar face, wound up sharing a flat over in Dowanhill when they went on to University. Martha paid no mind to the minutiae of other people's lives and offered scant information about her own. She liked her silences.

"So..." Gillian ventured in an effort to keep the conversation going. "How's the big search going?" Martha had begun unfolding a damp and mangled Evening Times produced from an inside pocket of her coat. Familiar black headlines: *Drugs, Death, Crazed, Cult*. Martha hesitated slightly as she attempted to carefully peel apart the pages. Possibly she even looked a little guilty.

"Well, em..." she muttered. "Okay, I suppose."

"Any success?"

A sideways glance – decidedly shifty.

"Sorry, what search was this again?"

Gillian laughed. "You remember very well. Hogmanay? Our place? On the kitchen floor to be exact. Your big declaration to the world..."

"Oh, right. That."

That was Martha's big resolution.

The New Year party had been fun for a change. After the bells had been seen in and the Bells had been swallied, and the last of the various friends had left, Gillian discovered Martha crouched under the kitchen table, cradling an empty litre bottle of Liebfraumilsch.

"Hey, you, everyone else's gone home. You want me to make you up a bed?" Gillian said casually, clattering cans and bottles into the first of many bin bags.

"Can't see me. M'invinsble," came a tiny voice.

"What?" she laughed, bending down to look at her friend.

"DON'T LOOK AT ME. I AM INVISNABLE!"

"Okay, okay." Gillian straightened up and sat on the table, her legs dangling over the side. "What's the matter, Mart? Why are you invisible?"

"Coz I'm not in a... a thingy!"

"Not in a what? A pvc catsuit? A major Hollywood motion picture?"

"Shu'up! This is seriousss." *This* punctuated by a sigh bordering on a sob. "I'm not in a rel.. .relashunship. You know? Like everyone else in the world. All of them making cozy little plans for the big Millennium thing next year."

So that was the problem. It had recurred more than once in the conversation. The speculations, both modest and wild, about how to celebrate the big one; the worries over whether it would already be too late to order enough champagne; the smart-arsed arguments over whether it was actually next year or the year after. At first, it was to be a big party, everyone and all their friends. But then Debbie and Paul piped up that, actually they had planned to go to Jamaica, just the two of them; then Andy and Elaine admitted to having a notion for renting croft in the Highlands. And so it went on, two by two, making private plans while Martha sat quietly in the corner.

This conversation was going to require patience.

"Oh, come on, that was all just talk. I guarantee you most of them will have lost the notion by the end of the month. And those that do end up in front of a roaring fire somewhere will last an hour together, tops, before they get in the car and try and find a pub with *other people*. Anyway, I don't think you'll find many people would say that being single makes you invisible, sweetheart. More likely the opposite."

"Well, it makes *me* feel invisible. How come you invite so many couples to your parties?"

"A lot of our friends are couples. But there were a few single men along tonight too."

Humph!

Oh, shit.

"They were *George's* friends, weren't they?"

"Well, yeah, but..."

"Well, *yeah*. Gill, George's friends think that changing' the topic of conversash'n means talking about how pish Celtic are instead of how 'mazing Rangers are."

"Come on, Mart, you didn't even talk to them. Some of them are really nice when you get to know them."

"Well, maybe, but George's friends aren't my type. There's no point in talking to them because it just wouldn't last."

"You don't know that."

"I do know that."

"Would it kill you to take a chance once in a while?"

"Yes it would. Soon as those meatheads even look my way I can feel this cold, clammy hand..." The words ended abruptly in a sequence of theatrical choking sounds. Gillian waited until they had died away and then tried again.

"Look at me and George, we started off with very little in common..."

"And you still don't. I'd want a better relationship than you and George!"

That stung the last of the Hogmanay cheer right out of Gillian. There was nothing wrong with her and George, she told herself. It was just Martha sniping again. Bitch. Hadn't they performed the host/hostess double act perfectly tonight? Complete with endearing looks and smartly executed two-handed gags. Gillian found herself glancing through to the darkened bedroom. She thought she could hear him snoring.

Eventually a meek voice from below said, "I'm sorry, Gill. Gill? I'm *so-rry*. I've maybe had a little too mush to drink." Gillian felt hands grab her ankles and swing her feet. "Gill? Gillian? I'm sorry okay?" She only smiled when Martha tried to lurch to her feet and clattered against the underside giving rise to an outpouring of sweary words. Eventually a rueful, blotchy face appeared above the edge of the table.

"Aw, Gill," the face said. "You don't know what it's like. You've always had someone there. There's always been George, or the guy before him – what was his name again? *I* need someone too, but it can't be just anybody. You know?"

Gillian kept a straight face, "So Ms McKinnes, what qualities do expect this special someone to possess?"

Martha grinned. "Haven't a scooby!"

"Well, who does?" Gillian said quietly.

"You know what my new year's resolution's gonna be?" Martha said after a while. "It's this. Next hogmanay, for the turn of the millennium, I am going to celebrate it with my partner. My perfect partner. Obviously, I've got to find him first, but he's out there somewhere. I just have to find a way of cutting through all the social shit and making him realise it's me he wants, and I have a year to do it."

Gillian smiled again, this time for Martha to see. "Good for you, Mart. I hope you manage it." Thinking, *Good, luck to you kid. Since he doesn't exist.*

Martha put on the kind of stupid grin only the drunk can manage. "I will. What about you? What's your resolution?"

"Oh, I'm giving up smoking for George. Same as usual."

Gillian lit a cigarette, avoiding Martha's sniffing disapproval by searching in vain for a bin for the empty carton. That conversation had stayed with her. It had been the first time Martha had talked openly about herself. Gillian had known that her outward air of diffident independence concealed a shyness concerning men, but had never realised the extent to which she yearned for a partner. Martha was so efficient and in control, Gillian had just assumed that on her own was the way she liked to live.

"So?" she said

"So what?"

"The search? How are you getting on? I haven't heard a peep about it since you were last round for dinner. You know, with George's mate from work."

"Mark." Martha had that look again.

"Yeah, right, Mark... Ooh, *Mark*!" Inviting Mark to dinner with Martha had been one of life's little disasters. Right from his bizarre opening conversational gambit: *If you're ever wanting a gun, there's this guy I know...* it had been all out war. George practically had to throw him out at the end of the evening. Mark had been the last of the available friends. The bottom of the barrel, so to speak.

"Sorry," said Gillian. "Again. But you shouldn't let people like Mark stop you from looking."

"I didn't." Martha's face was doing inscrutable to the max, but her voice had dropped just noticeably in volume. She cleared her throat. "I saw him again."

"You didn't."

She shrugged, "Just a couple of times. I was going through a perseverance phase."

"And since then?" Gillian was beginning to admire the determination on show here. When Martha made a resolution, she stuck to it.

"Oh, the usual desperate measures. I took some evening classes, went to a singles bar. Once." Putting on a comic shudder. "I practically lived in Safeways on Thursday nights. And I signed on with an agency, but I kept getting set up with someone else's idea of what would suit me." Big sigh.

"And still no luck?"

"Nope. Most of them were okay, but they weren't exactly right, you know?"

"Nothing like being a perfectionist, Martha!"

"I can't help it. And I can't explain it. That's just the way I am."

"So, what now?" Gillian, grinned, pointing to the newspaper. "There's always the personal ads."

Martha clutched the paper defensively. "That's not funny."

Gillian raised an eyebrow. Martha looked down, nodded. Gillian lowered the eyebrow and tried to think of something to say. She knew there shouldn't be a stigma attached to trying the personals. It wasn't as if there hadn't been times in her life when she'd casually considered what the people that placed these ads might be like. Lonely people, insecure, tired of rejection and frustration. And not at all like they sounded in their ads, where the women were beautiful, the men tall and professional, and everyone had a Good Sense Of Humour – let's face it, they needed one.

But that was the problem with personal ads. You only had twenty words to make yourself sound irresistible *and* describe your perfect mate. It couldn't be done. The result was an SOS crammed with buzz words and stock expressions, bizarre acronyms for mundane phrases, and everyone ended up sounding the same.

"A bit pot luck, isn't it?" Gillian ventured. "There's no telling what you might end up with."

"Doesn't have to be." Martha's smile was tight and secretive.

"What do you mean?"

Martha give Gillian a levelling look, as if evaluating how much she could tell her before she'd have to kill her for knowing too much.

"Well, there was this advert. A service to help you express yourself as well as possible within the space they allow you. And... Well, look." She flipped the pages and folded the paper back. The personals section, *Connections*, had a banner along the top. Incorporated into it was a simple text advertisement:

REAL YOU
Want to make the RIGHT Connection?
Find the words to describe the REAL YOU.
Call 338 1414

"Real You?" Gillian said. "You paid these people money?"

"I know what you're thinking," Martha gushed, "but I couldn't think of anything different, anything that would make me stand out, find me the right person. I couldn't see that it would do any harm just to call them."

"And?"

"And he invited me to an interview."

"He?"

"Yeah, turns out it's a one man outfit operating out of a bedsit on the south side. I know it was stupid going alone and everything, but Mr Bryden was really nice. He gave me a cup of tea and a sponge finger."

"Then I suppose he asked you all sorts of intimate personal questions?"

"Well, no. He just looked at me while I drank my tea and then he presented me with a tray and asked me to empty my pockets and my purse onto it. So I did, and he said, *everything*, and I fished out those dodgy passport photos and the emergency condom which is past its use by date anyway so I don't know why I still carry it."

"Embarrassing."

"You're not kidding."

"What then?"

"Well, he just stared at the tray and poked the stuff around a bit. It was mostly receipts and ticket stubs, that kind of thing, nothing interesting really. Then he passed me back the tray and said thank you and while I was jamming all the stuff back in my purse he wrote on his pad. When he was done he gave me what he had written and told me to copy it verbatim when I placed my advert. So I thanked him and paid him, and left."

"That was it?"

"Yep."

"What a swizz. How much did you give him?"

"Fifty quid."

"*WHAT?*"

"I know, I know. But he was just this wee old man with a wheezy chest. It's probably just as well he lives a stone's throw from the Victoria Infirmary. I felt sorry for him, okay?"

Gillian laughed. "You should be feeling sorry for yourself. You've been done."

"That's what I thought, at first. I was right in the middle of calling myself every kind of idiot when I remembered to read what I'd bought. Then I changed my mind. Look for yourself." She held the newspaper out. Gillian took it.

"So what exactly am I looking at here?"

"You'll see."

Randomly, she began to scan the columns: blocks of tiny text. each hanging off an emboldened first word like the drop of a cheap earring. "Beautiful, Beautiful, Beautiful…ahh, Stunning? No. Ooh, this is you isn't it? Balding Ugly Hunchback Dwarf!" Martha's smile remained in place.

"Keep going."

"I guess honesty as the best policy can be taken to extremes… Oh!"

"You've found it."

"I don't know, but… yes." Gillian pointed.

Messianic con brio
wilfully carnelian movietone Mahal wish taste melancohol.
Soulful detritus kingfish crepuscular sophist gillette melting
tsunami ska macaque.

Martha's eyes glittered. "Isn't it just perfect?"

Gillian was speechless. It hit her hard, deep down somewhere. She re-read it, lingering on each word. Really this was nothing but a random jumble of words, not all of them even real words. And yet something about them said Martha. Exactly and all of Martha, not merely the cipher of public face that Gillian had known all these years, but the essence of all that made her distilled into two stupid non-sentences. She didn't know how this could be, but that didn't change the certainty she felt. It was very spooky. And something about this ad left a nasty taste in her mouth.

Saturday afternoon. Martha buzzed the flat from the street, the insectile tinniness of the intercom doing little to disguise her good humour. Since when had Martha publicly displayed good humour?

"Gill? It's me. I got some replies."

Gillian, standing in the hall in her pj's didn't answer, just pressed the door release. She looked around. The flat was a mess. She had meant to have a bit of a clean this morning but the morning had dissolved into a haze of warm duvet and children's TV. George was out somewhere. She swore absently at him under her breath as she went about a half-hearted rearrangement of the clutter in the sitting room. Today's Times lay on the floor. She must have picked one up when she'd gone out for milk at midday. For the weekend TV listing. It lay open at the personals page. She slipped the paper under the couch and went to answer the door, wondering when she had changed back into her pyjamas.

Martha was smiling so brightly it hurt. Gillian made coffee so she wouldn't have to look at her. Placing the hot mugs down on the kitchen table, she said, less than enthusiastically, "Okay then, how many?"

"Two."

"A whole *two*?"

Martha refused to rise to the sarcasm. "It's not quantity..." she started good-naturedly.

Gillian stopped her. "Martha, why are you here?" The words were out before she even knew she was going to say them, and immediately she regretted the acid sound they made. The question had foundation though: Martha's personal life had always been a tightly closed book. This year's great campaign to find a partner had been undertaken with really only superficial help from Gillian and now here she was, all excited over a frankly amazing two replies to her whacko ad. Gillian supposed she must not have anyone else to share her success with. She took a deep breath and cursed the fogginess that seemed to have descended around her recently.

"I'm sorry, Martha. Forget I said that. Things are just a bit on top of me right now. You know." Her attempted smile felt transparently thin, but it seemed to do the trick.

"Yeah sure."

Gillian took a deep breath and indicated the A5 envelope clutched tight in Martha's hand. "Come on, then let's have them."

Martha's smile returned. She slipped a bundle of papers out of the envelope. Gillian looked at them – there had to be at least twenty pages there.

"That's two letters?"

"Well, they go into quite a lot of detail." Martha grinned, splitting the pages carefully into two lots. Placing a hand on each pile, she said, "Okay, there's the slightly loopy one. And then there's the totally bizarre one."

Gillian smiled too, infected a little at last by Martha's enthusiasm. "Slightly loopy," she said. "I think I'll have to work up to bizarre."

Slightly loopy was a systems analyst called Dennis from Drymen. His totally professional, word processed letter both started and finished by saying he didn't usually read personal ads, and had never answered one before, but had stumbled across the page while searching for the Dilbert strip, and her ad had just stopped him in his tracks. He included his address, phone number and email address, and begged her to call him. Please.

"Sounds keen," Gillian said neutrally, trying not to think the word *desperate*.

"You mean, 'sounds desperate'." Martha smirked. "Wait till you read the next one."

The writing paper was old, creased and faded. Vernon was even keener than Dennis. Gillian read thirteen pages of cramped old-fashioned script which amounted to a very detailed catalogue of a lifetime of true loves and amorous experiences. He was 93 and lived in a nursing home in Baillieston.

"Bit of a lad in his day, our Vernon," she said when she had finished, feeling her face slightly flushed. "And it seems he claims that all of this was..." she searched through the handwriting, "*merely preparation for my joining with you, My Angel.*" She giggled.

"Yes, that's what he says." Martha's expression was unreadable.

"Well, if you want my advice," Gillian said, "forget them both. It's early days yet. If you give it another week or so, you're bound to get someone slightly less wretched." Although, she thought, what kind of person answers an ad like this anyway?

"And if I were to choose one or the other to, say, take me out to dinner?"

"Oh, Martha, you can't be serious. You don't know what kind of people these guys might be." They were both certainly mad enough to mention words from her ad as if they meant something. *Soulful, sweet melancohol, I am your ska macaque.*

Martha frowned. "You don't feel it, do you? That's okay, I'd be a bit worried if you did, I think. These guys are reacting to *me*. They can't have any bad intent or they wouldn't react the way they did. They are harmless – more than that, they are right for me." She laughed. "Come on, help me choose. Which one."

Gillian couldn't be bothered to argue the any longer. "Oh, Dennis, for sure," she said. "If you went out with Vernon, I'm sure one of you wouldn't last the night."

The following Wednesday's paper ran Martha's ad again. Gillian's eye was drawn immediately to its shape, the distinctive pattern the black letters made crowding the allocated space. She looked, and then quickly looked away.

There were now other entries like Martha's. She devoured them, feeling oddly like a voyeur. Each set of words instantly conjuring a whirl of personality traits, flooding her with a wash of emotional colours. Reading this word, and this and this, she felt her stomach sour in disgust; but reading these five here, her heart leapt, compelled to read again and again, tracing them with a trembling finger. Taken as a whole, her mind extrapolated real people. This one – *inky moraine whisperbread* – she imagined a kind man, good with his hands and dangerously hopeless with his money; this – *belly gimcrack fritillary* – a nervous middle-aged woman with obsessive/compulsive tendencies.

In these oddly chosen words she heard hints of secret childhood dreams and minor sexual hangups; flavours of dark fears and unattainable ambitions.

They felt so real. Complete strangers, and instantly she felt knew them better than she knew any of her friends. Better than she knew

George. Maybe that was what spooked her so much – the thought of knowing Martha and a handful of strangers more intimately than her own lover. How would she and George exist together if they knew each other this deeply; if he knew the things about her she hardly dared admit to herself. How could anyone?

But how could any of this be true? It was just an idea planted in her mind by Martha and her imagination was doing the rest. An exercise in wishful thinking which she was particularly vulnerable to at the moment because she felt like shit and no one was on hand to cheer her up. Maybe she was coming down with a bug or something.

She read on. There were three pages of dense columns, attempts to connect by a lot of people who felt something was missing from their lives. Presumably many more read the entries on a regular basis. Two of these at least had answered Martha's ad, so there had to be something in it. Maybe it was the novelty, or perhaps without a face to pin the description to you read into it what you wanted to see. Gillian had seen Martha, because she knew Martha already, that was all.

Her eyes betrayed her and sought out Martha's ad. Once again she felt that sickening jolt of deep recognition. She snatched the paper off the table. It fluttered to the floor like some ugly, crippled bird. At the sink she gulped down cold water to sluice the foetid taste in her mouth.

The phone rang. It was Martha.

"I'm in the call box at the corner. I buzzed you but you didn't answer."

Gillian couldn't remember hearing the buzzer.

"I'll be there in a mo' okay? Gillian?"

"Huh?" She realised she'd been trying to think of an excuse to turn her friend away. Instead she said, "Yeah, sure. See you."

She hung up and stood by the intercom, counting the two minutes it would take for Martha to walk from the corner. At 45 seconds the buzzer sounded loudly in her ear. Startled, she stabbed the door release with an angry thumb.

Martha arrived, out of breath, clutching a heavy-looking bag and wearing a dress. It was pale blue with a floral print.

"What's with the get up?" Gillian asked.

"Eh? Oh, the frock." She had the decency to look a little embarrassed. "Well, I didn't think my usual clothes would be Vernon's type of thing. I'm going to visit him after this."

In the presence of Martha's new buoyancy Gillian's annoyance melted away, leaving her confused about why she had been angry in the first place. She smiled at her friend's determination, and felt a little sorry that whatever criteria were driving Martha in her quest for perfection, they were leading her on a date with a 93 year old Casanova.

"Sit down, Mart, I'll make coffee."

Martha sat herself at the table as Gillian went about finding clean cups and trying to think of the best way to phrase what she was going to say. Eventually she sat across from her friend placing before her a mug of hot black coffee, an offering of comfort. She cupped her hands around her own.

"Look," she said. "Try not to be too disappointed that it didn't work out with Dennis. Don't take this the wrong way, but I really think Vernon is a mistake. You have to draw the line somewhere, Mart."

Martha's mug stopped at her lips. She looked surprised. Then she laughed.

"Oh, Gill, stop talking mince. Saturday night couldn't have gone better. Dennis was perfect. In fact..." She finished the sentence whispering through a wicked grin. "He only left this morning."

After a stunned pause, Gillian managed, "Then... Why Vernon?"

Martha looked taken aback. "Oh for goodness sake. Credit me with some integrity. It's not going to be like Dennis. Vernon was nice enough to write to me, so I'm just going to say hello. That's all. If he proposes marriage, I promise I'll let him down gently. Besides," she lifted her bag onto the table, "Dennis hasn't necessarily won the race yet." She tipped the bag and a heap of unopened envelopes spilled across the table interspersed with the usual handbag flotsam.

Gillian was stunned for the second time in as many minutes. "How many are there?"

"Thirty-two."

"You haven't opened them yet?"

"Well it didn't exactly seem polite while Dennis was around. Do you want to help me?"

"I don't know. It's kind of a private thing, isn't it? Who knows the kind of thing these people might say? At least with the first two you had the chance to read them yourself first."

Martha's smile was big and open, "Aw, come on, Gill. You're my best friend. If it wasn't for you I wouldn't be doing this at all."

Martha thought of Gillian as her best friend. That surprised her. Gillian had never considered the idea. But faced with the notion, she realised that, regardless of how seldom they saw each other, outside of George the same was probably true from her point of view. At least at the moment. These days Martha was near enough the only company she had.

She hurried a smile. "Okay. If you're sure. It might be fun."

Martha grinned back. "Excellent!" She split the pile roughly in two. "You take this half," she said, pushing a heap across the table, "and I'll take the other. Then we can swap over."

And it was fun, at first. They read mostly in silence, occasionally laughing, exclaiming in disbelief, reading the choicest parts aloud. Martha found the first man willing to give up a happy marriage and family for little, old her. Gillian found the first woman. And they were among the more sensible ones. The majority, though, were less than inspiring – ordinary guys, apparently suffering from fits of histrionics as soon as they'd sat down to write their letters. In Gillian's pile alone there had been four threats of suicide so far. Martha sat glowing, beatific, reacting to them all as if each of them touched her most specially.

About halfway through her pile, Gillian found what sounded the best prospect of the lot. "Hey, Mart. How about this? A consultant paediatrician, thirty seven, single, big empty house out in Bearsden – he stresses *empty*, see? His name's Michael..." Martha was engrossed in the letter in front of her.

"What you got there? It must be a bit special to beat Michael."

"Huh?" Martha looked up, her face briefly a sketch of discomfort. "Oh, this isn't one of the applicants," she said quickly, folding the paper back into the envelope and slipping it into her bag. "It's from my mum, making plans for Christmas."

"You should get the phone reconnected."

"Maybe one day," Martha replied quietly, selecting the next unopened letter from her pile, studiously avoiding Gillian's eyes. "Tell me about... Michael."

Gillian passed her Michael's letter, aware of a change between them. The old Martha was back, defences up, shutting her out. She was surprised how much it hurt to be excluded.

She picked up the next envelope, tore it open with a rough tug. How Martha was going to choose one of these people, she didn't know. But eventually, she supposed, one of them would cut through all this mystic bullshit and connect with her on an old fashioned human level. It might be Dennis, who already had more than his foot in the door; or it might not, who knew? But sooner rather than later Martha would choose one and her time and attention would be consumed by her *perfect partner*. Gillian swallowed coffee, bitterly.

They read on unenthusiastically in silence for ten more minutes. Then Martha left.

She didn't work out that George was gone until Friday morning. He hadn't returned home the night before and a quick investigation revealed the disappearance of a few clothes, books, miscellaneous shit. Not much, but enough to indicate intent and not the dreadful technicolour accident she had been imagining as the reason for his no-show. She might have preferred the accident.

Gillian stood by the phone, unable to pick it up. Her mind filled up with details, the sorts of things she usually contrived not to think about. Her and George. Things said/unsaid. Countless small acts of ingratitude/laziness. She hated this. This thinking about it, the compulsive, toothachey exploration, the raw unravelling in her head. Having to think about it shocked right through the usual anaesthetic complacency.

She just hadn't expected him to leave. That was all. It wasn't like him. Okay, she acknowledged to herself that their relationship had been stretched a little thin lately. But not much more than usual, surely? She had vaguely expected they would go on this way until either they grew bored with being bored with each other and started talking again or she decided she'd be better off alone. *She* decided, not him. George had never shown initiative before. Why start now?

She would have called his work only it was the holiday weekend. She would have called their friends, but could not think how to ask casually about him without making it sound as if she did not know where he was. She would have called his mother, who had been certain they were set to announce a date for the wedding any day now for the last five years, but... She attempted to ring Martha, just to hear a sympathetic voice, but it went unanswered.

The phone rang the instant she put it down.

"George?" she said.

"No," came the reply, slowly. "Martha." Gillian's heart twisted.

"Where are you? I was trying to get you."

"I've moved, into Michael's place."

Shit. "Martha, don't you think you're taking this a little fast?"

"I know, I know. But you don't understand. We just have to be together."

"You think other people have never been in love."

"Not like this."

How could Martha call *this* love. Love grew over time. Love was intangible and non-verbal. Love was... Love *wasn't* instant. Feelings couldn't be declared like this over a bunch of nonsense words. She shivered, remembering the *frisson* when she had read those words the first time.

Gillian sighed. She had her own problems. Martha was big enough to make her own mistakes.

"At least with Michael you won't be short of a few fancy dinners," she said.

A pause at the other end, then, "It's not just Michael." There was an emotional catch in Martha's voice. Gillian couldn't believe what she was hearing.

"What? Dennis as well?"

"No. All of them. They're all perfect. I can't choose between them." She rushed on. "Look, Gill. I just wanted to say thanks, you know, for being a friend. And... I'm sorry. We're, all of us, much happier now." A man's voice, indistinct in the background.

Gillian couldn't think. What did that mean, *all of us?* "Martha? What the fuck are you playing at?" Almost screaming.

"I have to go. Bye."

Disconnected.

Gillian felt faint. She realised she was trembling all over, as if her body understood something her brain hadn't figured out yet. Something like rage coursed raw through her. She sank to the floor beside the little table the phone sat on. Underneath lay the newspaper. She saw the ad. The words jumped straight out at her, familiar now, each striking a nervy chord. What called her attention to it first though was the thick, black, felt-tipped circle.

Martha's envelopes were still in the bin. The one from Michael's letter had a neatly printed, gold return address sticker on the back.

She arrived at the house shortly after eleven the next morning. It was an elegant two-storey structure of grey sandstone, set back from the road and obscured by a line of dense conifers. She might have driven past it if it hadn't been for the crowd. After parking a little way down the road she approached them. Around twenty people, mainly women, some kids and a few lost-looking men, were standing in the driveway. The general mood was a mixture of bemusement and anger. Some were shouting abuse in the direction of the house.

Gillian approached a woman with short, dirty blonde hair.

"What's going on?" she asked.

The woman turned, her expression was hard and furious. "They've got my Davie in there. Kidnapped him or brainwashed him, no doubt." She added under her breath, "Not that he's got much of a brain, mind you, but what there is could do with a good scrub. Filthy beggar. You're man in there too, hen?"

"I think so."

"Bloody cults. How can they no just leave us normal folks alone? Thursday it was, he toddled off down the bookies as usual. From that moment on till this morning he's been all quiet. Not just no talking, but in a funny way. Today he gets this letter." She fished out a letter from her pocket. Gillian recognised Martha's handwriting. "Next thing I know he's offski."

"What are they doing in there?"

"Some kind of sex cult, isn't it? You should read some of the filth in here." She brandished the letter. "I seen the leader. She's an evil wee bitch. Right enough, she won't get much joy out of our Davie. It's ridiculous isn't it? I mean at his age."

"Maw!" A child of about eight came running up. She wore a Rangers sweatshirt with a badly printed Red Hand of Ulster motif. Gillian thought there might be worse beliefs to have than whatever Martha had stumbled across. "Maw, there's dad at the windae," the girl said. "He's crying."

Sure enough a scrawny little man was waving from a big ground floor window. His wife was already advancing forcefully on the window, "Hey! You! What the hell do you think you're playing at Davie Leggate." Gillian watched as the man was joined by another man and woman, hand in hand. She heard herself gasp and felt cold air stinging her lungs. George and Martha. They each put an arm around him, hugging him for a moment and then gently drew him away from the window. It was a scene of pure inclusiveness. Another gulp of air felt like a swallowed stone.

The police arrived just as the blonde woman started to throw clumps of hard earth at the windows. One or two of the others, spurred into action, began to follow suit, giving the officers a struggle as they attempted to restore order. Gillian half heard the conversation between the woman and the police sergeant. "Yes, a cult. In Bearsden. Do I have to repeat everything I say? You just do your job and get him out of there, pal, and I'll fucking deprogram him, so I will."

A man tapped Gillian on the shoulder, making her jump. She turned, backed half a step away from the dictaphone thrust towards her face. "Excuse me, madam" He smiled, eager. He looked pretty fresh faced, probably on loony cults and cats in trees detail for the local rag. It was nearly the Millennium after all.

"Uh-huh."

"What brings you here?"

"I... " The twist in her heart was tight enough to tug the muscles of her face in to a wince. "I don't know."

December had been wet. The kind of rain that stays in the air like a snapshot of grief and leaks slowly into your bones. Gillian was tired. Life had moved on but nothing had changed. The papers reported that the police had taken statements from everyone in the house affirming that they were there of their own free will. A number of divorce proceedings had started as a result. Since the household itself refused to give interviews, one had to assume that everyone in there was happy with the state of affairs. Every now and then a new snippet of information found itself fish-eye magnified in the tabloids. In the first week much was made of the fact that they imported a lot of beds – well where else would thirty five people sleep? More recently the house had been put on the market. They were looking for something with a little more room. She wondered if collectively they could afford a castle.

She scanned the papers hungrily for every snippet. She filled her life with imagining how they all lived. If they had fights like everyone else only more complex; if they staged great Bacchanalian orgies or if Martha had a rota worked out. She thought about it all the time. She thought about it even though she knew she could never be part of this, because it was better than thinking about her own life. Because it gave her a connection.

Hearing laughter in the garden, she rose from her crouch, wincing as blood reached her stiff extremities. She sidled along the fence she had climbed to get in and peered out of the undergrowth. There they were, standing around, filling the air with excited talk; words she could not understand. Someone went around lighting candles in glass bowls. She looked at watch – almost time. Inside the house, the radio or TV was turned up to a distorted blare.

They joined hands, forming a ring around Martha, a slender figure in a sparkling, black evening dress. Protective and exclusive. Gillian felt herself being drawn from her hiding place, coaxed towards them. If any of them were to look into the shadows now they would just about see her. She was lured by their warmth and happiness, could feel their inexplicable togetherness.

There was enough light now to read the rectangle of paper clutched in her left hand. All the time waiting the dark she had been dying to read it again. She held it up so that she could make out the words on the thin paper. The radio began to count down from ten and the people joined in. Trembling, she read.

Messianic Con Brio...

She wanted to walk ten paces forward, to join them. She felt their love roll out like heat in sickening waves, and could not get closer. So much love in these words.

...melting tsunami ska macaque...

And all they could make her feel was hate.

Neil Williamson

This is the oldest story in the book. We felt that it didn't really fit with the other pieces in The Ephemera *but I always liked it so I'm glad to find a space for it here. Really, this one springs from a joy of words, the sounds they make in our mouths when you strip them of context and meaning, and the power they hold when we are free to attach our own meaning to them.*

Last Drink Bird Head

There's little shelter on the Head. The wind plucks Margueritte's cloak like an aerialist's costume. Taunts her to fly. She's tempted, but won't be bullied. Not even by the wind.

Margueritte traces the black steps up the greensward into the cloud-dark twilight. At the summit is the inn, and inside: Oliver Waugh, wizard of flight, wisest barman in the world. Her saviour.

The wind stings. The sluggish sea below reminds her of the pursuit of happiness.

Margueritte reties her cloak, clutches the flask, and climbs. The steps are slick, but the tread is deadened with gravel and ash, supplemented by ropes of wrack, screes of shells and delicate bird bones.

Her steps crunch only softly. Buoyed, she runs, reckless of the wind, but as she ascends she gains gravity. Wrack pops, shells crack, bones snap. A gust billows the cloak into a sail, lifting her, but she is still too heavy. Margueritte's instinct is split: to control the cloak or to let it flap, allowing her to drink from the flask. Safety wins, and only once she is secure does she heft the flask.

Just a drop, and save what remains.

Beautiful, bitter aroma.

Two drops burn her tongue with cold.

Once, she was married. A ponderous husband who, on the advent of their albatross child, turned to drink. Terrified of petrification, a blasted stone woman rooted to the sofa, Margueritte ran away to join the circus.

The circus taught her the semblance of flying. It was a good simulacrum of freedom, at first, but it wasn't enough. Not with the faces of the ponderous husband and the albatross child staring up at her from the crowd.

That was when she had turned to drink.

Her feet hardly touch the gravel now. And this becomes the pattern: she drinks lightness and climbs until her gravity scares her. She drinks, climbs, all the while afraid that the flask will too soon be empty.

At the summit, the wind hurries her into the brick structure at the cliff edge.

The barroom is desolated. Its roof is gone. Where the rear wall used to be is now a vista of leaden waves.

"We're closed."

She can barely see him in that chair, surrounded by empty bottles.

She proffers her flask. "Please."

"I drank it all. Go away."

She can't believe it. All this way for nothing. "I can't go back."

"Then stay. I don't care."

Then Margueritte sees. Even here there are no wizards. Waugh is ponderous, concrete.

He's not slumped in the chair, he's part of it. And it's not balanced on the splintered pinions of the floorboards, it's an outcropping of the Head.

She cannot return, but gravity drags harder with every heartbeat.

Margueritte uncaps the flask for the last time. There is no liquid left, only vapour, so she drinks that. Gets drunk on the air itself. It fills her, feathers her skin, cores her bones.

And, for a time, she accepts the wind's dare, and flies out of the Head.

This story is exactly five hundred words long and it was written for an anthology created to raise funds for a literacy charity. The writers were tasked with deriving meaning from only those four words: Last. Drink. Bird. Head. Every story in that book was wildly different.

This is Not a Love Song

"There are three kinds of love song: the Fall, the Hold and the Breakup."

Tell me something I don't know, Michael thinks as the DJ who calls herself Heartbrkr leans back against the broken leather, stretches her legs on the seats. There is a motorcycle chain around one ankle below her shiny calf-length leggings. Grease on skin and spandex. The booth at the back of the pub reverberates to the *doof-doof-doof* of the electronica bleeding down from the club upstairs. The frosted partition glass rattles in its lacquered wood surrounds.

"Every day millions of people succumb to one of these. You probably have..." She says this dismissively, as if it's a fault, as if it's avoidable.

Michael doesn't like the DJ. She's too full of herself and this way she has of not singing her words is unsettling. But, if she can really do what she claims...

"Everybody has." His own words, properly intoned, sound old fashioned. Behind the thudding beats from above he is aware that *the* music is currently skittish. A disconcerting xylophonic rill. He tries to ignore it, to rid his own melody of its uncertainty when he sings, "It's the oldest cycle. But I was told you could break it."

She may be cocky, but Heartbrkr's smile has a gap-toothed charm. "Michael..." She sings this, completing his melody and metre in an almost patronising way. "It's *the music.* No one can break it. No one can hide. But if we're daring, baby we can ride." She reaches over, her arm rattling with dayglo bangles, the fingernails of her slender hand spangled with silver and stars.

The music swells when Michael extends his own hand, a threatening churn that increases his uneasiness, but then he shakes her hand and it's as if he's plugged directly into it. The beats from upstairs accentuate the churn, order it, turn it into a challenge.

"You in?" the DJ whispers.

Bang on the beat, Michael nods.

Michael got Insync from his parents for his eighteenth. Mum and Dad thought they were being terribly modern, giving their boy the latest thing. It had probably helped that his girlfriend at the time, Jennifer Philpott, already had one, and they had doted on Jennifer Philpott. Mum always a believed in good scansion as an omen in love and Jennifer's and Michael's names went together very nicely. They fit the music.

As consumer devices go, Insync – a perennially popular engagement gift – is not cheap. The surgical procedure is routine, though, and, once you've swapped your pin codes, the first time you feel the connection is an indescribable thrill: your heartbeats, directed by the implanted pacemakers, beating literally as one. After that it takes over your life. You get a late night text: *Insync tonight*, and lie in a state of unbearable anticipation, skin on fire, the music a roil of reverbed guitar teasing out the melody of your Fall, a grinding growl that you hope isn't loud enough to wake your parents. You feel your pulse twitch and kick on, and you know that she's thinking of you. You race and climax and sigh to rest. Beat for beat, together. Michael cannot deny that Insync makes the Fall really fucking intense. The problems come later, in the Hold.

They didn't have Insync when his parents were courting. Last year at Christmas he told them he admired them for staying in their Hold for so long, for resisting other Falls, for never tempting the Breakup. He didn't really think *admired* was the word, but it *was* Christmas.

"It's all part of growing up," Mum had sung, as if he was thirteen instead of thirty. "The music changes, and you change with it."

Michael had sipped his sherry with a nailed-on smile. "Next time, I think," he sang back. "Next time I'll kill it."

Mum had tried to disguise her disappointment. "You've just been unlucky. It'll come if you're patient, my lad. It's just not wise to tempt fate, like Jennifer. That little Fall-addict." Her frankness had shocked them all into silence. Dad had poured more sherry and turned on the TV for the Queen's Song.

Michael and Jennifer's Hold had lasted all of a month. Its melody was never convincing. During their Fall they'd got into the habit of Insyncing during college hours, so that they could be together while they attended classes. But once their Hold had settled in, Michael found his heart racing at odd times. Texting her to ask if she was skipping classes and did she want some company brought no reply. Then she started to forget to turn her Insync on, or else she claimed the device wasn't working properly. Then he simply couldn't feel her anymore and by then the music was already deep into the dour overture of their Breakup. Not that Jennifer Philpott noticed. Rumours had already reached him that she was well into a new Fall.

Michael had bounced back soon enough. It was what you did when you were eighteen. There was always another Fall stirring in the music's strings.

When Michael arrives at the club above the pub, attired as instructed in black, he exchanges his expensively-bought chit for an eye mask, which he slips on before pushing through the doors into a wall of sound. The room is dark, what little light there is coming in sweeps and stutterbursts that do little to actually illuminate the space. The air is soupy with pulsing noise and stewed heat, cut only slightly by the stir of electric fans. There are others here—he senses movement, glimpses outlines and features—but since everyone is dressed as he is, he has no idea how many there might be. As long as there are enough to make it work, he thinks. That's all that matters.

Michael finds a wall and leans against it, uncertain and jittery with anticipation. The music, which he had half-expected to be ringing with alarms, is biding its time, a barely discernible tick behind the electronics. It is the sound of Michael's parents' mantle clock.

The beats stop. In the sweating darkness, there is a moment of collective held breath, and then these things happen all at once:

– a figure, limned in luminescent pink and yellow appears high in the centre of the hall

– the beat drops, fat and booming, like a thunder peal as the opening salvo of Heartbrkr's set crashes from the PA

– a fist grabs hold of Michael's heart; he panics, but his pulse refuses to race – it is locked to the beat.

He has no option but to dance, so dance he does. They all do, all of the strangers cloaked in darkness, clustering by instinct below Hearbrkr's eyrie. Hips bump, arms and thighs brush, often eliciting a sigh. It's not sexual – or not *only* sexual – because arousal is only a small part of what is happening here, almost a by-product rendered negligible by the instant sensation of integration. With Heartbrkr, with each other, synched by their devices.

That's how it is after only ten, fifteen seconds under the DJ's control. And what happens next is so entirely unexpected that Michael shouts out loud. The music joins in. A sweet guitar strum bridges Heartbrkr's simple beats. It's joined by an irresistible bass groove, and then a synth melody that loops and climbs and soars. It's a *Fall*. It's a Fall that connects everyone in the room. And Heartbrkr is riding it. Driving it. She switches and mixes, ramps up the tempo, forces the music to match her. Michael's heart beats harder and he dances faster. He dances and he grins. Someone grabs his hand and pulls him into a spin and he laughs. He grins and laughs for the spectacular, swooping soar of the Fall, and for the knowledge that that's all it needs to be. There will be none of the usual awkwardness and appraisal to follow. No expectation of a Hold to come in the future.

This is exactly what the internet whispers told him that Heartbrkr would deliver, but it still shocks him that it is possible. Later, at home, once he and his tribe of infatuates have slunk off anonymously one at a time into the night, he lies in bed and his heart aches with the joy of it.

Michael has always been a fool for a Fall. No matter how often it happens, no matter how hard he tries to hold himself back, invariably the music sweeps him away. And the harder he falls, the shorter the Hold, and the more painful the Breakup that comes sniffing at its heels. As if, knowing that the Hold won't last, he actively seeks out its end. Several of his lovers have actually said as much. But what is there to explain? Nothing beats the excitement of a new infatuation. So, why not try and keep falling forever?

There is no pattern to their meetings. They've been instructed to leave their Insync permanently on in the evenings – contrary to the official medical advice – and to come when they feel the tug on their hearts. It's a lot like having a secret lover. Michael finds himself walking off the squash court, making up barely plausible excuses to leave dinner engagements, lying to his parents. Every now and then someone hears the tease of the Fall in the music when they're around him and tips him a wink. His mum asks him outright: "When are we going to meet her?" And, when he dissembles, adds with forced airiness, "or him, if that's what you prefer…"

They meet to dance three nights in a row and he's barely able to make it through the following work day, crippled with exhaustion, heartsore. Then they don't meet for three weeks and he aches for the communion of his tribe. Every time they dance together their Fall becomes more intense, and Heartbrkr rides it with masterful finesse, maximising the passion, the thrill, and changing things up every time the Fall feels as if it's going to settle and resolve into a Hold.

Michael is now pretty much convinced that he is not made for the Hold. There's something missing in him. Perhaps he just doesn't like people enough to want to spend what could end up being forever with them?

By the end of the third month of his Fall with the tribe, though, he starts to wonder how long it can last. Realistically, no one can fall in love indefinitely. And he is not alone in that thought. The next time they dance the lock on his heart is lighter than it was and he knows that the tribe has shrunk by one, maybe two hearts. A few days later, while grocery shopping, he becomes aware that there is a man following him around the store, making the same turns, aisle for aisle, putting the same items into his trolley. He's an ordinary looking bloke, straight from an office job where he wears a suit. A sales manager, perhaps an accountant. Michael ignores him until they get to the check out, then looks him in the eye and he knows for sure. The recognition strikes them both dumb. The music swells with their secret, shared theme, but Michael can't say a word, just pays for his food and then runs to his car.

It's different this time. He can feel it as soon as he enters the room. The sense of normalcy, of settlement, as domestic as the music's expectant mantle tick. Over the pre-gig beats he detects whispers, chuckles, conversation. The ambience is a mixture of familiarity and nervousness. There's a Hold coming, for sure this time. They all know it. Some of the tribe – less rebellious than they'd hoped to be – will welcome it, the rest are excited to see what magic Heartbrkr will work to lead them ecstatically back into their Fall. The tension, waiting for that moment when she appears, waiting for the heart-tug when she drops the beat and leads them one more time, is unbearable.

And there it is. The ambient cuts. The space of grace.

The lights come up. Uncertain fluorescents blinking on like a nervous cough before the announcement of bad news. And there are twelve assorted people standing around dressed like poor attempts at Halloween ninjas. Looking at each other in fear and disgust.

"Fuck," someone says, and they all feel it at the same time, the yawning, bottomless hole where there connection of their hearts used to be. Someone starts to cry.

The music counts in to a cheesy slow-rock piano ballad that is going to be the most sarcastic Breakup ever.

There are harsh words, recriminations and tears, although it's all somewhat pointless because no one is to blame. Michael is among the first to leave, dodging two women on the verge of coming to blows. The music follows him home, mocking what had once been a wonderful thing with saccharine hokeyness. He stops at the off-licence to buy whisky, and when he converses with the sales girl it minors his clichéd cadence. After that, he holes up at home, calls in sick and hides from the world, replaying it all in his mind: the half-suspicion that something was afoot, yet the complete shock at the clumsy, common manner in which Heartbrkr abandoned them. He has never felt so diminished. The pain of the shame is… exquisite.

Michael's hermitage lasts a week, by which time the edge of his hurt is sufficiently blunted to be able to interact with others. He answers his mother's calls, enduring first her admonishments, then her platitudes. He returns to work and suffers the discomfort of his colleagues. And he plans.

It takes months to find her because Heartbrkr covers her tracks well but there's another pub, another club above it. He arranges a meeting under a made-up name. She recognises him instantly, swearing and getting up to leave, but he stops her. Impressively, there's barely a note of the tribe's Breakup about her, as if none of it ever mattered.

Michael tries to match the DJ's cock and swagger, but he's shaking when he tells her: "Play it again."

All of the Musicals stories are, in some way, about how we interact with the music in the world. In some cases this means listening to our true nature, in others it's about rebelling against fate, bucking the narrative of conventionality. Along with "Arrhythmia", this story is very much one of the latter type.

The Golden Nose

Felix Kapel believed the sweet smell of success to be that of gold. This was his logic: Gold was the highest standard in the world of finance, and in Felix's own business as a globally respected olfactory specialist, a *nose among noses*, it stood to reason that any person who could discern the subtle smell of gold would rightly have attained the pinnacle of the fragrance world. Gold, Felix imagined, would have an aroma that was cool and warm, bright and mellow. It would be *rich* too of course but, at the same time... Well, it would be pointless to attempt to convey what the smell of gold was *like* because it would be unique.

Felix kept a South African Krugerrand in a velvet-lined box in his desk drawer. On days when business had gone particularly well he took it out, but as successful as he became – and during his career he had been on retainers with Parisian perfumeries and Assam tea producers, the cosmetics divisions of several famous multinationals and every distillery on the Scottish island of Islay – he had yet to detect even a glimmer of that elusive smell.

Now, sitting at breakfast – *linen with not too much detergent, a carbon scrape of toast, the earthy jag of espresso* – he was beginning to think he never would. Not the way the world was heading these days. All the computer modelling, nanoscale particulate sensors, and organic synthesis were pushing craftsmen out. Modernisation, his customers told him regretfully. The push for quality control and molecular copyright couldn't be guaranteed by human abilities alone any more.

Felix snapped shut his ancient laptop, hiding the latest missive of dismissal, and took his coffee to the window. Only a year ago his view had been of elegant Wipplinger Strasse, a quiet street, a block or so from a place that sold the best Kaiserschmarrn in Vienna. The new apartment in Ottakring offered a far poorer vista. Rain-dark and utilitarian, blare and grit. It wasn't a happy change, but one forced by finances. The only thing he hadn't had to compromise on yet was his coffee. He lifted the demi-tasse and breathed deep, let the aroma cloud about him, fill his passages. He did not waste the experience by drinking it. People who drank good coffee were, in Felix's book, degenerate criminals.

He turned when Joanna entered with the morning's mail and her yipping dog. She dumped most of envelopes on the dining table but retained one, waved it. He knew without looking that it was the revised quote from the decorators.

"I'll look at it later." Bijoux sniffed at his shoes, then looked up expectantly, all brown eyes and pink tongue. He nudged it away with a gentle kick.

"Oh, Felix, it's really not that expensive."

"Later, Joanna."

She stilled. "It's been nearly a *year*. And we're still living like this." Dramatically, she thrust out her hand. She could have been pointing anywhere, it wouldn't have mattered. Everything was shabby and none of it was chic. "You promised."

He scowled. "And you promised not to let Bijoux into the dining room. He stinks when he's been out in the rain."

Joanna ignored him and sat to butter herself some toast. He rejoined her and flicked through the rest of the mail. Bills mostly. He pushed them aside.

"What's that one from *Gustav & Jacob?*"

Her buttery knife was levelled at a cardboard box. Felix should have recognised the logo of the Czech chocolatiers immediately. He'd consulted on their aromatics for nearly fifteen years, until they too had taken the leap to automation and dispensed with his services.

Felix slit open the box – *hamster cage packaging, sex toy polyurethane* – and scooped out the shredded paper and a padded bag. Inside the bag was an arrangement of white plastic. A moulded respirator cup was attached by a neatly coiled tube to a box. Nestled into the top of the box was an ampule of amber liquid. Next to that was a switch.

The scribble, in English, on the *G&J* compliment slip was from their old production manager, Karel Bilek. Felix had thought he'd retired.

Felix

Good to hear from you before Christmas. If it were up to me I'd have you in like a shot, but you know the way the business is now. I'm truly sorry.

You and I were craftsmen, son, but the world has moved on. Did you know they can record smells now? Not perfectly, but it won't be long.

Do yourself a favour, give these guys a call and offer your services. They'll bite your hand off. Take their schilling for a few years and then enjoy a nice retirement when it comes.

Karel.

Underneath, Bilek had printed a company name, *Teleroma*, and a Swiss phone number. Felix vaguely recognised the name, but it took a moment to dredge up. On sufferance, he had been forced to converse via the odious Skype with the makers of a film-star-endorsed scent range in the USA, establishing a few details as a matter of formality before closing the contract, but when he raised the subject of when they wanted him to fly over, the young man in the little window had laughed. *No need, Mr Kapel. We can do all of that over the internet with the Teleroma.*

Felix hadn't known what Teleroma was, but he wanted nothing to do with it. He'd politely backed out of the negotiations at the earliest opportunity.

Now, he didn't know whether to be saddened or insulted. It was all right for Karel to talk about resting easy. He already had at least one foot up on the comfy cushions. Felix had fifteen years to fill before he could even consider retirement, and he had difficulty enough keeping Joanna and the dog under this roof let alone putting anything significant by for the future. And besides, while it was nice of Karel to acknowledge his craftsmanship, a little wider recognition would be nice too. By this stage in his career Felix should have been publishing books and giving lecture tours. There was still time to make his mark, and he wasn't going to throw away the chance of doing so by selling out to the very people who were killing his industry.

Felix crumpled the note in his fist.

"What is it then?" Joanna leaned over his shoulder. That terrible perfume – *crushed roses and children's candy* – that she liked made him gag.

He handed her the apparatus. "See for yourself." With that he stood, dusted the toast crumbs from his lap and strode towards the door.

"Felix!" The urgency in Joanna's voice made him turn. She was

holding the box in one hand, the mask in the other hovering in front
of a face that was stretched in uncommon delight. "Violets!" She
crossed the room, talking. "Is this new? Something you're working on?
You clever man." She kissed him on the forehead and pressed the
apparatus gently back into his hands. "Clever, clever man."

Once Joanna had breezed out of the room, her smelly little dog
trotting after, Felix closed the door and retook his seat. He placed the
device on the table, knowing he ought to toss it straight in the bin but
now curious. He had shared many examples of his craft with his wife
over the years. Some she had liked well enough, others she had not,
but he had never seen her express such delight in a scent before.

Felix pressed the sterile, soft plastic over his nose, closed his eyes,
flicked the switch, and inhaled.

"Fuck me," he whispered.

He had smelled violets in many forms over the years – crushed,
dried, distilled; violet water, violet powder, violet essence – but none
got close to this. This was fresh, living blooms of *V. odorata* growing in
a meadow at the height of spring. With his eyes closed even Felix
could not have told the difference between this synthesis and the real
thing.

He tore the cup from his face, pushed the device away. The
movement disturbed the pile of bills, exposing the corner of
something he had not spotted earlier. A postcard, plain apart from the
inked stamp of the shop that had sent it.

Antikzone
Gerhardt Zickler, proprietor

On the reverse, next to Felix's own address was a handwritten
message: *Herr Kapel, we have your item.*

The shop was above a café bar half way to the 12th district. The
barman directed him through the partitioned half of the room where
smoking students cast him looks that confirmed he was every bit as
out of place as he felt. By the time he had crossed the room, the
cigarette haze had entirely numbed his sense of smell, but on seeing
the piles of mouldering books crowding the wooden stairs, the reaches
of necrotic mildew crawling the walls as he climbed, he was grateful.

184

Herr Zickler, when Felix found the proprietor slouched at a desk at the centre of the maze of lumber like a torpid spider, was a surprise. From the tone of his emails, the sure, unfussy knowledge he had displayed on the Habsburg History site that Felix's ineffectual Googling had led to after reading about the artefact in the Karlheinz Kuntz biography, he had expected tweeds, greying temples, a professorial air. Not this...*loafer.*

Zickler acknowledged his arrival with a nod, but did not remove his headset or divert his attention from his laptop screen. "Five minutes, Herr Kapel," he said, covering his microphone. "Raiding on Warcraft. Dungeon boss. Have a look around."

Having no choice in the matter, Felix did as he was bid. He wandered curving aisles of casement clocks whose complicated faces once told who knew what manner of things in addition to mere time, but now were still and smelled of lacquer and dust. He brushed past rails of military coats pungent with moth balls. Teetering towers of books and sheet music and old documents of all sorts. Plastic tubs of spectacles and opera glasses, watches and hipflasks. Forests of walking sticks.

Old things for which the world no longer had a use.

"What a load of junk," he muttered.

"One man's junk, Herr Kapel." Zickler's beaky countenance appeared between two stacks of pulp science fiction magazines. "Is another's gold."

Felix reddened, but the proprietor did not appear to have taken offence.

"Come," Zickler said. "I'm printing out your provenance... such as it is."

Felix followed him back to the desk where a printer was spewing a sheaf of papers. "Such that it is?"

Zickler grinned good-humouredly. "As I explained before," he said, "with an artefact like the Nose, there's really no way to prove its veracity. I can tell you where I got it from, and where my vendors got it from, and so on. But there's no way of ascertaining that this is the *real* one. If indeed there ever *was* a real one. The Habsburg Nose is legendary, man. And legends, by their nature..."

"So you can give me no guarantee."

"Absolutely not." Zickler adjusted his glasses. "But I *can* guarantee that it's very old and a lot people have *believed* it to be the real deal down the years. Including Karlheinz Kuntz in the years before his unfortunate demise." Zickler folded the papers and placed them on top of the unremarkable cardboard box that had replaced his laptop on the desk. "I believe we said eight hundred and fifty."

Felix licked his lips. The money wouldn't have been enough to repaint the entire apartment, but it would have got a couple of rooms done. He was gambling it on what? A legend? And not just money, his entire career. He needed an edge, was hoping for a miracle. If it didn't work, he'd be out of business within the year.

"Will it really *do* anything?" He was surprised by the plaintiveness in his own voice. "I mean, *really*?"

"Who knows, Herr Kapel." Zickler tapped his nose. "I imagine you're the only man in Vienna who will be able to tell."

To the layman, Felix had always believed, real skill, real *art*, should be indistinguishable from magic. What else do you call it when another human being achieves something which, for you, would be impossible?

Karlheinz Kuntz had been a magician. A contemporary of Escoffier in Lucerne and a more than decent chef in his own right, he had been obsessed with the importance of aroma in cooking. *Without smell*, he said, *your soul is unnourished. You might as well eat air*. In pursuit of what started as a theory but quickly became an obsession, Kuntz had pioneered blindfolded tastings, then entirely dark restaurants. Towards the end of his life it was said he took to wearing a prosthetic nose made of gold. He died in a sanatorium in 1931 suffering from something called *psychosomatic putrescence*. According to the biography, the physicians had detected nothing physically wrong with the man. He had just wasted away, and near the end he had smelled so rotten the sanatorium staff had to be paid extra even to enter his room. A tragic and ironic fate for such a gifted individual.

Felix didn't open the box in the shop, or in the café downstairs or even on the tram home. While it sat heavy on his lap he distracted himself with Zickler's notes. They filled out the story that he already knew. The material was presented prosaically, but that in itself did much to restore his confidence that he'd done the right thing. He regretted now asking Zickler if the Nose actually worked. Of course it didn't *work*. However, it was a symbol, a talisman that had been owned by renowned olfactory greats over the centuries. The artists, the magicians. After Kuntz the chef, had come an orchid grower, an unassailable champion greyhound breeder, a wartime bomb disposal ace. Before, there had been a spice importer, a rose gardener, a mulberry horticulturist in the court of George III of England. The nose was like a badge of genius that cropped up now and then through history.

The story went that the Nose was made for a military officer close to one of the Viennese archdukes. The Hauptman, known only to history as The Bloodhound, had been famous for his ability to root out seditionists and spies, and the golden prosthetic, which he wore ostensibly to cover the syphilitic ruin of his face, was said to lend him the supernatural power of sniffing out plots against his master before they had even been uttered aloud. An ironically gruesome footnote claimed that the fellow had been murdered on Ottoman orders, his body dumped on an island in the Lobau, but discovered within a day because the stench of the corpse could be smelled from the city. The fate of the Nose was not recorded, but it had appeared a century later in the possession of a successful perfumer. The first links in the chain of ownership that continued now with Felix himself.

The apartment was empty but even so he went into the bathroom and locked the door before, with shaking hands, he unwrapped his prize.

Inside the box was a nest of straw. Buried within the straw, an object wrapped in sheets from a 1982 edition of *El Pais*. And then it was in his hands. The Golden Nose of the Habsburgs.

The Nose was an exact replica of a human nose, if perhaps a little large. It had a nobbled crook at the bridge and wide nostrils and had a texture that resembled pores. The colour of the gold was soft, dull, *almost* fleshy in tone. It was impressively heavy.

Felix brought the object up to his face and sniffed it, but the Nose did not smell of anything at all. He smiled ruefully. Then he tried it on. For such a heavy object, it was really rather remarkable how well balanced the thing was. How comfortably it sat on his face, even when he took his hands away. How natural it felt, encasing his own nose. Almost as if it wasn't there at all.

Felix looked in the mirror. The nose gleamed in the fluorescent light. When he had imagined this, he had thought it would look clownish, ridiculous, but no. The nose gave him gravitas. The man in the mirror was every inch the authority.

Finally, Felix gave in to curiosity that logic and common sense had been unable to kill, and drew in a full, deep breath.

Well, of course, there was no difference between that breath and the one before. *Does it actually work?* he'd asked Zickler. *Does it actually give you preternatural,* magical, *olfactory sensitivity? Will you be able to tell the difference between species of tulip from a mile away? Or inform the police what the victim's last meal was from the odour palette of their kitchen? Or tell whether your lover is true from the tang of her sweat?*

Felix laughed at himself. No, there were only the usual smells of the bathroom: soap on the wash stand, bleach from the floor, the slight odour of damp that told him Joanna had showered before she left. He could see the water droplets on the shower curtain, and a rim of mildew around the hem that had really quite a strong taint to it. It almost masked the sting of mint from the dried smear of toothpaste on the sink, and the fulsome guff of sewage seeping from the toilet, the lingering stain of farts too, and the cloying, complex melange of bathroom dust – talcum powder mixed with flakes of skin and tiny hairs and carpet fibres – and that dog really did stink, she'd been washing him in here, in their shower, that was disgusting, and their neighbours, the *vegetarians,* well she'd been cooking bacon again after he'd left for work and then doused the place in the most godawful aerosol freshener –

Felix removed the Nose.

And breathed out.

The effect on Felix's fortunes was immediate. He told no one but Joanna about the Nose, insisting on privacy while he worked, but it was difficult not to associate his ownership of the artefact with the sudden flood of work offers. And that initial flurry was nothing compared to what followed once word of his newfound abilities spread.

In a few short weeks there was enough money to completely redecorate the apartment. Joanna might have been a little more pleased, but her scowl over breakfast had not shifted one bit. Out of sorts, Felix had accidentally kicked the dog, which had taken to following him round, constantly sniffing at his legs and jumping up, and he and his wife had argued. "And give that thing a proper bath outside," he'd yelled as he rushed out to catch the flight to Strasbourg. "It stinks." Her reply had been a petulant mutter, but it had sounded like: *Look who's talking.*

Bernal et fils, was a gourmet provisioner. Having started life several generations back as two brothers with adjoining shops, one a *poissonnier,* the other a *volailler,* their main business now was in procuring expensive comestibles for the elite of Europe. However, they still kept their hand in with a range of home-smoked fish and meats.

"Monsieur Kapel." The woman's smile was professional, her handshake firm. "Welcome to Bernal. I'm Elodie Meilleroux. Thank you for coming all this way. We really hope you can help us make our mark in the smoked salmon market this winter season."

"My pleasure." Felix smiled too, simply because it was nice to be smiled at for a change. "I'd like to get going right away if that's all right. Although I have to say I still don't understand why you need me for this, don't you have tasting panels?"

"*D'accord.*" As Meilleroux waved him towards a door, she glanced quizzically at the carpet where he had walked. Felix looked too but if there was anything there, he couldn't see what it might be. "Well, that's our problem, you see," she said, holding the door and then following him through. "Our panels can't decide. And to be honest, Monsieur, the company can't afford to get this wrong." She shrugged apologetically then ushered him through another door. "So, we've called in the expert."

Felix was getting used to people saying things like this. It had taken long enough.

"Obviously, I'll do what I can," he said.

"Thank you, Monsieur." Meilleroux beamed and stopped before one more door. "Well, here we are. The room has been prepared as you requested. Spotlessly clean, fragrance-free detergents, no background odours."

"Very good." Again Felix tried to match her smile. "Then I shall get started."

When he raised his hand to push the door, though, she stopped him. She looked embarrassed. "Monsieur, I'm sorry but, have you perhaps *stepped in something.* There are a lot of dogs in the area..."

"Stepped in something, you mean like –?"

"Oui, *merde*, Monsieur Kapel. Can't you smell it? It's really quite strong."

Kapel shook his head. Without the Nose on, he could smell only the things you'd normal expect to smell in an office building. Sterile carpet, stale recirculated air, a lingering chemical taint of air freshener. Nevertheless, he lifted first one shoe, then the other. His soles were spotless. Meilleroux's brow creased. She checked her own shoes, then she shook her head. "I must be imagining things."

"It's not a problem. The nose sometimes plays tricks on the best of us."

She shrugged again. "I'll let you get to work then. When you're finished, press zero on the phone and ask for me."

The room was empty of everything apart from the table, the sample containers and the clipboard and pen. Felix placed his briefcase on the table and retrieved the velvet-lined box that used to contain his krugerrand. He took out the Nose, and began his work.

Business boomed. Felix travelled constantly, all over Europe, to the Americas and throughout Asia. First class every time. He passed the travelling time writing guest columns for a variety of trade magazines and Sunday supplements and responding to requests to give informative talks. At least to begin with. The columns continued, but the public appearances dried up pretty fast. He tried not to feel personally insulted. Same as when the customers, delighted with his work, nevertheless tried to persuade him not to visit in person in future. *We don't want to inconvenience you. I'm afraid our budget won't stretch. We'll send the samples to you. Don't you use Teleroma?*

He did not, would not, could not use Teleroma. His laptop barely managed email. And besides, he told them: "Why would you buy a greyhound and make it run in shackles?"

Return visits were to deserted parts of buildings accompanied by a single green-faced employee. Even though Felix had bathed that morning, was wearing clothes fresh out of the drycleaner's wrapper, and brand new shoes.

At first he thought it was his imagination, but the evidence mounted. What he had thought at first to be room accorded by the public to a person of obvious status became naked avoidance. People crossed the street to distance themselves from him. Shop keepers asked him not very politely to leave. Children jeered, or cried.

He thought of Karlheinz Kuntz. Of *psychosomatic putrescence*. Well, what else could it be? He was certain he gave off no particular smell – he of all people would detect one, surely – but everyone he came into contact with acted as if he were the skunk from those old cartoons.

Even Joanna was sleeping in a room at the opposite end of the apartment now. The only person who enjoyed Felix's company these days was Bijoux. When he came home, the little bastard was waiting at the door to snuffle at his ankles, happily licking its chops.

Joanna was sitting in the kitchen typing on her computer. When she saw him she looked cross, then guilty, then nauseated. Like the rest of the flat, the kitchen was full of fresh cut flowers and the windows were wide open.

"What are you doing here? I thought you were in…" She trailed off because he knew she had long since ceased to care where his travels took him as long as it was out of the house.

"Change of plan," he said. "I'm conducting a telephone interview with *Spice! Magazine.*"

Joanna sneered. "Oh, they're not coming to do it in person? I wonder why."

"Well, the drains…"

"It's not the *drains*, Felix. Have you seen the doctor again?"

"He maintains there's nothing wrong with me a good bath won't fix. And he won't let me make another appointment."

Joanna *hmphed*. "There's another letter from the landlord. The neighbours have got a petition together. It's got nearly four hundred names. Who would have thought your fame would have spread so far?"

Felix took a step towards her. "Joanna…" But she held up a hand, so he sat meekly at the opposite end of the table. "What are we going do?"

"Perhaps you could consider getting rid of that bloody *thing*?"

It wasn't the first time she'd mentioned it, and he'd promised to think about it…but he knew in his heart he couldn't. The Nose made him who he was. It completed him in a way she could never understand. He made no reply.

"Well, I know what *I'm* going to do." She closed her computer and came around the table where she hovered for a moment, perhaps considering touching his cheek, even kissing his brow like she used to, but her face blanched. "It's all in the email," she said as she rushed from the room. Moments later Felix heard the delicate sounds of retching from the bathroom.

Felix made coffee. Quadruple strength. The warm aroma from the cracked African beans filled the room, welcoming and lovely and surely stronger than any imaginary odour. He made two cups. Both went untouched.

These were the sounds of her leaving: the busyness of bottles and jars in the bathroom, the firm shutting of the bedroom door followed so quickly by its re-opening that he knew she must already have been all but packed, the rumble of case castors, the whispered imprecations to the bloody dog, the beep of the taxi horn. The slam of the door.

Felix counted one minute, then another, calling her bluff and waiting for the sound of her return, but the only thing he heard was his own voice and that only emphasised her absence.

He stopped counting and walked the length of the empty apartment to his office. Bijoux was there, gleefully humping his laptop. The casing was gnawed and covered in saliva.

"Bijoux!" The dog perked as soon as it saw him, tripping itself in its haste to scurry over. He lifted it up. It got a couple of licks in at his face before he stretched it to arms' length. "So she abandoned you too?" The dog gave no reply, but seemed happy enough with the situation. It certainly smelled as if it had just farted with delight. "To be honest, I'm not surprised," he told it. "You're an obnoxious little bastard." And, with rare physical dexterity, he calmly drop-kicked the ball of fur through the open window.

Felix went through the flat with a refuse sack, shoving the flowers and air fresheners and bloody scented candles into bags, closing and locking the windows, drawing the curtains. Then, when he was ready to find out her reasons, he returned to his office and switched on his laptop: *hot metal, burning plastic, wisps of toxic smoke.*

With a bellow of rage he reopened the window and tossed the computer after the dog.

It took three days before he gave in. On the first day he went to the kitchen and made a wonderful-smelling meal out of all the things that

Joanna didn't like. Not so much out of defiance, or even because he was hungry, but because on that side of the apartment he could barely hear Bijoux's howls. The dog was unharmed, just pissed off. The laptop had not fared so well. On the second day, both dog and wrecked device were gone. Felix threw himself into work, or at least tried to. Every phone call was met with excuses. They even seemed to object to talking to him, as if merely the sound of his voice conjured the imaginary smell. *All of this could easily have been discussed by email,* one customer said. *It'd have been so much more convenient if only you would use Teleroma.*

That night he went to Joanna's bedroom and donned the Nose to see what lingered: *sickly perfume, unlaundered sheets, the musk of sex that hadn't involved Felix.* Then he looked at himself in her mirror.

"Look at you," he said. "You're a master of your profession, and yet no one will have anything to do with you. You could still get by if you weren't so afraid of the future."

"You're right," he replied to himself. "If the old world doesn't want me, perhaps after all I can make a place for myself in the new one. How bad can it be, really?"

He really had no option.

On the third day Felix went to an electronics store and asked for their top-of-the-range computer. Pretending not to notice the fleeing customers, he cornered the clerk who had been slowest to escape. The girl rattled through the features in a blur of words. Felix cut her off: "Teleroma."

She nodded, swallowed. "Comes as standard on all new models, sir."

"I'll take it."

Pink relief coloured her pallid cheeks. She told him how much it cost.

Just because he was feeling spiteful at the world, he said: "I want a discount. Otherwise I'll have to have a good look around."

Felix wrote that afternoon to those clients with whom he still had some tenuous relationship and informed them that he might after all in some circumstances be willing to work remotely using the Teleroma service. He intended to spend the subsequent hour learning how Teleroma worked but the help document confounded him and the number of results to his Google search for something simpler was so bewildering that he only got as far as understanding two things. Firstly, that Teleroma was a mechanism for transmitting scent over the internet, which he'd already surmised. And secondly that it was hugely popular. People used it for everything: cookery videos, perfume advertisements, porn. He scowled at the little grill in the laptop casing, his finger poised to click play on a coffee ad, but he couldn't bring himself to do it.

Outside, the sound of people laughing passed and faded. The bark of a distant dog made him wonder where Bijoux was. His apartment was still and silent.

Occasionally the phone rang, but after the third call from a newspaper wanting to talk to the *incredible stinking man*, he switched it off.

Going through his emails, Felix discovered an invitation to join a dating site. He stared at it. Even he knew better than click on unsolicited links. But this one was personally addressed, and very welcoming. He stared some more, and then he clicked on it. What was the worst that could happen? The site offered him with a bunch of forms. It took some time to list all of his achievements before his application was ready to send off.

He had a reply within the hour. Her name was Ania, and she was Polish. In the subsequent exchange of emails, she came across as cultured, understanding and not lacking in humour. When she asked if he would like to Skype, he cringed but in for a penny… Besides, he was still handsome, and he had no intention whatsoever of switching on the Teleroma, even if he was able to work out how.

Ania had a strong face, a broad mouth with nice teeth when she smiled, which was often, and a sexy nose. Could a nose be sexy? Hers was. It had very wide nostrils. She was a partner in an accountancy firm. She worked late and was divorced. In what little free time she had she drank vodka and torrented HBO shows and chatted to men from dating sites. She winked when she said that.

Felix didn't know what torrenting was. He didn't understand the wink either. But Ania proved a good person to chat to and he told her about his work (she was impressed) and his recent singledom (she was sympathetic). While they chatted his eye was drawn repeatedly to her nose. The gorgeous nostrils flared, as if inhaling deeply, and when she breathed out it was through her mouth. Heavily, a little shaky. There was a flush in her cheeks. He'd not seen her hands for some time.

"Are you – *touching*, I mean are you –?" he blurted.

Ania grinned sheepishly. "I'm so sorry. I couldn't help myself." Her hand came up into view. She licked her fingers. "You smell unbelievably good. I've never –" She suppressed a shudder. "Oh, God, *never.*"

Felix's heart tripped over itself in panic. "You can *smell* me? That thing is on?" He clicked wildly at icons on the chat window. Ania disappeared but he could still hear her.

"Of course. Teleroma is on as standard, you have to opt out. But please. *Please*, don't."

Don't? She could smell him, and she wasn't repulsed? He relaxed a fraction. "Well, why can't I smell you?"

"I'm sorry, I'm being selfish. I didn't want my feedback to contaminate you. It took so long to track you down." When she reached forward to click something on the computer balanced on her lap he noticed that her blouse wasn't tucked into anything. The taint of soap mixed with the faint but unmistakeable odour of female arousal leaked from his computer. "Felix, I've got to see you tonight."

"But aren't you in Poland?"

With a smile, she shook her head. "Please."

He told her his address. She closed the connection.

While Felix waited, he went over what she had said. She genuinely found his odour attractive? What was she, some sort of freak?

Ania almost knocked him over when he opened the door. Then she was kissing him, licking his face, yanking off his robe, popping buttons from his pyjamas. He smelled the rain on her hair, the sweat from her run up the stairs, the edge of something else – *alcohol?*

"The Nose," she breathed. "Put on the Nose."

She followed him through to the office. "I smelled you in the drop off zone of Frederic Chopin Airport. I *had* to have you," she told him as she unlocked the desk drawer and retrieved the box. "I've bribed people. Coerced them even. Eventually I got your email address. Thank you for replying." She nodded at the golden gleam in his hand. "Put it on." Felix did as he was told, and immediately his visitor shuddered.

"I smell worse when I'm wearing it?"

195

Ania licked her lips several times before finding the breath to reply. "Oh, God, a million times better." With the Nose on, her arousal was overpowering, her sweat almost as erotic, and that other smell was stronger too. Not alcohol, but familiar. Something medicinal...

She pushed him back against the desk, tore off what remained of his nightwear, and then came at him. It was only when the damp cloth was clamped over his face that he finally recognised the smell.

Of course, *chloroform*.

The house was very nice. Spacious and sparsely, but tastefully, decorated. Clean walls, stone floors, functional furniture, plain accessories. Sterile. It was not in Vienna. There were no mountains high enough for the air to be this pure in Vienna. Felix didn't even think it was in Austria. The German the housekeeper spoke was different. He suspected Bavaria perhaps.

He thought of himself as a prisoner. But he found he didn't mind so much. He watched HBO and played Warcraft (his goblin avatar was called Stinky Bill) and read from a well selected library of books.

And three times a day he got naked, put on the Nose and broadcast himself in Teleroma for an hour.

Occasionally, Ania visited. They had exhausting sex and then lay in bed and talked. She told him, to his surprise, that he was not in fact a prisoner in the house. Rather, he owned the place, having paid for it outright in the first two weeks when they'd broadcast him sedated as "proof of concept" to their backers. It would be unfortunate if he was to leave, but he could do so if he wanted. He thought the distinction was a technicality, but stopped worrying about it when she showed him his bank balance.

And so it went. To keep things interesting for the punters, they varied his diet: Spice Time! Umami Hour! Apparently that made a difference to his odour. Sometimes, they gave him things to smell with the Nose – orchid blossoms, durian fruit, cow shit – because that made a difference too. Felix did as he was told. He chose early on not to watch them watching him – the myriad white faces in dark rooms, many with Teleroma masks squashed against them as they struggled to breath in everything he had to offer, the orgiastic groaning; it was all too much. Much better to content himself with the ever fluctuating, but overall steadily rising, visitor stats. To think of the money.

One time he asked Ania: "Am I famous?"

Her smile was broad. "In the greater world, no one has a clue who you are," she said. "But to the people who matter, you are a god."

They fed him exquisitely but he knew he was losing weight. "Am I going to die?"

Ania kissed his brow. "We all die," she whispered. "Surely all that matters is that, by the time we do, we achieve the things our hearts wish for."

Felix stroked the Nose, heavy and solid and cold. He breathed in and smelled, faintly, an entirely new smell. It was warm and cool, and bright and mellow. It was rich, and it was oh so very sweet.

I fell in love with Vienna on a footballing trip. Scotland Writers vs Austria Writers, a wonderful weekend of cultural exchange (in which the cunning gifts of Ottokringer beer and Viennese wafers for our half-time snack failed to derail an excellent away win for the visitors). I adored my time the city, and this is my attempt to capture it within a sort of European fable. It is also kind of icky in places. You might want to hold your nose.

The Death of Abigail Goudy

Guilt and blossom chase me along the mausoleum path. The guilt because I'm late, but not only that. Coming here makes me realise how badly I've neglected a friendship. The blossom sticks to my shoes, already fringed with brown corruption before it left the tree.

It's been too long since I last saw Abigail Goudy.

The building is an impassive example of Scottish masonic Victorian death fetish. The square sandstone base is adorned minimally with simple pillars and arches and topped by a squat tower. It's a monument to the fundamental truths of life and death constructed with absolute precision from the simplest geometries, and built to last eternity. As I near the doors, an usher slips out. Extracting a roll-up from his pocket, he cups his hands to light it. He takes a draw, then nods companionably and steps aside to let me enter.

"How much have I missed?" I listen for music.

The usher cocks an eyebrow. "Not a thing, mate. They've only just finished tuning up." He waves me inside. "Sit anywhere. There's plenty of room." I duck past him and his voice follows me inside. "Mind and take the bumf from the table."

The exterior wall is thick, the ceiling low; the echoes of shoe-scuffs on stone startlingly oppressive. At the other end of the entrance passage there's a sign:

QUIET PLEASE

TALKING IN THE AUDITORIUM IS FORBIDDEN

Next to that, a rosewood table that wouldn't have looked out of place in my granny's hall. It holds a stack of leaflets.

"Brochure, sir?" The words are whispered but the closest person to the table is another usher standing a good fifteen feet away. She smiles, lips glossed with cherry smugness and, maybe, an ounce of flirtation. I'd consider asking for her number, something to pass the time while I'm back in town, but she's probably an undergrad and I can just hear the scorn in Abi's laugh when she finds out. It's not worth the effort. "This part of the room is a whispering gallery."

Again, the words are ear-intimate. "You can read all about it in the brochure."

I take one of the leaflets. Single-page; the first usher had it right with *bumf.* On one side: a photograph of Abi, badly shot and too formal; it makes her look ill. Under the photo, a crush of text. I barely glance at it, taking in only the highlighted phrases: *Ground Breaking* and *Daring* and *Rewriting The Rules Of Classical Music.* At the bottom, in larger type: *World Premiere.*

A world premiere classical music performance in a nineteenth century mausoleum could, generously, be described as fairly daring, for anyone but Abi at least. The rest is crap. Typical university production, the pamphlet clearly rushed off by some clueless intern at the last minute. Those aren't Abi's words. It all feels a bit... *desperate*, but then it's been twenty something years since *Alpine Pasture* earned her the wunderkind tag and she always took the expectation that came with it hard.

I gift the usher a smile, turn to survey the rest of the mausoleum interior and realise that the tower that sits atop the square base is hollow all the way down. Cresting it is a dome and I can see the clouds through the cupola. Once again I'm impressed by those simple geometries. Back in the day, Abi and I would have taken much puerile glee in the fact that it looks like a stubby cock.

"Alessandro Stradella was chased through the streets of Genoa by a love rival's assassin and brutally stabbed to death."

This was on the smoking deck of the Chip. A June evening swelter. We'd been baking ourselves since lunchtime, guzzling lager to chill down. Roz had gone for a pee and then it was her turn at the bar. The pub was crowded. She'd be a while.

Abi was my new girlfriend's music student flatmate. Quiet, I thought. Not the easiest to make small talk with. Maybe even a bit strange. Now, she looked pleased with her pronouncement, even if it was apropos of fuck all.

"Okay..." I didn't know who Stradella was. I rolled the heel of my glass across my forehead. It wasn't cold enough. I wished Roz would hurry up. Not for the first time that day, my thoughts turned to fucking her when we got home.

Abi scooted closer. She was wearing a high-necked retro top, and a floaty skirt that displayed her skinny legs. She slapped my leg just below the hem of my shorts. Her fingernails were painted green. *Just like Sally Bowles*, I'd told her earlier but she'd dismissively claimed not to know who that was.

"Old Allesandro was a philandering bastard. Are you saying philandering bastards don't deserve to be punished?"

Unsure where this conversation had come from, and wary of where it was heading, I opted for non-specific agreement. "Well, within the law of the time, of course," I ventured. "I suppose that happened a while ago, eh?"

"Sixteen eighty two. He composed a lot of well-regarded work, but he fucked around just a bit too much. Naughty boy." It happened in a single movement: one second she was sitting next to me, the next she was straddling my leg. Her face was inches from mine, her eyes sparking and, when she pushed herself against my bare thigh, I could tell she wasn't wearing knickers. Abi kissed me, a slack smooch that tasted of beer. When she disengaged, she was smiling. "Poor Alessandro," she whispered. "Who knows what great works he might have left us if he'd lived out his natural days. But he just couldn't keep it in his pants." She settled back into her original seat and smoothed out her skirt just before Roz returned with the beer.

I didn't get to fuck Roz that night. We had a row that was probably more about the heat and the drink than anything real. Certainly, Abi's name was not mentioned, but I couldn't help being convinced that Roz suspected something. It was that or my own guilty conscience.

I never asked Abi why she did it. The more I got to know her afterwards, the more I learned that was just the sort of thing she did. Even so, Alessandro, and my own name, Alastair, were too close for me to accept as coincidence.

Beneath the tower, the square mausoleum floor is made into circle by a beautiful geometric mosaic. The intricate black and white pattern is currently obscured by folding chairs. In the very centre are four grand pianos, set nose-to-nose like compass-point jigsaw pieces.

The improvised auditorium is far from full. Nearest the door are a clump of journalists, identifiable by the tablets and netbooks they fuss with while they wait. As an insider I can tell you that it's never a good sign when they begin their copy before a performance has even started.

I'm supposed to be covering this too, in the hope that I can flog it to some online arts blog or other. I used to get commissioned for this malarkey but times move on, don't they? The rest of them will hustle to get their pieces posted. I'll at least do the composer the decency of waiting until the performance is over. My byline still carries some weight. My expertise in the subject. I didn't even bring a notebook. For once, this is easy money.

Further round the room are the students and academics. Among them I recognise Abi's old tutor, a spectacularly unkempt man whose name I can't for the life of me recall. He sits with his eyes closed, as if he's already hearing the music although, most likely, he's napping. I don't recognised any of Abi's family among the remaining singletons dotted around the space. Those must be friends, maybe even fans. There aren't many.

I take a seat. The chair scrapes, an ominously loud rasp that booms around the room, turning heads and raising a few smirks from others who have previously made the same mistake. The reverberation persists as I remove and fold my coat and then carefully sit down. And then, to my surprise, the noise of my *faux pas* washes back again. This impressive echo certainly explains why everyone is obeying the sign at the entrance so diligently. And it gives me the first real hint as to why Abi picked this place.

"Jean-Baptiste Lully died from a conducting injury." She offered me this while clambering upon the outcrop that she'd gleefully christened *the clit* for the way it protruded at the base of the narrow vee-shaped pasture and overhung the gushing waterfall below.

"Really?" The rock was slick with spray but I refrained from warning her about it. I'd already made that mistake once. She said I sounded like her dad.

Abi reached down for the flags. "Lully was a court composer for the Sun King. In the days before they had conductors' batons, they used a heavy staff to keep time." She stepped onto the highest part of the rock, wobbled, and then righted herself, with the furled flags outstretched to the sides like a tightrope walker. She grinned down at me and I was momentarily dazzled by the spray and the alpine sunshine. "So there he was, beating away on his big gilded staff, and he only went and bashed his foot. The wound festered, then duly turned gangrenous. *Fin de Lully.*" She had her poise now, like a gymnast about to perform some feat of acrobatics. "Well...?"

"What?"

She nodded towards the recording equipment waiting up the hill and I scurried off obediently. When I was in position, she raised the flags above her head. The silk fluttered like emerald sails. Then she waved them and that was the signal for me to set the recorder going, and for the tenor and the violinist a little higher up the meadow to begin their performance, and for the patient, bemused Austrian farmer way up in the high pasture to start bringing his herd down the mountainside.

Once everything was underway we lay in the grass and listened to the birdsong and the rushing water and the approaching clatter of cowbells, and to the twin melodies of Abi's music rising into the spring air, shimmering off the mountains that ringed our little valley, colouring the air with echoes.

We weren't a couple. We never were that. But lying in that field with the wildflowers and the insects and sounds of nature and music mixed together in that huge, natural echo chamber, we were happy.

Something hovered and droned near my head until Abi swatted it gently away. "Did you know Alban Berg died from a bee sting?" she whispered.

It says on the back of the leaflet that the mausoleum is thought to have the longest echo of any man-made building in the UK. It's the old obsession, then.

The hoo-hah over *Alpine Pasture* had barely died down, its incredible twin melodies, famous already, appearing in adverts and sampled in chart music, when Abi went public to declare them worthless. "It's not the music itself, Al," she told me over the last of the champagne. "It's what the music creates, what it leaves behind. They can play *Alpine* in the fucking Carnegie Hall from now until judgement-day-hallelujah, but they'll never get it. The only people that ever heard it properly were you, me, Herr Krankl and twenty four cows. Listen..." She played me the recording I'd made that day in Austria, skipping to the soft tailing off of the voice and violin. She made me listen until the sounds had become echoes, and then even less than that. A delicately stained atmosphere. A hue.

Abi called this the *persistence of echoes*. Said it stayed in the place long after the reverberations had dwindled beyond human hearing. "Music is *situational*, Al." She was drunk by then but she meant what she was saying. I just didn't know how much.

I've been hoping that the gap between her last outing and this new venture might have meant a rethink – the reviews of *Priestland Beach* had, with gleefully childish irony, labelled it a *dull echo* of what had gone before – but it seems not.

I look around, surprised that the composer herself hasn't put in an appearance yet, scan the interior for that slight frame, those sparky eyes, that dirty mouth that will smile sweetly and then utter a public reprimand. "Who fucking invited you, cocksucker?" Something like that.

I'll take it. I deserve it, half of it at least. I'm looking forward to seeing her.

For now, though, there is no sign of her. Instead, without further preamble, a young Japanese woman dressed in ubiquitous orchestra black walks along the central aisle, sits at the closest of the pianos, and begins to play.

They did perform *Alpine Pasture* at Carnegie Hall. By that point Abi was deeply disinterested, calling any performance of the piece pointless. I persuaded her to at least take advantage of the paid-for trip to New York for the opening night. As hoped, she took me along as her plus one.

Neither of us saw much of the city. At that time, perhaps inspired by her success, I was still trying to be a novelist, making a point of bashing away on the laptop the whole day while Abi was dragged around a succession of interviews and associated obligations. I couldn't have left that hotel room if I'd wanted to. Writers talk about the *white heat*, when the hold their entire world in their head and the words simply flow. That was me that couple of days. A genius in nova. I pounded away at it until she appeared at my door in her party frock and demanded to know why I wasn't ready.

While I washed, she hovered at the bathroom door, nosing through the running order for that night's programme. "Alexander Scriabin died from septicemia resulting from a sore on his lip, you know." She looked at me in the mirror. "Is your novel done yet?"

"Nearly," I replied sulkily, unwrapping my rented tux.

I remember very little about the performance. Both of us felt restless and out of place, Abi twitching and tutting, and me frustrated at being separated from my book. I do recall very clearly the applause at the end of *Alpine*. A rapturous wave that stilled her for the only time that night. I think it was with terror. Later there was a reception. Abi was whisked around the gushers and the glad-handers while I made friends with the booze table. I lasted an hour before grabbing a bottle and sloping off back to the hotel.

I was still up writing when the knock came, and there was sufficient fury in it to make me jump up to answer it.

"Where the *fuck* did you go?" Abi stormed past me, kicking aside the suit trousers that lay on the floor. "I needed you there."

"Sorry..." I was taken aback by the force of her obvious hurt. "I was just hanging around looking stupid..."

"No." She spotted the champagne and necked a long swallow. "You were *being* there. Did you think I brought you along for *your* good?"

"I *was* there." I folded my arms, aware that wearing only boxers and a Motorhead t-shirt undermined my attempt to prove my commitment, but determined to try anyway. "But I got bored, and I needed to write my fucking book."

"This?" Abi kicked off her heels and climbed onto the bed. She dragged the laptop over and glanced at the text on the screen. "Is it brilliant? Because there's really no point if it's not. Brilliance is all those tossers are interested in."

I grabbed the laptop off her and closed it. "How the fuck do I know if it's brilliant or not?"

Abi laughed then. She could use laughter cruelly and often did, but this laugh was one of recognition. Something that came from deep inside. She got off the bed and gently took the laptop back from my petulant hands, placing it on the nightstand. Then she took another long swig of the stolen champagne and kissed me. The cold fizz that filled my mouth in one moment was driven from it in the next by Abi's tongue, and when she pushed me back onto the bed there was such energy in her that her face glowed.

It wasn't the first time we'd fucked, but those other occasions had been out of boredom, a need for companionship. This was something else entirely. It was sex as narrative, a savage-subtle exploration of themes of defiance and insecurity. It was sex as performance, a nuance choreography of physicality, of touch and timing. It was sex as communion, a blurring of the roles of artists and audience. Of person and person. It was physically and emotionally exhausting. I had never had a night like it, and don't ever expect to again. Not with her, not with anyone. Abi was a virtuoso that night, and when we were done I finally fully understood what she meant when she described herself as a situationist creator. That art is its time and its place as much as it is its content.

"Do you ever worry that you'll die before you create your masterwork?" She said this into my chest, as she curled against my side.

I don't remember what I answered. I was preoccupied with the knowledge that she'd addressed me for the first time as an artistic equal, and I felt anything but that. I knew that I had nothing like Abi's passion. I never would.

"I can't decide if it would be worse dying with your greatest art still inside you," she was mumbling now, almost asleep, "or getting to the end of your life and realising that your best came right at the beginning."

The melody is picked out slowly, metronomically methodical. For the first ten minutes it could be something by Erik Satie, but the tune lacks the sweet delicacy of his *Gymnopédies*. I recognise it as a moodier – *doomier* – rendering of the main theme from *Alpine Pasture* played without character or inflection like the flattest recording of the piece. A *dull echo*. But that's not all: the tempo has been chosen so that the notes mesh precisely with the mausoleum's long echoes, the tones coming ghosting back down the chamber, layering behind the melody like contrapuntal memory. Washes of harmonics lying on top of each other like geological strata.

It's a beautiful effect, and a clever one. It's certainly enough to hold the attention of the audience. Looking around, I see eyes closed, half-smiles, heads nodding in appreciation. I still can't see Abi, though. For all my laxness in keeping in touch, she's been partly at fault too – dropping off social media, making herself hard to reach short of an actual phone call – but that's quite different from snubbing your own premiere. Having created something this intricate, this unique, I can't believe she wouldn't attend the performance, but that seems to be the case. It saddens me.

The pianist repeats a cycle of interpretations of the themes, drawing different moods and colours from the space, but it becomes apparent that there's no development going on. Just the tune and its echoes. I can hear the audience becoming restless. Someone is whispering, then someone else suppresses a sneeze and rummages in a bag for a handkerchief. There are scrapes, shifts, rustles. From the area that the journos are sitting in I hear a clear mutter: "…well it's just substandard Cage, isn't it, really…?" In answer, someone laughs. And all of these sounds come back again five, six, seven seconds later. Through the growing susurrus of impatience, the pianist keeps playing.

At almost an hour into the performance, something new happens. A second pianist, a bearded man this time but dressed identically to the first, walks down the central aisle. He sits at the opposite instrument in the cloverleaf and begins to play. The effect is shocking. An intentional, cacophonic grinding of musical gears that silences the room instantly. Not only is the new pianist playing a different tune but he is also playing out of time and, worst of all, his piano is maybe a quarter tone out of tune with the first. The two players continue as if oblivious to the music each other is making for perhaps a minute, and the relief when the female instrumentalist stops, stands and leaves is palpable. There's a ripple of laughter in the room, but I'm listening for the new melody and am unsurprised to recognise *Hangar No.1*, her second major piece.

What is this Abi? A greatest hits tour?

Hangar No.1 did not play at Carnegie Hall. Given that it involved a piano and string quartet played while suspended thirty five feet up inside an aircraft hangar, and ended with all of the instruments being dropped onto concrete, it was amazing that it was ever performed more than once.

"Well, they wanted an ending," Abi said. This time the hotel was a B&B a few miles from the Norfolk aerodrome where the premiere had taken place. One of Abi's irks from the continuing commentary about *Alpine Pasture* had been the grumblings over the ninety seven seconds of silence following the final notes that she insisted must be observed as part of the performance. Apparently audiences wanted to know when to clap. She looked at me levelly. "*Gimmick* or not."

"I said I took that back." I'd tried to make a joke of it since that unguarded word had escaped my lips but she refused to let me off the hook. "It's quite the fucking finale." Then I realised that despite her bullishness she was looking for reassurance. It's hard to gauge an audience reaction that consists mainly of shrieks of alarm. "It was amazing. Really."

And then I went to hold her. Partly because I had no more words to give her and partly because I was afraid that if we continued to talk she would start nagging about the novel again. When we saw each other, she'd stopped asking about how I was; just the book, like art was the only thing one could value.

By that weekend, we'd not seen each other for a while because I was being offered increasingly steady, and lucrative, work in the south. It was my reason and my excuse. To my surprise, though, I'd not completely given up on the book. I still tooled away at it in the evenings and had even managed to interest a literary agent, but he'd had fuck all luck in selling it. I knew it wasn't brilliant. I didn't even know how to make it good.

We made love for the sake of it. It had become a habit of affirmation, nothing more than that. About as far from the fireworks of that night in New York as it's possible to get. Afterwards way lay apart. Not speaking, not touching. I don't know if she knew I was awake to hear her whisper into the darkness: "Bedřich Smetena contracted syphilis, and died in an asylum of a progressive paralysis."

There was no exploding piano at the end of this rendition of *Hangar No.1*. Just another jarring, out-of-tune changeover to the next pianist. The following hour was variations on the melodies from *Celestine*, which I knew to be an achingly gorgeous thing that flowed like water, but was now rendered heavy-handed and robotic.

We're now well into the fourth hour. The journos are long gone and more than half the audience too. A while ago I heard someone whisper something to the attendant. Some seconds later, the building's echo relayed it to my ears among the piano reflections: "How long does this thing go on for?"

"They haven't told us, sir," came the shimmering reply. "The mauseoleum is booked indefinitely."

I, though, know it won't be long. They're on to *Priestland Beach* now. The fourth and last of Abi's major pieces and, while as gorgeous as the rest, my least favourite because it's the one we'd rowed over. *Hangar No.1* came out a year after *Alpine*, but there was then a gap of several years before the world saw *Celestine*. Abi had filled her time with short pieces, with theatre music, scores for friends' indie films. None of these she put her name to. Sketches, she called them. Which was all very well, but she had a label with a schedule to fulfil, publishing and distribution deals. She despised it all, *the industry*, but promised to deliver more promptly in future. When *Priestland Beach* was ready, she made absolutely sure that her already all-but-burned bridges were reduced to smoking rubble by declaring that there were to be no recordings or concert performances of the piece. There was no point, she said. They could never replicate the experience of being there, the echo profile of those towering slate cliffs.

As a friend, I'd tried to reason her around. "What are you going to do for money?"

"Money?" She was genuinely astounded that I should ask such a thing. "Hark at you, Mister Work-for-hire. What are you going to do for *time?*" She screwed her face up, suddenly pugnacious. "How long do you think you have to dick around? How many tries to get it right? You want to be like poor old Alkan? His fucking coat stand fell on him."

We'd already begun to, but after that we drifted increasingly apart. At birthdays and Christmases, I used to send her those hideous cards that played tinny little tunes when you opened them. They transmuted into e-cards, and then Facebook messages. After she moved off of social media, with no one to nag me, I quietly and conveniently forgot I'd ever attempted to be a novelist. This is the thing Abi never understood. It's how most attempts to make art end. Failure, or, at best, mediocrity – which in her eyes was the same thing.

Listening to *Priestland Beach*, its echoes washing back and forth like the sea waves on that bitterly cold day when it was first, and last, performed, I acknowledge that I've missed Abi like fuck. I've *always* missed her. Every single day. The guilt gnaws at me afresh, and I discover that I'm also mightily pissed off. At myself, at her, at both of us for letting this happen. I want to take her by the arm and usher her outside right now and tell her that I'm angry and I'm sorry, and that we should both make a bloody effort to spend more time together. But she's not here, is she?

I extract the leaflet from my coat pocket and smooth it out, thinking perhaps that I've missed some detail, like this is a second performance and I should have been here for the matinee instead when the room was a sell-out and ovations echoed up and down the length of this odd, old building. I scan the blurb and then I see the thing I missed before. In my arrogance, my familiarity. In my expectation that she would always be there when it suited me to look for her.

The past tense.

The prose is ham-fisted but it clearly mentions an illness – an impressively rare one, apparently borne bravely, and alone, while she worked to complete this final composition. I drop the leaflet on the floor and bow my head into my hands and, while it sinks in, the pianos continue to play. And play. Sometimes it's two of them together, sometimes three, sometimes all of them. It's no longer noise to me, it is memory. Echoes, layers and hues.

—We're in the hangar, laughing at the pianist's fear of heights.

—We're noisily manhandling the tubular bells down the cliff path to the beach, gulls wheeling around us.

—We're setting up seventeen glockenspiels along the length of a road tunnel at four in the morning.

—We're holding each other hard in New York. She doesn't know that I'm crying into her hair.

—We're lying in the alpine grass, holding hands under the bluest sky.

—She's chiding me about Ravel, Chausson, Purcell. *Taxi crash, rode his bike into a wall, drank bad chocolate.*

The music, *her* music, all of it. Mechanised, dehumanised, rolling on relentlessly, perhaps forever, but I remember how it really was.

"Abigail Goudy died of a broken heart."

This is not a memory. It is sung. A soft, mezzo line that weaves through the melee like a silver thread, riding the echoes once, twice, three times until it is inaudible. I snatch my head up but there is no singer. Just the four pianists, the bored attendant, and me. It's got dark. Everyone looks tired. I realise I'm shivering, shaking. There's a blanket around my shoulders and a prepacked egg sandwich on the chair next to me. I have no idea how much time has passed.

I look at my hands. They're the hands of someone who has drifted into middle age unaware. Something at floor level catches my eye. Something white on my shoe, a perfect blossom flower. It is ringed with brown corruption.

Without a word I rise and leave the mausoleum and, as soon as I am outside, the music ceases.

But the echoes linger.

This is a story about the secrets in the hearts of all artists. In some senses I've been writing it for a long time and, like Abigail Goudy, I've been putting off committing to it because I really wanted to get it right. Of all the stories in this book, this is one with fewest filters. And it gets truer every year.

About the Author

Neil's debut novel, *The Moon King*, was nominated for the BSFA Award and the British Fantasy Society Holdstock Award. His short fiction has been nominated for the BSFA and British Fantasy awards and, with Andrew J Wilson, he edited *Nova Scotia: New Scottish Speculative Fiction*, which was nominated for the World Fantasy Award. He lives, works, writes and makes music in Glasgow, Scotland.

The Moon King
Neil Williamson

The stunning debut novel from one of Britain's finest writers of genre fiction. Shortlisted for both the BSFA Award for best novel and the Holdstock Award.

All is not well in Glassholm. Amidst rumours of unsettling dreams and strange whispering children, society is disintegrating into unrest and violence. The sea has turned against the city and the island's luck monkeys have gone wild, distributing new fates to all and sundry. Turmoil is coming…

"*The Moon King* is adult, literary fantasy at its best."
— *Eric Brown, the Guardian*

"*The Moon King* is a mysterious, luminous read, full of intriguing characters... Beautifully written and thoughtful. Sure to be one of the best debuts of this or any other year."
— *Jeff Vandermeer*

"The sort of book that creeps into your dreams."
— *Chris Beckett, winner of the 2013 Arthur C Clarke Award*

"*The Moon King* has you hooked from the start."
— *Edinburgh Book Review*

"An intricately constructed, heartfelt novel that does its author proud."
— *Nina Allan, author of The Race*

Available now in paperback, and e-book
http://www.newconpress.co.uk

Splinters of Truth
Storm Constantine

Cover art by Danielle Lainton

Storm Constantine is one of our finest writers of genre fiction. This new collection, **Splinters of Truth**, features fifteen stories, four of them original to this volume, that transport the reader to richly imagined realms one moment and shine a light on our own world's darkest corners the next. A writer of rare passion, Storm delivers here some of her most accomplished work to date.

"Constantine's talent for twisting the mundane and making it dark and delicious shines out on each page"
– Starburst

"Storm Constantine is a myth-making Gothic queen. Her stories are poetic, involving, delightful and depraved. I wouldn't swap her for a dozen Anne Rices." – *Neil Gaiman*

"Storm Constantine… is a daring romantic sensualist, as well as a fine storyteller." – *Poppy Z Brite*

"Storm Constantine is a literary fantasist of outstanding power and originality. Her work is rich, idiosyncratic and completely engaging. Her themes have much in common with Philip K Dick – the nature of identify, the nature of reality, the creative power of the human imagination – while her sensibility reminds me of Angela Carter at her most inventive." – *Michael Moorcock*

Available now from NewCon Press
www.newconpress.co.uk

NEWCON PRESS

Publishing quality Science Fiction, Fantasy, Dark Fantasy and Horror
for eight years and counting.

Winner of the 2010 'Best Publisher' Award
from the European Science Fiction Society.

Anthologies, novels, short story collections, novellas, paperbacks,
hardbacks, signed limited editions, e-books…
Why not take a look at some of our other titles?

Neil Gaiman, Brian Aldiss, Kelley Armstrong, Alastair Reynolds,
Stephen Baxter, Christopher Priest, Tanith Lee, Joe Abercrombie, Dan
Abnett, Nina Allan, Sarah Ash, Neal Asher, Tony Ballantyne, James
Barclay, Chris Beckett, Lauren Beukes, Aliette de Bodard, Chaz
Brenchley, Keith Brooke, Eric Brown, Pat Cadigan, Jay Caselberg,
Michael Cobley, Genevieve Cogman, Storm Constantine, Hal Duncan,
Jaine Fenn, Paul di Filippo, Jonathan Green, Jon Courtenay Grimwood,
Peter F. Hamilton, Frances Hardinge, Gwyneth Jones, M. John
Harrison, Amanda Hemingway, Paul Kane, Leigh Kennedy, Nancy
Kress, Kim Lakin-Smith, David Langford, Alison Littlewood, James
Lovegrove, Una McCormack, Ian McDonald, Sophia McDougall, Gary
McMahon, Ken MacLeod, Ian R MacLeod, Gail Z. Martin, Juliet E.
McKenna, John Meaney, Simon Morden, Mark Morris, Anne Nicholls,
Stan Nicholls, Marie O'Regan, Philip Palmer, Stephen Palmer, Sarah
Pinborough, Gareth L. Powell, Robert Reed, Rod Rees, Andy Remic,
Mike Resnick, Mercurio D. Rivera, Adam Roberts, Justina Robson,
Stephanie Saulter, Gaie Sebold, Robert Shearman, Sarah Singleton,
Martin Sketchley, Kari Sperring, Brian Stapleford, Charles Stross, Tricia
Sullivan, E.J. Swift, Adrian Tchaikovsky, Steve Rasnic Tem, Lavie
Tidhar, Lisa Tuttle, Simon Kurt Unsworth, Ian Watson, Freda
Warrington, Liz Williams, Neil Williamson, and many more.

Join our mailing list to get advance notice of new titles, book launches and
events, and receive special offers on books: www.newconpress.co.uk